THE RELIC BOND

The Lost Riders

Book 1

JASPER ALDEN

D.K. HOLMBERG

Cover art by Damonza.com

Prologue

General Kolass Jeniq was not one to worry about the details in life. And it wasn't simply because he was a General of the Malarsan Army, either, which basically forced him to focus on the bigger picture, often leaving the smaller details to his commanders, captains, and lieutenants to figure out on the battlefield.

It was a philosophy that Kolass had picked up during his initial war training some twenty-odd years ago now. His instructor, a tough old veteran of the last Dragon War thirty years ago, had told Kolass that one should never miss the war for the battle.

Privately, Kolass had assumed this was the main reason he'd been so much more effective at killing dragons than the other generals. Most people, even trained and hardened veterans, panicked in some form or another. Those who didn't often tried to kill them by focusing on the wings or the claws or the eyes, thinking that going for the tiny details would make it easier.

But Kolass had found that dragons *expected* you to go for their so-called 'weak points' and adjusted accordingly. The dragons rarely knew what to do or how to react when a puny human went straight at them, no-holds-barred, with everything they had.

That was why Kolass had killed two dragons so far … and was in the middle of slaying his third. Which made this a momentous day.

The harsh wind of the Southern Plains swept through Kolass's hair as he jumped backward to avoid a desperate slash from the claws of the dragon before him. Landing on his feet, Kolass thrust his hands toward the earth, sending green moulash into its depths.

The effect was immediate. A massive spear of rock exploded from the ground, striking the dragon in the chest. The dragon, however, was swifter than it looked, staggering backward at the last second to avoid getting impaled in the heart, which Kolass had been aiming for. Still, the spear struck its chest and smashed through its thick scales, causing red dragon blood to leak out from the new wound.

The dragon didn't let the injury slow it down. It opened its mouth wide and unleashed a torrent of red-hot flame toward Kolass, the flames moving too fast for Kolass to dodge or deflect.

Instead, Kolass ran his hands through a series of complicated gestures, pouring more earth moulash into the ground under his feet. A thick barrier of stone erupted around Kolass, forming a dome of rock and dirt that instantly shrouded Kolass in midnight darkness.

A second later, Kolass heard the roaring dragonfire as

it slammed into his barrier. Fortunately, his dome held, although it was already starting to heat up. Sweat broke across his brow. The dragon was clearly trying to cook him alive.

Let it think that. Kolass slammed his hands together again. *And let that be the last thought it* ever *has.*

Once again, Kolass drew upon the earth moulash within his soul, channeling it through his battle boots and into the ground itself. The ground suddenly became as soft as water, and Kolass, taking a deep breath of air, fell into it.

More darkness. More rock and earth everywhere. Rough. Solid in some places.

But Kolass was already pushing himself through the ground, using his earth moulash to make the ground as malleable as water. At the same time, he paid attention to the vibrations in the ground overhead, trying to sense where the dragon was. It was difficult as the dragon had not been moving very much last Kolass had seen.

But then Kolass felt it. A soft *boom* as the dragon slammed its tail against the earth. Although Kolass was about six feet underground, he could feel the vibrations even from here.

Gotcha, Kolass thought with a grin.

Stopping in roughly the right spot, Kolass thrust his hands up. At the same time, he channeled more earth moulash through his feet, creating a force that sent him rocketing up through the ground until he launched into the air.

Light. Sound. The harsh and shockingly cold winter breeze of the Plains. A bird's eye view of the charred, torn battlefield below. Bodies of his soldiers scattered everywhere while the remnants had retreated to the far side of the field on the other side of some hills. The lesser war mages had cast glowing magical barriers over them and their allies.

Good. That meant they were following his orders.

And below Kolass—its back to him, seemingly ignorant of his presence—was the dragon. A medium-sized beast, the dragon had scales as red as fire. Many of its scales were scarred and broken from Kolass's prolonged battle with it, threadbare wings torn in several places. It was still breathing fire on the dome, perhaps under the impression that Kolass was still in there.

It was about to be proved lethally wrong.

As Kolass reached the peak of his flight, he drew his preferred weapon from his side: A steel-tipped drill sword. Normally helpful for tunneling through particularly thick rock or dirt, Kolass had learned that it could pierce the skull of a dragon quite well and double as a sword in a pinch.

Pulling the trigger on the drill's handle, Kolass yelled at the top of his lungs, channeling earth moulash through the drill to make it stronger. His yelling startled the dragon. It looked up at him in surprise, smoke drifting from the corners of its mouth.

And then Kolass slammed his drill directly into its forehead.

The impact sent the dragon's head, perched on top of its lengthy neck, crashing to the ground. Kolass stumbled a little, but he didn't stop drilling deeper and deeper into its skull. Bits of scale and flesh shot past Kolass's face as the drill dug deeply into the dragon's skull, until he felt the tip strike something soft and tear it apart.

Without warning, the dragon—which had been flapping its wing incessantly in a futile attempt to throw Kolass off—went limp under him. Its wings twitched once or twice before stopping entirely.

With supreme effort, Kolass yanked the drill out of the dragon's skull and stood up. As useful as his drill was for killing dragons, it did have a tendency to get stuck inside the dragon's brains if it went in too deep. A quick glance at his weapon told him that it had largely survived the encounter, although it would definitely need to be cleaned by his attendant later on.

But Kolass forgot all about his weapon when a loud cheer suddenly erupted all around him. Slightly startled, Kolass looked around at his surroundings.

The other members of Kolass's troop had left the safety of the camp to come out and cheer Kolass's victory. Soldiers with broken or cracked armor chanted his name over and over again while mages in dirty black and brown robes clapped and cheered.

"Dragonslayer! Dragonslayer! Dragonslayer!" the soldiers and mages alike cheered.

Kolass smiled tiredly. He just wanted to rest, but he knew that his men expected at least a short victory speech from him, if nothing else.

Raising his bloody drill high above his head, Kolass declared, in a loud voice that carried across the crowd, "Soldiers and mages of the Slayer Squad! Let it be known that I, General Kolass Jeniq, have slain my third dragon! Send a message back to the capital, informing the queen and the other generals of this amazing victory for the Kingdom of Malarsan!"

Kolass paused. He could have left it there—it would have been more than enough for his soldiers—but Kolass was feeling rather victorious himself, so he decided to end it on a higher note.

Bending over, Kolass ripped off one of the dragon's head scales and held it up for everyone to see. "And I promise that one day, we *will* win this war and we *will* destroy the dragon menace once and for all! On the names of the gods themselves, I promise this!"

The soldiers and mages went positively wild at Kolass's ending speech. Another chant of *Dragonslayer, Dragonslayer, Dragonslayer!* started, but fortunately, Kolass spotted his captains already breaking up the crowd, telling the injured to return to the camp and rest or barking orders at the uninjured to help with the cleanup. A few soldiers, he noticed, quietly picked up fallen scales and other bits from the dead dragon, no doubt intending to keep them as trophies of the battle they participated in. Likely they would flash the scales to attractive women to try to win them over or bring them out anytime they had a disagreement with their male friends over who was the toughest.

Not that Kolass minded. He already got his palm-sized scale, after all. He made a mental note to add it to his necklace containing the scales he'd picked up from the last two dragons he'd slain.

But the real prize was the fireproof armor that could be crafted from this dragon's scales. It was well-known that dragon scales were practically immune to dragonfire.

After killing a dragon, it was common to strip the corpse of all usable scales, melt them down into liquid, and then mold that liquid to make special fireproof armor designed to handle dragonfire. Kolass himself wore armor made at least partially from the scales of the last two dragons he'd killed.

It was a long and messy process, though, so Kolass was relieved when he saw the scalpers—the men whose primary job was scaling the scales from a dead dragon—already rushing out from the camp to start their work.

"General Jeniq!" a familiar voice called out.

Kolass spotted a young fire mage clad in bright-red robes with a fiery design etched into their chest scurrying across the battlefield toward him. She was rather short with long brown hair flowing out freely behind her. She almost stumbled over the holes in the earth created by Kolass and the dragon during the fight.

"Shalla?" Kolass frowned at his personal attendant, lowering his red scale to his side. "What is the matter?"

Shalla stopped about a dozen yards from the dead dragon, which she eyed nervously as if it was still alive. "A message for you just came in from the queen."

Kolass's frown deepened even more. "The queen? What is it?"

"She didn't say," Shalla said with a gulp. "Her Majesty merely demanded your presence."

Kolass raised an eyebrow. It was rare for the queen to directly communicate with Kolass or any of the other generals directly on the battlefield. It was even rarer for it to be an emergency which immediately required Kolass's presence.

Shaking his head, Kolass waved his hand, and a set of crude but effective stone stairs rose out of the dirt from the dragon's head to the ground below. He marched down the stairs easily and walked past Shalla, who scurried to keep up with his longer strides. A handful of scalpers ran past.

"Who else will be at the meeting, Shalla?" Kolass asked without looking at his attendant. "Did the queen say?"

"She did not," Shalla said. "But I think she'd summoned all four of the generals."

Kolass nearly missed a step. "Then it must be important indeed."

"It is," Shalla said. "Sorry for not getting you more information. The queen—"

"Can be *very* difficult to deal with sometimes, I agree," Kolass said with a smile. He gestured to the right. "Gather the captains in the officers' tent for the usual debrief. I'll aim to be there in twenty. And then I'm off to meet with the queen."

As Shalla nodded and scurried off, Kolass tried to puzzle through what the queen might want but had no answers. At least he would have a prize for her. That would limit her temper, though if she summoned all the generals, there must be something significant at play.

More than a dragon?

He wasn't one to question. He would serve as he always had.

Chapter One

THE AIR HAD A MUSTY STENCH THAT LINGERED, THOUGH Hal Norath didn't find that unusual when it came to places he was sent to find relics. They usually stunk. Some places were worse than others, but almost all of them had a certain foulness to them that left him wishing he'd gone into a different line of work.

The valley stretched in front of him. Trees towered overhead, most of them strange jungle varietals that he wouldn't be able to identify if he were pressed, but scattered among them were smaller shrubs, most with thorns that tried to snag his cloak and tore at the fabric. He lost track of how many pieces of fabric he'd left behind. Probably enough to weave a new cloak.

Stop dallying, Hal.

He ducked under one branch. It seemed as if the branches swayed with an energy all of their own, though Hal knew that couldn't be the case. The one above him looked like it was moving, as if there was something that slithered along the branch itself…

There *was* something that slithered along the branch.

He darted forward. It wouldn't be the first time he had to deal with creepy crawlies, but he would *love* not to have a snake drop down on him from above and bite at him like some demon from stories of old. When he was free of the branch, he crouched next to a small boulder, looking around the jungle.

A simple job, he'd been told. Find the lost tomb, grab the relic that was there, and he could return for some well-earned rest. The general had said nothing about *snakes*.

You should've known better. You're in a jungle.

Those were his father's words that rang in his mind like a warning, though Hal tried to ignore them right now. Were it not for his father, Hal might have taken a different line of work, but he wasn't upset that he ended up as a Relic Hunter. Just that he was here.

He pushed a cobweb-covered vine out of the way, ducked underneath a vine, and glanced around. He wasn't supposed to be alone here, but there were certain things that even the mages refused to come along for. Not that he'd put one of the mages through anything like this. What would they do—burn the forest down just to get past the cobwebs? Maybe they'd use the wind and lift the branches for him so that he wouldn't have to duck beneath them.

I wouldn't mind them keeping the flies away.

He swatted at his arm, trying to keep one of the dozens of flies that had been circling him ever since he had descended down into the jungle from biting. It seemed as if every strip of fabric that ripped away from his cloak had given the flies another target. More exposed skin made it so that he was little more than a walking buffet.

And worse.

He'd plucked a few multi-legged creatures off his arms and his cloak. After the third one, he'd pulled the hood of his cloak up so that he wouldn't have to worry about any of them dropping down passed the neckline. One had still managed to get down along his chest, and the memory of it crawling along his flesh—as if it were looking for someplace to burrow *And probably lay eggs*—left him shivering.

A small clearing opened before him.

At least the directions he'd been given had been accurate about that.

Hal slowed, looking around the clearing. The tomb shouldn't be far from here, though he wasn't sure why *he* had been sent. Something that one of the mages had spied, most likely, and he was the nearest of the Relic Hunters so that he could come. It certainly wasn't that he was the most skilled of them. Not that Hal was unskilled —his time with his father and his first mentors had taught him enough to be more than competent—but Hal knew he was inexperienced. That was part of the reason he hadn't objected when he'd been asked to come on this assignment.

A snapping branch caught his attention, and Hal turned to see what caused the sound. He was supposed to be the only one sent on this assignment but that didn't mean that others wouldn't be out here. Once relics were discovered, it wasn't unusual for others to make a run at them, thinking that they could then resell them to the kingdom—or worse, outside of the kingdom.

When convinced there wasn't anything behind him, Hal tore his attention away and focused on looking for a way to get into the tomb. That was the reason he was here, after all. Get the job done, then he could deal with getting back. If there were other relic chasers, then he'd have to be quick.

A pile of moss-covered boulders drew his attention, and he made his way over to it. The tomb was said to belong to an ancient warlord, so someone of power, but had been lost to time long ago. He was far enough on the fringes of the kingdom now that he wondered if the warlord who'd once been here had even reached the lands that Hal considered his home. Probably had. That was in a time of the dragons, a time when the war did not rage as it now did, and when the dragons had not fought mankind the way they did now.

When Hal reached the rocks, he slipped among them until he found a small opening.

Really?

There were times when relic hunting was not something he wanted to spend his days doing. Most of the time, he loved it. It gave him a chance to get outside of the cities in the kingdom and gave him a chance to test himself, but he *really* didn't love dealing with caves or enclosed spaces.

Too bad. That's a part of what you have to do.

He slipped into the opening, following a series of

stairs down deeper into the earth and into what he believed was the tomb. The walls opened up, which suggested that he was right and that this *was* the tomb, but the heavy humidity in the air and the stench of the valley itself didn't lift at all.

The stairs were slick with moisture, and the walls looked as if they would cave in at any time. The remnants of an ancient lantern hung on one wall caught his attention, but he had to be careful with his footing. One wrong step and he could tumble down into the darkness, never to be heard from again.

The relic had *better* be valuable.

Most were. Hal never learned what they were *all* used for, but most of the relics he'd been sent to acquire were used to defend the kingdom against the dragons. Many of them were made by the first mages when they'd been forced into fighting creatures that were much larger and more powerful than them. There were stories about incredibly powerful relics, dragon killers and those that would even tame them so that they wouldn't have to be killed, though Hal didn't know if those stories were real or something that his father had made up.

At the bottom of the stairs, Hal paused.

The air had changed. Now it didn't have the same foulness to it. There was a heavy dampness, that of moisture that had to have been trapped into this space. When a bit of a breeze drifted toward him, he paused and looked up. There *had* been the sound that might have meant someone following, though he hadn't seen any evidence of them.

And it wasn't as if Hal got challenging jobs.

When he was sent for relics, it was because there had been something discovered that *might* be useful, not because there was something that was *definitely* useful. Unfortunately. He never got the challenging assignments.

The wind persisted.

Just a breeze from above.

He had to remind himself that he was down in a tomb. There might be all sorts of strange breezes here—or maybe worse. relic hunting had taken him to tombs before, though not often tombs that were underground like this. He hadn't found the crypt yet, but that was where he figured he'd need to go so he could find the relic.

Hal hurried forward, gaze skimming the walls for unseen traps. Many of these ancient tombs liked to have traps placed to keep out anyone who might wander in, though Hal had trained to pick up on most of them.

A small dimple along the wall caught his attention, and he paused.

He reached into his pouch and pulled out a small fistful of sand. When he tossed it, the sand rippled along something before falling to the ground. Then a spike of pale white bone went shooting across the hall, embedding in the far side.

Clever, but not unique.

Hal had seen traps like that before. That didn't change that he *was* impressed by the ancient engineering that went into making such traps. He slipped forward, crouching down briefly to look at the space where the spike had shot out. The trigger was a strange opening that he found impressive.

Using a bit more sand, he tossed it forward, staying back.

Another spike shot across the hall.

Hal stood. Now he knew what they looked like, it would be easy enough for him to avoid the dangers. Not that there wouldn't still be *some* danger, but most of these ancient places had distinct signatures to how they created their challenges, so Hal didn't expect anything more than this.

Taking a long, slender rod of metal in hand, Hal tapped on the ground in front of him. He could use that to determine if there were other dangers. The rod triggered two more spikes—though, both of them had been from places along the wall that he had seen before they were triggered.

The hall changed. The stone no longer had the irregularities along it that were likely going to lead to spikes shooting at him. He straightened and probed nonetheless, pushing forward to see if there were any other triggers that he needed to be careful around, but found nothing.

The hall ended.

There had been no doors, which meant that now he had to find his way past the wall. And there *would* be a way past. Hal traced his hand along the wall, probing for any irregularities. He felt nothing.

A shuffling came from somewhere behind him.

Hal jerked his head around. A body lay motionless on the ground, one of the spikes sticking out of it.

A Relic Hunter chaser.

They were uncommon, but Hal knew to be careful as

there were a few who would follow Relic Hunters and track them until they found the relic. Occasionally, they would even track them until the Relic Hunter managed to acquire the relic they had been sent after and then attack them. Several hunters had been killed that way. It was part of the reason most Relic Hunters had protection.

Hal should have brought his protection down into the tomb.

There's no reason to think like that now. Find a way in, and finish the job.

How was he supposed to get inside, though? He had to find his way through, and so far, had not uncovered anything along the wall that would show him how or where he could get in.

What if it wasn't on this section of the wall?

There might have been other places that went through. Hal ran his hands along the neighboring wall, testing for any cracks or irregularities that might reveal some sort of triggering for a doorway. There was nothing.

There had to be something more. The tomb had led down…

Down.

Hal smiled to himself, then he dropped to the ground and began to search the stones. He found one with a small hole in the center of it abutting the wall at the end of the tunnel.

Hal shook his rod and pressed it into the hole.

A shuffling from behind him caught his attention, and Hal looked up.

Two others were coming down the hall, creeping past the body.

It was time to move. He shoved the rod down into the opening and heard a soft click.

As soon as he did, he paused and looked around. He wasn't sure what caused that shifting, but he was uncertain if it was a door opening or if there was something else happening here. Hal knew to be careful.

The footsteps were louder.

Hal waited until the wall pulled up enough, and then he rolled underneath it.

Now he was inside of the smaller chamber. The crypt.

The air stunk, centuries of age and rot and moisture all building up into a foulness. He scrambled to his feet, looking around. The light in here was dim enough that he couldn't see much, but he knew this had to be where he was going to find the relic. He just had to get to it.

The wall continued to rumble upward.

Even if he got to the relic, there was no guarantee that he was going to be able to get back out quickly.

He might be able to find something that would help keep the chasers from getting the relic from him.

And there was something else he might be able to try. There was the possibility that there might be other protections here. He just had to find them.

As he moved forward, he noticed a section of stone that was more irregular than others, and slipped around it. One of the figures came through the now wide-open doorway and raced after Hal, who tossed the rod at the man's feet.

The man looked down at the same time a spike shot up from the floor, catching him in the midsection.

That left one chaser.

Now he just had to figure out what else might be here.

A pedestal in the center of the room caught Hal's attention. On top of the pedestal rested a golden, circular object. It glowed, reflecting some unseen light. Hal approached it carefully, sweeping his gaze around the inside of the crypt, but he didn't see any other triggers that he needed to be concerned about. Which meant that the relic itself would have been booby-trapped in some way.

"Leave it, and I'll let you walk out of here alive," a voice said from behind him.

Hal spun, holding out a knife. "It's just the two of us. What makes you think you are the one to negotiate?"

The man slipped forward. He was a little shorter than Hal, with coarse black hair, a prominent brow, and a sharp nose. Not from Malarsan, then.

"These are not your lands."

"I think the queen would argue with that."

"The queen can burn."

The way that he said it suggested a longing for the queen to burn. Hal noticed a branding on the back of the man's hand, and he understood. He was one of the Sishan, a tribe of people who celebrated dragons. Hal couldn't imagine anybody celebrating or worshiping dragons. They were brutal and violent creatures that had destroyed so much of Malarsan that Hal could not imagine anybody wanting to protect them.

"Listen," Hal said, "maybe we got off on the wrong foot here." He had to be careful. He didn't know if the Sishan had mages, but there were stories about how they had embraced fire and used it in their celebrations. It would make sense if they somehow had a way of controlling it. Hal didn't have any protection against that. If he were attacked with some sort of fire magic, he would definitely burn.

All for a relic?

The queen would like that way of thinking, though. Hal served the queen, and as one of her Relic Hunters, it was his obligation to do whatever was needed.

The man held his hands up. They were both raw and red, as if the skin had peeled off of them. He began murmuring something, though Hal couldn't make out the words. Heat began to build in the air, radiating from the man's hands, forming a glowing fireball in between them.

Then the wind swept through the tomb, catching the man — and his flame — and sending him staggering. Hal darted forward and drove his elbow into the man's temple, and he crumpled.

The wind continued to spill into the crypt, now with a violence that swirled, until it suddenly fell still.

"That's enough, Fralia."

His mage protector stepped forward, the wind that had been swirling holding onto her dark hair. She remained in the shadows near the doorway, but her blue eyes shone with amusement. "I thought you didn't need protection on this job, Hal."

"I guess I made a mistake. I didn't think we had any chasers here."

She looked down at the ground at the fallen man. "Not the typical chaser, though. Most don't have access to power."

"I think he was one of the Sishan."

She sucked in a sharp breath. "Really? They should've warned us if this was a dangerous job."

"Dangerous jobs come with the best reward," Hal said, turning to the relic resting on the pedestal. "Now. Since you are here — finally — you might as well be ready to sweep us out of here the moment I lift this relic. Everything else here has been booby-trapped, so I suspect this will be, as well."

"You are the Relic Hunter. You get us out of here." She flashed a slight grin at him.

Hal reached the pedestal, looked over to her, and lifted the relic.

As soon as he did, the entire crypt began to tremble.

Fralia let out an exaggerated sigh. "What would you do without me?"

"Well, today, I probably would have burned."

"Probably. You should know not to play with fire, Hal."

He raced toward the entrance to the crypt. The door had already started to slide closed. He grabbed Fralia around the waist and slid forward, beneath the doorway, just before it crashed down.

Out in the hall, he looked over to Fralia. "I got the relic. Now you can get us the rest of the way out of here."

"You'd better report that I helped."

"Why would I do that when I can take all of the credit?" She glowered at him, but the wind picked up, and it carried them along the hall before settling them near the stairs. Together, they raced up them, and back above ground.

Another successful job.

Chapter Two

Hal stopped at the edge of the jungle, looking down into the valley. The relic weighed down his pack, as if it were made of gold, though it had turned out to be only gold-colored, not solid gold as he had initially thought. The air still stirred, swirling around him and tugging at his cloak, as if a reminder of Fralia's help escaping from the Sishan.

"Would you come on?" she said. "You've been looking back there as if you're going to find some answer by staring into the jungle."

"I'm still trying to make sense of the Sishan. We've never seen any of them before."

She shrugged, and jerked on her cloak. "We've not seen a lot of things, but that doesn't mean anything. Besides, how do you know that I haven't seen one of the Sishan during my travels?"

Hal shifted his pack. It was *heavy*. Fralia could offer to ease the weight. Her magic could certainly do that, though she'd never offered it. It was almost like she enjoyed making him suffer under the burden. Which she probably did.

"I'm sure you have. Your father probably helped push them back from these lands."

At the mention of her father, Fralia's face darkened for a moment. Hal knew to be careful about that with her. They weren't on the best of terms. "Yes, well I'm sure he did. I can't imagine what it would be like to think that you needed to serve a dragon." She wrapped her arms around herself and shivered. "That's what they do, you know. They give themselves over to the dragons. They serve them."

"If I never see a dragon myself, that will be fine with me."

"Why would *you* ever see a dragon, Hal Norath? You're a Relic Hunter. You'll never be tasked with fighting along the front line."

Hal shrugged. "I don't know why I would. I was just saying that I don't want to."

They started walking. It wasn't a long way back to the encampment from here, but it would take the better of two days. Then he could hand over the relic, hopefully get a bit of a bonus in compensation having dealt with the Sishan, and learn his next assignment. That was the way it worked for him.

"I should've seen some sign of them," Hal muttered.

"What if they didn't leave anything for you to find? Besides, in the jungle that dense, it would've been difficult for you to have seen anything, anyway. You're lucky that they came rushing at you."

"Actually, I'm lucky that they weren't smart enough to test for any traps."

Fralia laughed. When she did, the wind swirled slightly as if she were calling it to her. "About that. How did you manage to miss one of the traps? Wait. Not just that. How did you manage to get past it without triggering it?"

"I *did* trigger all of the traps. Makes me wonder if there was some way that they reset."

"You've never seen anything like that."

"Not in most of the places we've gone, but this was a bit more out of the way than usual." He shifted the pack and pulled the relic out. The sunlight shining overhead reflected off the gold. Flakes of it peeled back, making it look as if it were starting to fade, though beneath the gold paint, it looked to be bronze. "What do you think this was once?"

Fralia took the plate from him, and she turned it over in her hand. "I don't know. It feels heavy. Like there's something inside." She held it up to her ear and shook it. "Maybe there's something stored in here. Those ancient engineers might have known something, especially with what we saw of how they managed to set those traps."

"Doubtful," he said, but didn't know.

As a Relic Hunter, Hal visited many different places throughout the kingdom and had come to learn that their kingdom had once been settled by many different peoples—and had served many different gods. Most of the relics represented some way for those ancients to serve their gods, though Hal wondered if there might be something more they had hoped to do with the relics.

"What do you think this will help the queen understand?" Fralia asked.

Hal took the plate back from her and stuffed it carefully into his pack before slipping it back onto his shoulder. The pack dug down into the skin of his shoulder, almost painfully so, but he tried to ignore that. "I don't even know anymore. I wonder if it is the queen or if it's one of her historians, as they all have their own reason for us gathering these things." Hal shrugged. "And this one isn't quite as special as some."

"Think about that tomb. I wish we would've had more time to explore it. We haven't seen anything quite like that before."

"You mean buried underground? You might not have, but I certainly have. The last time I went down into a tomb like that I almost didn't make it back." Hal shivered. That had been in the northern section of the kingdom, and had not been a tomb so much as it had been a cave, marked with ancient symbols, some carvings that represented dragons, and a series of letters. That had been an assignment that he took on his own, only after having learned of the possibility that there might be something found in that cave that could be of use. Most of the time, Hal got his assignments from his superiors.

"Not like that," she said, shaking her head. "Besides, I think you're overreacting. You were never in any real danger."

"That's news to me. I thought with one of the Sishan forming a fireball in his hands that I might have nearly died. My apologies for mistaking my near-death for something serious."

They started up a hillside, and Fralia started to laugh at him. "You were the one who told me I didn't need to come with you."

"For jobs like that, you generally don't. Besides, you've made it quite clear that you are only there to accompany me to reach the relic's location, and have no interest in going inside those kinds of places."

"Well, can you blame me?"

Hal snorted. "I don't know if I can blame you, but I certainly wouldn't mind your help. Anyway, why did you come down?"

"I felt something." She frowned, her brow furrowing. "And to be honest, I don't really know what it was. Maybe it was just the heat of the fire. Of course, I don't know that I would've identified that. That isn't my affinity, so unless it were drawing upon the wind, I may not have noticed anything."

He was thankful that she had. They had been traveling together as a team for long enough now that Hal knew she was incredibly skilled, though he had rarely needed her to protect him. Relic Hunters traveled with mages for such things, but most of the time they served as a deterrent for chasers, keeping them from losing the relics that they managed to acquire.

"Now that we've got it, where do you think we will be sent next?"

Hal shrugged, shifting his back again. "I don't know. You know the general. Probably someplace like this."

"Only if you get rewarded. I could pass on word that you overlooked warning signs of an impending attack, and it was only through my heroics that you managed to acquire the relic you were sent to find."

"And I could make it clear that my mage protector was unwilling to come with me through the jungle where I found the clearing that led down into the tomb because she's afraid of creepy crawlies and enclosed spaces."

Fralia stuck her tongue out at him and marched ahead. Hal laughed and hurried after her.

They traveled quickly and reached the encampment midday on the second day after having acquired the relic. Hal nodded to the soldiers inside of the encampment and headed straight toward the command tent. It stood taller than most of the others, a large, square structure with a central peak that bore the flag of Queen Bariwa waving in the wind. As they neared, Fralia looked over to him. "I'll let you have the honor here. I'm going to try to reach my father."

"Are you sure about that?"

"I need to know what he's been doing. He's been quiet lately. Anytime that he goes quiet like that, I start to worry."

"He *does* have other responsibilities," Hal said.

"I know. Anyway," she said, glancing at the activity in the encampment, tilting her head as she frowned. Wind swirled ever so subtly around her. "After I speak to my father, let's get some food, and see if we can't get word of what's happening along the front."

"You mean the place that I never intend to go."

"Exactly," Fralia said.

She started away, and Hal stood in front of the command tent for a moment. There were no guards, though there were never any guards around the tent. There was no need. The tent was empty save for a small stone circular platform that probably weighed an incredible amount — something Hal was thankful that he never had to learn on his own — and a few other small sculptures that would probably be considered relics in a few decades.

Hal approached the central stone platform. He shifted the pack, pulled the relic out of it, and held onto it as he stood in place for a moment. Then he stepped forward onto the platform.

"General Mokoa."

He waited. It could take moments, or much longer, something Hal had come to learn that he had to deal with. These communication devices were meant to ease the distances felt within the kingdom and were his way of reaching his commanding general, though Hal preferred face-to-face communication.

He didn't have to wait very long. There came a surge of pale light from around the platform, something that seemed to surround him, as if he were bathing in that light, and then it swept upward, the light taking on a shape, forming the outline of a figure. General Mokoa stood in front of him.

"Report."

The general was little more than a figure of light and not clear enough that Hal could make any details out, though his mind filled in the details. He had only seen the general in person a few times and didn't even know if his memory of the general was accurate or not. She was a distinguished older woman, though incredibly muscular, who had strange tattoos on all of her exposed skin. Her eyes seemed to burn with a vibrant intensity. At least, that was the way Hal remembered her, and the way that his mind filled in the gaps in what he saw before him.

"It is Hal Norath reporting. I acquired the relic I was sent to find." Hal held the plate out and then set it down. That was the only way the general would know what he had brought her. The light swirled around the relic. It seemed to hold it for a moment, before it faded, drawn back down into the stone, and the general surged a little brighter.

"Excellent. You did well, Halar. Did you have any difficulty with it?"

It was more questioning than Hal was accustomed to when it came to the general. Most of the time, he handed off what he had acquired, and then they moved on to the next assignment. He wondered why the general would begin to question more.

She knows something. There must be some reason the Sishan attacked.

"There was a little difficulty," Hal began, and he explained the attack. "Thankfully, my mage protector was there, and she incapacitated the Sishan. It went smoothly after that."

There was a moment of quiet, and in that moment, Hal began to wonder if perhaps he had said something that upset the general. He didn't think he had, but the generals could be a bit touchy, especially when it came to the relics. He wasn't sure how the assignments to search for relics were handed out, but he suspected there was some measure of prestige to it. Each general would want their Relic Hunter to be the one to find each item.

"Unusual," she said. "You did well succeeding in securing it. I will send a courier to bring the relic to me quickly."

That was even more unusual. Often times, after Hal or the other Relic Hunters secured the relics, they were left to linger inside of the encampment. For the general to send somebody suggested this relic was even more important than Hal had known.

"You will be compensated for the time and difficulty, and I will even pass word to the queen that you should receive special recognition."

Hal bowed his head. The idea that the queen would recognize him left his heart hammering. Only the most prized Relic Hunters were ever acknowledged by the queen. It was a great honor, and one Hal didn't expect to have bestowed upon him.

"I'm only doing what I can to serve the throne," Hal said, knowing that was the expected response.

There was another moment of silence. It seemed as if the general were distracted.

"I have another assignment for you," the general finally said, and her voice sounded strained. It was times like these when Hal wished that he had a more direct line of communication to the general, but then again, having any way to communicate with the general was an honor. It was something that very few soldiers in the army ever were permitted. It was only because Hal was a Relic Hunter that he was given this honor to speak directly to the general. "You are the closest hunter to what we need, and so I would ask for you to make the journey as quickly as you can. What I'd like for you is to head to the Tops, and from there, there's a temple I'd like you to find. I will send directions, but you may need to find local resources to help assist in this journey."

Local resources meant they'd have to hunt down anyone local to help guide them. It wasn't usually very difficult, especially if people were committed to the throne, but the Desolate Tops were near the edge of the kingdom, and a place that Hal had never visited.

"Of course. And this relic?"

"*If* there is a relic," the general began, now her voice sounding even more faint and even more strained, "it will be unique. I would have you secure it and keep it hidden. Then I would have you return as quickly as you can, and I will send further instructions."

Hal bowed his head in a nod. "Of course."

"Do this well, and you will be rewarded."

The glowing started to fade, and the shape of the general began to flutter, before finally disappearing altogether.

The plate rested on the stone circle, and it felt strange for Hal to leave it there, but he wasn't about to remove it, not unless he was told to bring it somewhere else, and given that the general had told him to leave it for her courier, Hal would do just that.

He reached the entrance to the tent, and then outside. Fralia was waiting for him.

"How did it go?"

"Surprising," he said, and described what the general

had said. She frowned as he spoke. "And we got our next assignment."

"Why do I get the sense that I am not going to care for this?"

Hal flashed a smile. "Why wouldn't you enjoy taking a journey?"

"Because I know you, Halar. And you look like you're keeping something from me."

"The Tops," he said.

"There's nothing there," she said.

"That's not what she thinks. That's where we're supposed to go."

"Great. I don't have clothing for the cold."

"Well, then first we gather supplies, and then we can set off."

"Do we have directions or details or anything to help us know what we'll find?"

"Local resources," Hal said.

"Even better. We get to go to the Tops, and we get to ask people who are naturally suspicious of us to help. I wonder what we might find."

"It's the job, Fralia."

She snorted, then let out a long sigh. "Sometimes I wonder why we do it."

Chapter Three

"I COULD'VE DONE WITHOUT THIS JOB," FRALIA SAID, raising her cloak up to cover her face against the howling of the wind. "I might even be convinced to return to the jungle and face the Sishan. At least they were warm."

When Hal laughed, his breath plumed out. They were both dressed as well as they could be for the cold, though that was not saying much. The wind tore through even the warmest of their clothing, making it difficult for them to keep constantly warm.

"You can head back there. Once we get to the Tops—"

"We don't know what we'll find when we get to the Tops."

It was called the Tops because it was far removed from the rest of the kingdom, situated in a part of the mountains that was otherwise impassible. Hal had never visited, but now that he had been given one assignment out here at the edge of the kingdom, he might as well have more. Besides, if he did this — and if he did it well — he knew that he'd be rewarded. And at this point, that was all that Hal wanted.

"We know we are going to find more of the same. Cold. Wind. And we don't know what else is there. There might not even be anybody local that we can use to help us find anything else."

"You're far too pessimistic about all of this."

"Not pessimistic. Realistic. Gods," she swore, wrapping her cloak around her face for a moment and turning so that she could get out of the wind. "What kind of relic do you think we are going to find here, anyway?"

"I don't think it's always this cold," Hal said.

Then again, he didn't know. He didn't have any experience up at the Tops, other than to know that it was widely regarded as a desolate place. Remote. Even the people who were said to live there were wild. It was what made this job a bit more interesting than some of the others. He had to use local resources, but Hal didn't know what that would involve.

"We can go back," he said, looking over to Fralia. "I'm sure we can just return to the encampment. I can head into the command tent and let the general know that my mage protector didn't want anything to do with the cold."

"You can tell her that all you want. It's not going to change anything. You're the Relic Hunter."

He started to laugh, but she wasn't wrong. She didn't have to do the job. He did.

Which made it all the more difficult for him.

He flashed a smile. "Come on, Fralia. It's not so bad."

She looked over. "It's not all bad? No. It's worse."

The wind howled, and they picked their way along the path, falling into a comfortable silence.

It was late on the third day after leaving the encampment when they found a streamer of smoke swirling against the wind. The air was biting and cold, but so far, they hadn't seen any snow. Hal considered that a victory, especially given that with as cold as it was, it wouldn't take much for snow to fall, which would make it even more difficult to make their way up.

When he pointed, Fralia nodded, but her pace picked up.

They reached what was little more than a shack and stopped in front of it. He looked to Fralia. "We haven't seen much."

"You mean other than the abandoned homes that we have passed on our way here?"

Hal shrugged. There had been three such buildings so far, so not enough to be much of a pattern, but certainly enough to make it clear that anybody who had lived here had decided that it wasn't worth the struggle. One of the homes looked as if it had been recently abandoned, though it had been cleaned of furniture — probably burned for warmth, Hal had figured — and had no personal belongings. One of the buildings had been made of stone, and when they had come upon that one, Hal had thought that maybe it was the temple they were assigned to find, but it was too small, something that temples were almost universally not. Besides, there were no markings on it, and as he had picked his way through the stone rubble, he had found no sign of anything to suggest that it was the temple.

"At least this one looks occupied," Hal said.

He stepped toward the door, following a path leading toward it, and paused. The door was a stout wood, though the rest of the building was made of stone. It was small, cozy even, and the smell of smoke drifting up gave off a comforting aroma.

Considering what they had gone through, he thought that having a warm place to stay might not be the worst thing in the world. Besides, maybe whoever was here could point them in the right direction.

Before he had a chance to knock, the door came open.

A thin, elderly looking man looked out at them. He had wild gray hair, and his wide eyes stared at them, first at Fralia, and then at Hal. "What are you doing out here? Did you come to rob me of my chickens?"

Hal resisted the urge to look over to Fralia. "I don't know anything about chickens. We didn't see any, so I don't know what to say if they have turned up missing, but we aren't at all interested in them. We are just travelers, looking for a warm place, if you could be so kind. We can pay."

He had a little discretionary money that the general provided for such circumstances, though it was unusual for him to actually have need of spending it. Most people were accommodating, especially when they found out that they served the crown.

The old man looked over to them, before wrinkling his brow. "How much?"

"I can offer you five coppers," he said.

The man scoffed and started to close the door. "Not worth my warmth for that. I can't even buy a chicken."

Hal looked over to Fralia. "How about a silver?"

"I suppose for a silver, I can make sure that you have a place to sleep, but I won't have enough food for you. Now, if you have a couple silvers…"

"I do," Fralia said.

Hal wanted to caution her against spending her own money, but Fralia was stubborn, and likely wouldn't be deterred.

"Fine," the old man said. "Come in. You can't let the wind in, because you'll never get it out."

He waved for them to step inside, and Fralia followed with Hal only a few steps behind.

The inside of the home was every bit as cozy as the exterior seemed to have promised. A warmth radiated outward, and Hal immediately let out a relieved breath. Maybe he had been colder than he had let on. He shivered and pulled his cloak around him as he followed Fralia into the home. It was simple. There was a table, a stove with what looked like a boiling pot of water or hopefully something more on it, a hearth — which was where the warmth radiated from — and several chairs all lined up near the hearth. A single room led off of the main part of the home, where Hal suspected the old man's room was.

"I've got some stew. Now, I can't have you eating too

much, as I don't have that much to share, but I'm perfectly content to let you have a bowlful."

He made his way over to the stovetop and scooped out a bowl of thick stew. He handed it to Fralia, who took it and waited until Hal was given his own bowl. He looked up at the man. "Let me guess. Chicken?"

The man snorted. "I don't eat the chickens. I need them for their eggs. Rabbit."

Hal took a seat at the table, took the spoon offered to him, and began to hungrily eat. They had food that they had packed, but nothing hot like this, and though the vegetables were a bit stringy, much like the rabbit, it still tasted perfect.

"What are the pair of you doing up here?"

Hal finished his bite before resting his arms on the table and glancing over to Fralia. "I'm sorry. We were so hungry that we forgot our manners. I'm Hal Norath, and this is Fralia Jeniq. We are working on behalf of the Queen Bariwa and have been sent here to investigate an ancient temple."

The old man looked at them. "You don't look much like a Hal. Besides, what kind of name is that, anyway?" He turned to Fralia before Hal had a chance to respond. "And what is a Jeniq?"

"That's my family name."

"I see. Well, interesting enough. You can call me Old Snow."

"We can?" Fralia asked, a hint of a smile playing on her lips. "You don't have another name that you'd like us to call you?"

"Not any longer. Do you have any other name that you'd like me to call you?"

"I wouldn't mind the Great and Powerful Fralia Jeniq traveling along with her annoying sidekick Halar."

Old Snow looked over to Hal. "That's a better name. Why don't you go by that?"

"Well, it is my name," he said.

Old Snow snorted, pounded the table, and got to his feet. "Can't say that I know much about what you're looking for. Can't say that I don't, either." He looked over, and a hint of a smile curled his lips. "But if you keep climbing, you can follow a path around to the west side of the mountain as you make your way along the Tops, and maybe you'll find something there. Plenty of old temples and ruins there. This place was once a bit different, you know."

"Well, we don't really know," Fralia said.

She was always better with people than he was, especially people like Old Snow, somebody who seemed more crazed than sane. Hal figured that it might just be better for her to take the lead here. And she was usually perfectly content doing so.

"Oh, place like this has history. Even this home has a history, though you could probably tell that just by looking at it."

"You didn't build it?"

"You think I could build this? I'm an old man, Jeniq."

"My name is Fralia. My last name is Jeniq."

Old Snow laughed, waving his hands before scrubbing them through his hair. His eyes widened even more, making him look fully crazed. "That's right. You go on and tell me what to call you."

"You were saying about your home?"

Hal shot her a look. She was actually encouraging him.

She suppressed a smile. She had to know just what it was that she was doing, and likely enjoyed every bit of it. Mostly because Hal was forced to sit through it alongside her.

"An old place. It was something of a fortress, though it's changed over the years. Didn't have this kitchen. Had the hearth," he said, waving his hand over to it. "And the roof was once a bit more stout. Had to be, given what it was built to withstand." He flapped his arms and danced around.

Hal looked over to Fralia. "He's crazy," he mouthed.

"I like him," she whispered. She turned to Old Snow. "You were saying? Your home was meant to withstand dragon attacks?"

"Oh, I don't know. Maybe it was meant to house dragons. They could roost here, you know."

"I would imagine dragons like warmer weather," Hal said.

Old Snow stopped moving, everything within him going suddenly still, and he turned his attention to Hal. "Do you know dragons?"

Hal started to smile. "I don't, and am quite thankful that I don't. I can't imagine what it might be like to run across one. Probably terrifying."

Old Snow nodded, and he scrubbed his hand through his hair again, before moving his arms as if he were a dragon trying to take flight. "Terrifying. But could you imagine having that fire?" He stopped and went to the stovetop, and then to the hearth. "Now I'm tired. You can sleep. Don't let the chickens out."

He headed to the back room, leaving Hal and Fralia standing and looking at each other. Fralia grinned, though of course she would. She probably thought this was all too amusing.

"We should get some rest. We don't want to let the chickens out."

Hal took her bowl, and he stacked it in the wash-basin. He took a seat in one of the chairs near the hearth and rested his head. It didn't take long before he was asleep. When he awoke, Fralia was sitting next to him. He got to his feet, went to the door, and pulled it open to see the daylight had started to break, before waking Fralia. He checked for any signs of Old Snow, but the old man was not anywhere to be found.

"Maybe he's checking on his chickens," she said with a smirk.

"We should go." He started toward the door, when Fralia shook her head.

"We told him that we would pay."

Hal wanted to argue, but she wasn't wrong. The kindness of strangers, and the locals, was how they managed to survive for as long as they had. He couldn't betray that trust, even to a crazy old man like Old Snow.

"Let me cover this one," he said.

"Good," Fralia said, pulling open the door and stepping outside. "I was going to let you."

He stacked the coins on the table and looked around

the home, before joining Fralia outside. The wind had settled down somewhat and wasn't nearly as violent as it had been earlier. They started up the mountainside, and at one point, he saw a scurrying of movement and turned to see a chicken darting off into the brush. He laughed.

"Look at that. He wasn't lying about the chickens."

"Did you let them out?"

"Would you stop?"

Fralia grinned. They picked their way forward, and when they found the path splitting, he remembered what Old Snow had said. "Do you think he knew where we should go?"

"Well, I get the sense that he's lived up here a while. Probably on his own," Fralia said. "People like that tend to know the area. You have to. And besides, that side of the mountain is likely to be shielded from the wind. It would be the more sensible place to build a temple."

"No place up here is a sensible place to build a temple," Hal said.

"You might be right."

"And no place up here is sensible to keep chickens."

Fralia started to laugh. "I bet they don't like the cold."

"Let's get this over with. Find the relic and get back to the encampment. I'm ready to return home and have a little rest time."

"I don't know," Fralia said. "The last two assignments have been very unpleasant. It wouldn't surprise me if we were given another one as unfortunate as this one."

"You could always talk to your father."

Her brow furrowed. "He doesn't answer. And I'm not going to involve him in this, anyway. Let's get going. I want to find this temple just as much as you do. Mostly because I want to get out of the cold and back someplace warm."

"Maybe Old Snow will welcome us on our way back down."

"Why do you think I wanted you to pay him?"

The wind suddenly whistled, and he pulled his cloak tight around him again, trying—and failing—to ignore the bite of the wind.

Chapter Four

As Hal walked among the crumbling remains of the grounds surrounding the Forgotten Temple, he found himself wondering, again, what sort of god had been worshiped here. He saw no statues, no idols, no altars or symbols to indicate who the object of worship here had been.

The once paved ground was rocky and uneven from lack of proper care, forcing Hal to tread carefully. And although he didn't think there were any dragons here, the place was not entirely devoid of living things. A mountain snake eyed him beadily before slithering into a pothole. He gave it a wide berth; his last bite had taken him out of action for a week. The descent from the Tops was perilous, and he doubted Fralia had the skill to airlift a diamond down without it ending up in pieces.

Like father always used to say, Hal thought as he approached the tower, *it's okay to make mistakes, but it's* not *okay to make the same mistakes twice in a row.*

Hal sighed at the thought of his dad. Ten years. It had been ten years since his dad had died, but it still felt like yesterday to him. He didn't cry as much anymore, but a swell of emotion would rise up in his chest anytime Dad's old sayings popped into his head. But Hal had learned to control his emotions and pushed them down. He'd already mourned his father enough at this point.

And if I want to make sure that other peoples' fathers don't keep dying in this awful war, then I need to get as many relics as I can, Hal thought.

With renewed determination, Hal made his way across the rocky, barren landscape, passing empty building after empty building, ignoring the dark-gray clouds in the distance. They didn't have much time remaining before the storms hit, so he knew he needed to move quickly. Then he reached the front doors of the Forgotten Temple itself.

Up close, the building looked even worse than it did from afar. Most of the windows had been busted out, while much of its outer facade had been stripped away entirely, revealing the old, crumbly stone support structure underneath, essentially the building's skeleton. Hal assumed that the Forgotten Temple must have had a gold or silver exterior, which had probably been stripped by robbers in the years since the Temple was abandoned.

Or, more likely, dragons have stripped it, Hal thought with a scowl. *Stripped it of its gold and silver to add to their hoards. Seems like the sort of thing a dragon would do.*

The doors were made of wood, rather than stone, and they were missing their handles. Hal assumed those had been stolen by human thieves, if the handles had been made of some sort of precious metals as well. Hal's relic hunting had taken him to many places all over the kingdom, and most of these places had been stripped of anything of value by various thieves and robbers. He had yet to find ruins that had been left intact.

Even out here, the dragons and thieves have no respect for our ancestors and their work, Hal thought, rubbing the stubble on his chin that he had not bothered to shave yet. *Greed, it seems, has no limit.*

Shaking his head, Hal walked up to the doors and tried to push them open. They wouldn't budge at first, partly due to old age, partly because of the building's angle, which meant they were pressing against each other.

So Hal stepped back and looked for another way in. He immediately spotted an open window to the right of the doors. It was a little high up for him, but part of the Malarsan Army's training involved scaling large, seemingly impossible surfaces. He was able to climb through the window with ease.

The broken window allowed a single stream of daylight to enter, illuminating a wall of holes where torches had also been stolen from. He pulled out his own torch and, banging it against the wall, was answered with a roar of flame as the fire on his torch came to life in his hands. Raising the torch high above his head, Hal was astonished by what he saw.

The Forgotten Temple's central lobby was bigger than it had looked on the outside. A sprawling marble floor, pockmarked with holes and burn marks, supported what appeared to be ancient statues of mythical creatures. Some of the statues had been knocked off their pedestals, shattering to pieces against the floor, while others were missing heads, tails, and other assorted body parts that would have helped Hal identify them, though he felt grateful that he couldn't. He found the statues disturbing for some reason he could not quite articulate, and he was glad that Fralia wasn't with him, otherwise, she might see him trembling and tease him about it.

What really disturbed Hal were the human skeletons lying underneath many of the fallen statues. They were mostly adult-sized, their clothing disintegrated, other than a few scraps of leather armor and metal helmets. The soft stench of dirt and long-decayed bodies entered his nostrils.

What happened here? Hal waved his torch back and forth to try to see more of the area. *Was the temple abandoned because of … this?*

Hal's curiosity was definitely piqued, but he was reminded that his job title was Relic Hunter, not physical historian, when his torch reflected off of something shiny in the darkness ahead.

The relic. Hal's pulse quickened with excitement at the thought.

Deciding that whatever had killed the humans was probably long gone at this point, Hal made his way across the massive floor toward the center of the room. The relic in question was sitting on a stone altar covered in a thick layer of moss, and just like Old Snow had said, the relic was a helmet.

But Old Snow didn't *say that the helmet looked like a dragon's head.*

The top parts stuck out like dragon ears while the helmet itself was elongated into a snout. The front part was open with a chin strap hanging underneath it. He briefly checked behind the altar but found nothing except another altar with a stone bowl full of worthless sticks standing atop it.

Hal picked up the old relic. Despite being made of metal, it was warm, although Hal was not surprised by that. The relics, despite being thousands of years old, were all said to have been crafted from dragon bones and steel. That explained why they allowed humans to control dragons, though Hal suspected they were magically enchanted as well.

Either way, he couldn't wait to show it to Fralia and see the look on her face when she realized that the crazy old man living by himself in the Desolate Tops hadn't been so crazy after all.

Mages never get humiliated enough, in my opinion. Hal turned around, intending to leave through the way he came. *And Fralia definitely deserves to be knocked down a—*

Hal's thoughts were interrupted by movement in the shadows just beyond the ring of light from his torch. There was a sound of claws against stone. And then a dragon stepped into the light.

His mission had just gotten a *lot* harder.

Chapter Five

HAL HAD NEVER SEEN A DRAGON IN PERSON BEFORE, BUT he knew not to expect this. Dragons were bigger than his cottage, they'd said. Some were as big as mountains. The creature before him was… small.

Not tiny, by any means, but this dragon was only about as tall as a horse. Perhaps he was mistaken and this was some kind of overgrown lizard rather than a dragon. He'd heard of the king lizards of the Southern Plains, creatures said to prey upon unwary travelers and their horses, but he didn't think they traveled this far north.

Then Hal spotted the dragon's golden-yellow scales, its far-too-intelligent bright green eyes, and especially its wings, which were currently folded against its body. Its claws were as sharp as knives, and wisps of smoke rose from its nostrils. Its spiked tail lay on the floor behind it, barely visible behind its bulk. The creature seemed to be watching Hal as carefully as he was watching it.

No doubt about it: This was a real-life dragon.

But why is it so small? Hal thought. *Is it still a fledgling or something? And if it is, does that mean its mother is somewhere close by?*

Hal shuddered at the thought of running into a mother dragon. They were said to be the fiercest of all, at least when their young were threatened or in danger. He dared a glance around the room.

How in the world did that thing sneak up on me? Hal thought. *Or maybe it was always here? Perhaps this is its den and I woke it up somehow. If so, why hasn't it killed me yet?*

Of course, if it was a fledgling, like Hal thought, then maybe it didn't have the same instinctive hatred of humans that all dragons were said to have. It might not even know what to *do* when stumbling upon an intruder in its nest. If so, that gave Hal time to figure out his options.

I could fight it, Hal thought, aware of his sword sheathed at his side and his shield hanging on his back. *It's small enough that I might even be able to win or at least scare it off.*

That would be stupid. While all Malarsan soldiers were given basic training in anti-dragon combat techniques, Hal still had no experience fighting them. He'd heard plenty of stories from the older soldiers about how even baby dragons could still be a threat. In particular, he was thinking of a story where a war mage ran headlong into a seemingly unprotected dragon nest all by himself, only to get slaughtered by the ravenous newborns in a gory fashion.

No, Hal thought. *I'm not a dragon hunter, but a Relic Hunter. The point of my mission is to get this relic out of here safe and sound. And for the sake of the kingdom, I* cannot *fail this mission.*

As if reading his thoughts, the dragon's eyes darted down to the relic in Hal's hands. The dragon snorted, sending up a few more clouds of smoke.

It occurred to Hal that he did not know when baby dragons developed the ability to breathe fire.

But how do I flee?

It seemed that Hal's best option was to distract the fledgling and then make a break for the window he'd used to enter the Temple. Food might work, and he had just the thing.

Before Hal could pull out the salted meats from his pocket, however, the dragon rushed toward him. It moved surprisingly fast for a creature of its size, smoke streaming from its nostrils.

Without hesitation, without thinking it through, Hal lifted the dragon helmet relic and slammed it onto his head.

The second the relic touched his head, Hal felt a strange jolt of power shoot through him. He groaned. The initial jolt—similar to being struck by lightning—had passed, and suddenly, a sense of mastery fell over Hal that he'd never felt before.

The dragon was more than halfway toward him now. If anything, it sped up when he put on the relic, a seemingly worried expression crossing its reptilian features.

It knows, Hal thought. *It knows what I'm wearing. And how it is going to lose.*

Remembering what his relic mentor had taught him, Hal focused intensely on the dragon rushing toward him.

He delved deep into his heart's desire to *control* the creature, to make it his own, to make it *stop*.

Then he felt a shudder of power leave him, and a tendril of energy lanced out from his head toward the dragon. The tendril connected to the dragon's forehead, causing it to come to a complete stop less than five feet away from him. The dragon became as still as a statue, save for its eyes, which moved and blinked in fear and confusion at what was happening.

Hal couldn't blame it. He, too, was not entirely sure what was going on. His relic hunting training had focused more on finding and gathering relics, not actually using them.

Perhaps that was why Hal felt an irresistible desire to look into the dragon's eyes. The dragon must have been compelled by the same unknown force, because it, too, met his gaze.

And the second Hal and the dragon's eyes met, Hal's world changed.

Gone was the chamber of the Forgotten Temple. Hal was standing in a cave. The floor was covered in tree branches smeared with blood. Bones were strewn amongst fallen leaves.

At the center of the nest, six young dragons circled a seventh. It was smaller than the rest, its yellow wings underdeveloped. A sleek black dragon with red eyes stepped forward and slashed the yellow one, which yelped and staggered to the floor.

The scene changed, and Hal stood on a cliff. Half a dozen dragons soared through the rocky valley below.

The yellow dragon paced beside him, its scales now

tinged with gold. After a moment's deliberation, it launched itself through the air, wings flapping desperately to stay afloat. But it was plummeting too swiftly.

Hal winced and braced for it to smash into the boulders below. Instead, his surroundings reshaped themselves, and he was in a cave once more.

A reddish-white dragon slept amongst a pile of gold, its body larger than the cottage Hal had grown up in. The smaller yellow dragon briefly opened a sleepy eye before nuzzling into its mother's red-veined wing.

Memories flew past Hal like scattered paper. A lifetime of loneliness, breeze, and forest filled his heart.

Then he was back in the temple.

Hal did not, however, fall forever and ever. His eyes snapped open and he found himself face-to-face with the yellow dragon, which lay on the floor of the Temple less than a foot from him.

Startled, Hal rolled away from the yellow dragon and sat up. The dragon shook its head and slowly rose to its feet. Hal reached for his sword, but just as he rested his hand on the hilt, the dragon opened its mouth and spoke a single word.

"Stop."

Hal froze. Maybe it was the shock of hearing the dragon speak the Mara tongue—the primary language of the Kingdom of Malarsan—or maybe it was some sort of spell cast by the dragon itself. Could dragons even *cast* spells?

He gripped the rough leather handle of his sword and, drawing it out in one smooth motion, rushed toward the dragon, yelling at the top of his lungs, hoping to startle it before it could react.

The dragon leaped backward, well outside of Hal's range, just as Hal brought his sword down on where the dragon had been standing previously. The sword clinked uselessly against the stone floor, but Hal pulled it up and held it before him defensively again.

"Are you afraid of me, beast?" Hal demanded, glaring at the dragon. "If so, then perhaps you should go back to the cave you crawled out of."

"I'm not afraid of you," said the dragon. Although its words were surprisingly clear, there was still a distinct, inhuman growl underlining them. "But I don't want to kill you, either."

Hal raised his sword up to shoulder height, pointing the blade directly at the dragon. "Then why did you charge me earlier? And how do I know this isn't some kind of draconic trick to make me lower my guard?"

The dragon raised one of its front claws as if trying to reassure Hal. "Trust me, Halar Norath, if I wanted you dead, you'd be nothing but blackened bones and melted flesh right now."

Hal's eyes widened. "How do you know my name? I didn't tell you that."

The dragon blinked. "You mean, you don't sense our bond? Listen closely to your soul and you will see. You will even find out my name that way."

Hal scowled. "Listen to my soul—? I didn't realize you dragons spoke such silly riddles."

"It is not a riddle," the dragon insisted. "Close your

eyes and listen. And, because I know you don't trust me, I'll even turn around so I am not facing you."

To Hal's surprise, the dragon turned its spiked back to him.

This would be an excellent opportunity to attack it while it's not looking. Hal gripped his sword tighter than ever. *Strike it in the back and cripple, or maybe even kill, it. I'd get revenge for what those monsters did to my dad all those years ago.*

Yet Hal's sense of honor did not like doing a sneak attack on an enemy who had already kept his word. One of the virtues taught to soldiers of the Malarsan Army was that they were to behave honorably to everyone, even to their enemies. Granted, such rules were usually lifted during conflicts with dragons, but Hal thought this dragon wasn't quite like the others.

Hal closed his eyes without lowering his sword and did his best to 'listen' to his soul. He didn't quite know what that meant, but decided to just focus and meditate. He felt a bit foolish at first, as he heard nothing in his soul, and he also felt defenseless, worried that any second now Keershan would turn around and attack him.

Wait a second … *Keershan*?

Yes, that was the dragon's name. Keershan Clawfoot. Hal knew that as well as he knew his own name, but he didn't know how he'd learned it. Keershan certainly hadn't introduced himself during their short conversation.

Does that mean Keershan is right? Maybe he even knows how we both learned each other's names without telling each other. Worth an ask.

Hal opened his eyes and found himself face-to-face with Keershan again.

Acting strictly on instinct, Hal swung his sword at the dragon's face. The dragon ducked and backed away quickly, an alarmed and sheepish expression on its dragonic features.

"What the hell was that about?" Hal demanded, pointing his sword at Keershan again. "Did you *want* me to gore your eye out? Or did you think you could sneak up on me and get me while I wasn't looking, Keershan Clawfoot?"

Keershan held up another claw. "So sorry. I just didn't know if you'd fallen asleep or—Wait, did you use my name?"

Hal nodded, though without smiling. "Yes. And I don't know how."

Keershan gaped at Hal for a second, which was a rather comical expression on a dragon, before his face split into a big smile and he clacked his teeth together excitedly. "It worked! The legends are true. There is hope for the world after all."

Hal stepped back in alarm. "What worked? What legends are you talking about? And what hope for the world?"

Keershan, who had been flapping his wings in excitement, suddenly stopped and looked at Hal apologetically. "Sorry. I forget that very few dragons know about the old myths and even fewer humans do. I should start from the beginning. And when I say the beginning, I mean the Fall. The event that separated humanity and dragonkind and led to the eternal war between our once-united species. Legend says it happened about five thousand years ago. And I even have some proof."

Keershan raised his head and started spitting fire at the walls, lighting the few torches that had not already been stolen by thieves. One fireball even soared over Hal's head and struck the bundle of deadwood set in the stone bowl he'd noticed earlier. The fire behind Hal roared to life.

But it was not the fire, swelteringly hot and bright, that caught Hal's attention. His eyes were drawn to the murals on the walls of the Forgotten Temple all around him. The murals were old and many of them had faded to nonexistence, but most of them were surprisingly well-preserved.

They showed humans riding dragons. They were rather simplistic drawings, admittedly, but he couldn't deny the images they displayed. He saw a male human wearing a helmet very similar to the relic on his head sitting atop a golden dragon with half a dozen similar human and dragon pairings behind him. The human and dragon duos were flying into battle against strange furry black creatures that looked like a mixture of bears and goats with bat-like wings protruding from their backs.

Similar murals covered the other walls as well. Painted depictions of humans and dragons walking and living side by side, and an ancient human king sitting in a throne room with a large green dragon by his side. Images of humans protecting dragon eggs and dragons defending baby humans from predators and more of those frightening beasts above. Even an image of a dragon that had obviously died in battle, surrounded by humans who were clearly holding a funeral for it, their heads lowered and hands clasped together in some sort of group prayer.

"What …" Hal's breath caught in his throat. "What am I looking at, Keershan?"

"You are looking at the *true* history of our people," said Keershan in a serious voice. "The hidden history of the Dragon Riders."

Chapter Six

FRALIA DID NOT LIKE WAITING.

As a child, Fralia had often been praised for her patience by her father—at least when he wasn't too busy being the army's greatest war hero. Fralia had always been able to patiently wait for things, including presents, days off from her mage lessons, and so on. Her teachers and mentors had often noted it on their reports to her father or would even outright mention it to him in person when they spoke with him. It helped that patience was the Virtue of her patron goddess, Waroness, which made it even easier for her to practice that Virtue.

But there was a difference between being patient and liking waiting. Fralia had always told herself that waiting for something meant something would eventually come, and so she would just not worry about it unless it was late or something.

But Fralia did not like waiting right now. It wasn't just

the storm threatening in the distance—though that irritated her as well. She did *not* want to get drenched on the journey back. It was more that Hal had been gone for nearly half an hour at this point. She'd seen him disappear into the ruins of the Forgotten Temple below and had not heard anything from him since. She was even considering using her communication necklace to find out how he was doing, even though doing so risked drawing attention to him.

Come on, Fralia. She brushed her dark hair out of her eyes. *He's clearly another one of those macho soldiers who obviously doesn't need the help of a useless bookworm like you. Definitely the type who thinks he can solve all his problems with his sword and his muscles and doesn't understand that magic is the main reason the dragons haven't burned the entire kingdom to ashes yet.*

A cold blast of wind shot through just then, making Fralia shiver and pull her green mage robes tighter around her body. It was times like these that she wished her Affinity had been fire, rather than air. Fire mages had higher body temperatures than mages of the other five Affinities, which meant they could handle both cold and hot weather better than most people.

Fralia, however, was an air mage. While that came with plenty of its own advantages—such as enhanced speed, the ability to create mini tornadoes, and even fly at higher levels—air mages were infamous for being more fragile. They tended to be less tolerant of extreme weather, which meant they had a reputation for being the weakest Affinity of the six.

I should have brought my winter robes this time, but how was I supposed to know it'd be so cold today up in the Tops?

She remembered, cringing, that her mentor, Deman Ulto, had stressed the importance of using air magic to study the weather and get an idea of what the weather would be like in a given area over the next couple of days. Unfortunately, Fralia had always struggled with that aspect of air magic. Her fellow students teased that she couldn't predict snow while standing neck-deep in it.

Not my fault the weather likes to change its mind on a whim. I just can't wait until we're back in an actual city. Or heck, even the Outpost would be better than this.

In fact, the weather was Fralia's biggest concern. Heavy storm clouds were gathering, and the temperature in the Tops dropped correspondingly. Even Fralia could tell that it would not be long before the rain started.

That's it. Fralia reached for her communication necklace. *Unless Hal wants to camp among the ruins tonight, I need to find out what he's doing before we get caught in a thunderstorm.*

That was when Fralia heard, above the roaring wind and rumbling thunder overhead, the sound of hooves clopping against the rough stone ground of the hill she stood upon. Turning around to see who it was, Fralia frowned.

Several Malarsan soldiers—bearing the army's flag, which depicted a sword thrust into the skull of a screaming dragon—were marching up the hill toward her. They rode on warhorses and wore steel armor that was designed to protect them from dragonfire. Yet their armor was a strange black color, instead of the usual green and silver soldiers of the Malarsan Army typically wore.

The dragonfireproof armor seemed odd to Fralia, but she forgot about it when she spotted a seventh figure riding among the soldiers.

The figure was smaller than the soldiers and wore a thick, heavy-looking black cloak instead of armor. His horse was also smaller, darker, and more sickly-looking than the warhorses, yet it kept up with no issue. Only the figure's hands, thin, skeletal, and deathly pale, could be seen, gripping the reins of its steed with surprising tightness.

Fralia instinctively created a pocket of air between her and the man. As the soldiers had already seen her, Fralia saw no reason to hide. She held out her hand in greeting.

The small band of soldiers, plus their mystery escort, stopped several feet away from her. The lead soldier—a middle-aged man with an eyepatch over his right eye—nodded at her. "Greetings, young air mage. Identify yourself and your purpose for being here."

Fralia was taken off-guard by the soldier's unexpectedly harsh tone. It reminded her too much of her father. "I'm Fralia Jeniq, escort to Halar Norath, who's searching for a relic in these ruins."

The lead soldier raised an eyebrow. "Jeniq? Any relation to General Kolass?"

"He's my father."

The soldiers shifted, though the hooded man appeared distracted by the ruins below.

"It's an honor," the lead soldier smiled. "My name is Lieutenant Ajon Bana. We were given direct orders from Queen Bariwa herself to escort this man here to these ruins, but we did not know a Relic Hunter was in the area."

One of the soldiers behind Lieutenant Bana, who had a ferret-like face, snorted. "You mean those 'soldiers' who go around playing treasure hunter all day while the rest of us do the *real* work of fighting dragons? What a joke."

Fralia raised an eyebrow. She had believed that some soldiers were jealous of the Relic Hunters. She'd always assumed that most soldiers wanted to be Relic Hunters due to the importance and prestige of the job. Then again, Fralia rarely interacted with non-magical soldiers.

But Lieutenant Bana waved dismissively at the soldier behind him. "Calm, Surrels. Relic Hunters may not be on the front lines fighting against the dragon menace, but that does not mean the role they play is unimportant or even easy. Very few relics even still exist, after all, and most that do are in out-of-the-way locations such as this."

Fralia nodded, looking at Lieutenant Bana curiously. "You seem very well-informed about the relics, Lieutenant."

Lieutenant Bana shrugged. "I once applied to become a Relic Hunter. I even got as far as the practical exam, but didn't meet the high expectations of my instructors."

Fralia nodded again. She found herself liking the Lieutenant. He seemed a reasonable man, although a small voice in the back of her head still warned her about this troop. Or, rather, about the mysterious hooded man on the sickly horse beside Lieutenant Bana, who had been as silent and still as a statue the whole time. His gaze was still fixed on the ruins behind Fralia.

"So you are on a quest from the queen?" asked Fralia, impressed. She looked at the hooded man. "May I ask your name, sir?"

The hooded man finally turned his face toward her. Instinctively, Fralia wanted to step away from the man as soon as he looked at her, but she didn't.

Then Lieutenant Bana and his horse stepped in between Fralia and the hooded man.

"Apologies, Mage Jeniq," said Lieutenant Bana in the same polite, professional tone he'd been using this entire time. "But our guest is a shadow agent of the queen whose identity—and mission—must remain a secret. Can you share with us the approximate location of the Relic Hunter?"

Instinct told her to lie and point somewhere else. She didn't know *why*, though, other than it had something to do with the silent hooded man.

Stop listening to your easily frightened instincts, Fralia. Just because he looks like one of the demons of old doesn't mean he is. If he's an agent of the queen, then he must be good.

Steeling herself, Fralia pointed at the Forgotten Temple which dominated the center of the ruins. "There. He should be in that building, searching for a relic reported to be in this area."

Lieutenant Bana nodded and glanced over his shoulder. "Did you hear that, Hood? The Relic Hunter is—"

But Hood was nowhere to be seen. Only his horse remained standing where it was, though now it was pawing at the dirt, looking for grass to eat.

The stench of blood-soaked mud filled Fralia's nostrils briefly, and she thought she felt *something* pass her. She looked over her shoulder in time to see a formless dark shape moving down the hill and across the rocks with the grace and speed of a living shadow. The dark shape disappeared into the ruins, heading toward the Temple in the middle.

Lieutenant Bana chuckled. "Looks like Hood is already on the move. He's very impatient, that one, and quiet, too."

Unnaturally quiet, Fralia thought, but did not say that aloud.

Instead, Fralia said aloud, "So you think Hal will be safe? He doesn't know you guys are here, you know."

Lieutenant Bana gave Fralia a surprisingly cool smile. "So long as the Relic Hunter does not interfere with Hood's quest, he should be just fine. Do you have some way of communicating with him to let him know that Hood is coming his way?"

Fralia glanced at the communication necklace hanging off her neck. "We have a two-way communication necklace. I'll give him a glow and let him know Hood's coming."

As Fralia stepped away from the soldiers—who fell into chatting and gossiping with each other now that they had nothing better to do—Fralia did not say the word she had really meant to say. She had said she would 'let

Hal know' about Hood, but she *meant* that she'd warn him.

Because, despite Lieutenant Bana's assertions that Hood was working for the queen and was of no threat to either her or Hal, Fralia's instincts were screaming at her that Hal was in trouble.

Chapter Seven

HAL LOOKED OVER HIS SHOULDER IN SURPRISE AT Keershan. "The Dragon Riders? What are you talking about?"

"Legend has many names for the Dragon Riders, but that is the name they are best known by. They were the perfect unity of human and dragon, forming relationships between the human Rider and his dragon Steed that would last a lifetime, almost like a marriage bond, but not quite."

Hal turned to face Keershan, still pointing his sword at the dragon. "Back up, dragon. Why would any human even attempt to form some kind of relationship with a dragon? For that matter, why would a dragon feel the need to become a human's mount?"

Keershan gestured with his head at the paintings on the walls of the Forgotten Temple. "Five thousand years ago, humans and dragons were once friends. A threat to humanity was considered a threat to dragonkind, and vice versa."

Hal stared at Keershan in utter disbelief. "Humans and dragons. Friends."

Keershan nodded quickly. "I know how crazy it sounds, but trust me, it's—"

"The biggest load of dragon shit I've ever heard," Hal interrupted. He took a step forward. "If we were friends, why would your kind slaughter so many innocent people? Why would you dragons kill parents' children or leave their children without … without their parents?"

Hal had a hard time saying that last sentence. He kept seeing his father's identification tags, the only thing that survived his body being burned to ashes. He saw his mom on her knees at the entrance to their house, bawling her eyes out while he tried to comfort her as best as a fifteen-year-old boy who had just lost his father could. Even the smell of the chicken soup they had been about to have for dinner that night was still strong in his memory as if carved in stone. And so was the vow he'd made that day, that when he grew up, he'd avenge his father. He'd find the dragon and end its sorry life.

Before Hal could take even one step further, however, Keershan gave him an apologetic look. "I am sorry about your father, Hal, but I didn't kill him."

Hal froze. "My father …? How did you know about him? I didn't even mention—"

Keershan tapped the side of his head with his left front claw. "Because we're bonded, remember? I saw everything, Hal, as you saw all of *my* pivotal life moments."

Hal remembered those three strange visions he'd had of the dragon runt that had been bullied by its siblings, but he didn't realize … "That was you?"

"It was said that certain humans could form special bonds with a particular dragon that were deeper than that of a mere rider and his mount. By wearing special relics, humans and dragons could form psychic and spiritual links with each other that would allow them to know each other's thoughts and feelings, work together as one, and even supposedly gain unique powers and abilities."

"Like magic?" Hal said. He scowled. "Sorry to disappoint, but I'm Affinity-less."

"But that's the amazing part," Keershan said. "According to legends, humans did not need an Affinity to access these abilities. It's less clear about what dragons got out of the deal, though my current research suggests that dragons may have learned the ability to speak human languages through these bonds. Either way, it was a mutually beneficial relationship, and such humans were called Dragon Riders, while the dragons they rode upon were called Steeds."

Hal's eyes narrowed. "Dragon Riders … I've never heard of them."

"Nor have most dragons," said Keershan. He winced. "And they don't *like* hearing about them, either. Trust me on that one."

That was when Hal noticed a rather thick scar running along Keershan's face. It went from the top of his head to his jaw and looked like it must have been a terrible wound before it healed. "I believe you."

"Dragons are … prideful," said Keershan, "and we

don't like being told we let humans ride us. But like I said, it wasn't some kind of master and slave or even human and horse relationship. It was more like a really deep friendship, and it couldn't work if one or the other tried to dominate or control their partner.

"Why all the war and conflict and … and death?"

"Hal, do you see those demons?" Keershan was looking at the paintings of the bear and bat creatures. "They were evil creatures said to have crawled up from the darkest depths of our world's core, with the intent of spreading misery, hatred, war, death, and disease wherever they go. They invaded the surface world ages ago and would have conquered the entire planet if not for the combined efforts of humanity and dragonkind who killed their god, the Nameless One."

The darkness seemed to become a little blacker when Keershan mentioned the Nameless One, and even Hal shivered slightly. "The Dragon Riders killed a god?"

"Only after a long, grueling fight in which hundreds of brave Dragon Riders and their Steeds perished," said Keershan grimly. "After, the human and dragon army was able to wipe out the remaining leaderless demons. But it wasn't a happy ending, because, with his dying breath, the Nameless One cast a curse on both humanity and dragonkind. No one knows what words he used—at least, I haven't been able to find a source—but the gist is clear: The Nameless One cursed humanity and dragonkind to turn against each other and wage war perpetually for as long as either species continued to exist."

Hal glanced at the demon paintings on the walls.

"You expect me to believe that humans and dragons were separated by a curse?"

"Curses are not unheard of," said Keershan, "and demonic curses are supposed to be the worst. His words seeped into the hearts and minds of the remaining Dragon Riders, who eventually turned against their Steeds, which caused a domino effect over human and dragonkind. And things have been that way ever since."

"Even the most highly-educated mages in the Hallowed Halls have never mentioned this history. Is this what you dragons tell each other?"

Keershan lowered his head to the floor, looking a bit like a dejected puppy. "Actually, dragons don't believe this, either. That's why I came out this way to territory that even the other dragons don't care about. The others … they have a similar attitude toward you regarding the idea that dragons ever let icky human beings ride them like some kind of horse. And some of them get so offended they get violent."

Hal again took notice of Keershan's facial scar. "So you're an outcast among dragons, then."

Keershan nodded, still without raising his head. "I wouldn't be so blunt about it, but yes. Most dragons are too focused on hunting, survival, reproduction, and killing humans to research anything. Research, in general, isn't held very highly among my kind. They think that because we dragons live ten times as long as humans, we can just pass down any important information orally. But even our ancestors kept records and left paintings and statues, although there aren't too many around anymore and, those that do exist, are in constant danger of being lost forever."

Hal blinked. "You really *are* a strange dragon, aren't you?"

Keershan finally looked up at Hal. "And you are a strange human. Most humans would have tried to kill me already or at least run away. But you stay and listen to my ramblings. Because on one level, you *do* believe what I just told you," said Keershan, pointing a single claw at Hal. "You know—just as I do—that something is not right in this world, and that we need to do something about it. It's the relic, isn't it?"

"relics are tools," said Hal. "Said to have been crafted ages ago by the gods themselves. They're the key to ending the war between humanity and dragons. It's why I'm a Relic Hunter."

Keershan tilted his head to the side. "No, it's not. The real reason you're a Relic Hunter is because you want to avenge your father, who was killed by dragons. I saw it in your mind. And you, presumably, saw my memories."

Hal put a hand on the relic on his head, which felt oddly warm to the touch. "So we really *are* bonded, then?"

"Yes," said Keershan. He shook his head in disbelief. "Never did I think I would end up being the first bonded dragon in Salard-knows-how-many years. It's an honor, but also scary. Even with my research, I don't know the full extent of what being bonded means. It will be interesting to explore."

Hal raised his sword again, pointing the sharpened

tip directly at Keershan. "You're assuming I even *want* to be bonded with you in the first place. For that matter, you're assuming I believe your story, but maybe I don't. Even if it was a long time ago, surely someone would have mentioned it to me at some point."

Keershan's smile faded into a soft frown. "That's the thing. There used to be a *ton* of evidence of our true history together, but over the years, most of it has faded into irrelevance. In fact, I came to these ruins because my research indicated that this entire location had once been either a Dragon Rider base or a place where the Dragon Riders were worshiped. Hence the paintings on the walls behind you, which are ancient."

Hal glanced over his shoulder at the wall paintings that depicted humans riding dragons. "Some figment of an artist's imagination, perhaps."

Keershan shook his head. "If humans are as anti-dragon as you say they are, Hal, then why would any human choose to paint pictures of them living in peace with your sworn enemies? Plus, as I said, the fact that we bonded at all is proof enough that Dragon Riders once existed."

Hal could not argue with that last point, largely because he couldn't explain the bonding process without it. He wondered if Fralia, being a mage, would be able to explain it differently, seeing as she had a deeper understanding of magic than he did.

But Fralia isn't here. Hal glanced at the necklace hanging off his neck. *I am still not sure I trust Keershan enough to glow Fralia. Better to wait.*

"How did *you* find out about Dragon Riders?" Hal asked.

Keershan cracked his teeth together in what looked like an unconscious habit. "My mother. She was an ancient dragoness and the granddaughter of one of the Steeds that fought during the Dragon Rider War. She passed the knowledge down to her children, but none of them listened to her, save me. The rest… well, they didn't like the idea that we might be susceptible to riders. She passed away about ten years ago due to scales disease, which prompted me to seek the truth of the Dragon Riders and share this information with anyone who would listen, human or dragon."

Hal had no idea what 'scales disease' was. "Did she ever give you proof?"

"Some," said Keershan in a slightly defensive way. "She showed me some old ruins near our nest, which had engravings of the Dragon Riders that the other dragons could not explain. But … she also said that there were some who did *not* want humans or dragons to know. She said there were beings—not people—who benefited from the division between humans and dragons and even went around deliberately destroying any and all evidence of the Dragon Riders for fear of people discovering the truth and ending all conflicts between humanity and dragonkind."

Hal slowly lowered his sword again, though the frown on his face deepened. "A conspiracy, in other words?"

"Not like that," Keershan added hastily. "And even if it was, I've seen evidence of these beings myself. They're the reason why most of my investigations have proved fruitless. Anytime I find a hint of some old ruins or paintings somewhere, maybe an old book that describes the Dragon Riders, they are always defaced if not outright destroyed by the time I get there. It's why I am frankly excited to see these intact paintings and carvings. It means that I'm finally, finally a step ahead of our real enemies."

Hal rolled his eyes. "Who in the world would waste time and energy trying to locate and destroy long-forgotten paintings, carvings, and books that no one even cares about anymore? It's far more likely that time and decay have destroyed most of them."

"Maybe," said Keershan, "but if you'd seen what I'd seen, you'd believe—"

Hal's communication necklace started shining brightly and vibrating against his chest.

Keershan's eyes widened in surprise. "Is that a real communication necklace? I've heard of humans using them, but never seen one myself. So pretty."

Ignoring the research dragon, Hal picked up the necklace and held it close to his mouth. "Fralia, this is Hal. Glad you glowed, because right now I—"

"You've got visitors coming to the Forgotten Temple," Fralia's voice crackled through the green gem embedded in the necklace. "Or one visitor. And he doesn't seem friendly, either."

"A visitor?" Hal said, exchanging quick confused looks with Keershan. "But we're the only people in the area."

"Not anymore," Fralia said. "Get out of there as soon as you can, and I'll meet you at—"

A snapping sound could be heard and then several other deeper, male voices could be heard in the background, while Fralia said, "Hey! Give me back my necklace, you—"

Hal's communication necklace suddenly stopped glowing and he could no longer hear her words.

"What was that about?" asked Keershan in evident confusion. "A friend of yours?"

"A mage assigned to be my bodyguard while I hunt relics," said Hal. "Sounds like she's in danger."

"We could help—"

Keershan's sentence abruptly turned into a scream of pain as something dark and quick darted out of the shadows and slashed at his back. Keershan abruptly collapsed onto the stone floor of the temple, blood leaking out of his back.

And standing atop Keershan, bent and twisted in a distinctly inhuman way, was a dark, hooded creature, its thick, long claws dripping Keershan's blood.

Chapter Eight

Keershan was alive. Hal knew this because he could feel the agony of the creature digging into Keershan's back as if it was his own.

As for the creature, it reminded Hal of a lizard attempting to do a very bad impression of a human being, not helped by its green eyes glowing from within the hood.

"Relic Hunter," said the hooded creature in a voice that was *almost*—but not quite—human, "did the dragon harm you?"

"No," said Hal, trying to hide the pain in his voice. "You got here just in time. Otherwise, it would have gotten me for sure."

No … I wouldn't have … said a voice in Hal's head that was definitely not his own. *We're … bonded …*

Trying to hide his startled feelings, Hal thought back, *Keershan? Is that you? Or am I going crazy?*

It's me, Keershan said, his voice strained. Speaking

was a great effort. *Legend spoke of a Rider and his Steed being able to … communicate telepathically … decided to test it out … would be happier to see it worked if I hadn't been nearly killed …*

Hal gulped, pulling the relic off his head and tucking it under his arm. He did not dare exchange a look with Keershan, even though the hooded creature had turned its attention from him to the paintings on the walls behind him.

"Good," said the creature. It stood up straight, or straighter than it had before, anyway. It still wasn't looking at Hal. "I am a servant of the queen, much like yourself, though my mission is different. Rest assured that you are safe so long as you stay out of my way."

Hal raised an eyebrow questioningly. "What is your quest, exactly? Killing dragons?"

The creature lowered its bloody claw to its side, droplets of blood falling onto Keershan's nearly unconscious body. "No. I'm here for those."

The creature pointed its bloody claw at the paintings on the walls behind Hal. He glanced at the Dragon Rider paintings himself again, his eyes lingering on the one depicting the Dragon Riders fighting against a seemingly uncountable number of demons.

"What are you going to do with the paintings?" said Hal, looking at the creature again. "The queen's love of ancient art is well-known, of course, but I fail to see how you will transport these."

The creature made a noise like broken glass, though it was probably supposed to be a chuckle. "The queen is not interested in collecting this art. She wants it destroyed."

He's one of them ... Keershan said in Hal's mind, his voice even weaker than before. *One of the Defacers ... you must stop him, Hal ... stop him before ...*

Hal ignored Keershan. Anything that could mortally wound a dragon, even a runt like Keershan, was not a creature to be taken lightly. And this creature was what Fralia had likely been warning him about before her communication necklace mysteriously cut out.

"I see," said Hal, shifting the relic under his arm. "Far be it from me to stop a fellow servant of the queen from doing their duty. I've already gotten what I was looking for. Do what you must."

The Defacer seemed to freeze. "You carry one of the relics."

Hal looked to where he held the relic under his arm. He'd allowed himself to forget about it until now. "Yes, but only to defend myself from the dragon. Otherwise, it would have mauled me to death."

The Defacer did not respond at first. It tilted its head to the side, a move which looked unnatural to Hal, before nodding once. "Very well. If you wish to have my advice, however, I would not wear that too long. Relic Hunters are supposed to *hunt* relics, not wear them, and certainly not use them. Do you understand?"

Hal tried not to scowl, but it was difficult. Although Relic Hunters were far from the highest-ranked members of the Malarsan Army, they were certainly above the common soldier in terms of authority. The Defacer, however, gave him orders as if it were one of the four generals itself.

Still, Hal nodded. "Of course. I understand that

humans and dragons are not meant to be friends. Dragons are creatures to be dominated by humans. That's the way the world should be."

The Defacer, again, was silent, though even if it had spoken, Hal would not have paid any attention. His focus was back on Keershan. He could feel Keershan's surprised feelings at what Hal had just said.

"Very well," said the Defacer. It hopped off of Keershan's body and stalked toward Hal. "Move aside. I have a job to finish."

Hal did not argue. As the Defacer passed, Hal caught a strange stench.

If the knowledge of the Dragon Riders is lost to history, you'll never find out who really *killed your father.*

That got Hal's attention. He risked a look over his shoulder at the barely conscious Keershan, who still lay flat on the floor, covered in dried red blood. Their eyes met for a fraction of a second.

What do you mean, who really killed my father? It was a dragon, wasn't it?

Keershan, however, shook his head. *I saw your memories of your father's death. And he wasn't … wasn't killed by a dragon. He was killed by one of them. A Defacer.*

Hal turned his attention back to the Defacer. It was now running the tips of its claws along the surface of the painting before it, as if admiring the artist's attention to detail. Or perhaps simply trying to decide exactly how much force would be necessary to ruin the painting entirely.

How do I know I can trust you? Hal said. *What if you're lying?*

Hal … look with your own eyes, Keershan said. *Every single thing I've told you about the Dragon Riders has been corroborated by your own experience. Every. Single. Thing. Yet this Defacer … it has offered you no proof that it wants to help you. It's lying. It will kill both of us once it is done with its task. Queen Bariwa … she clearly wants to leave no survivors.*

Hal stiffened. *But it already said it would spare me if I kept out of its way, which I have.*

I forgot … forgot to mention one last thing that my mother told me about them … Keershan paused a moment, perhaps briefly overwhelmed by the pain he felt. *She said she found bodies of humans before the paintings they destroyed. Soldiers of the Malarsan Army, who escorted and protected them. The Defacers have gone unnoticed as long as they have precisely* because *they leave no survivors. Including their fellow soldiers.*

How do I know you aren't just saying this for your own benefit? Perhaps you're planning to kill me next.

Keershan chuckled painfully. *If I wanted you dead, you would be* dead. *Magic-less humans like you stand no chance even against runts like myself. Besides, our bond would prevent it. That's what being bonded* means.

Hal licked his lips uncertainly. Part of him told him not to listen to a dragon. Dragons, after all, were the enemy. For thousands of years, dragons had rampaged across human lands and kingdoms, senselessly killing any humans who got in their way. Dragons were the monsters under the bed, the bedtime stories that parents told naughty children to get them to behave.

And dragons had killed Hal's father. What more reason did Hal need to ignore Keershan?

But the Defacer seemed distinctly unnatural. From

the moment he saw it, Hal's instincts had told him he could not trust the creature.

By contrast, Keershan *had* been right so far about the Dragon Riders. At least, Keershan's explanation helped Hal make sense of the strange things he'd experienced since putting on the relic. And it was true that Keershan had not tried to kill or even harm him yet. The dragon seemed fairly harmless as dragons go. There was also the fact that Hal did not know what the Defacer had done to Fralia, though he doubted it was anything good.

Meanwhile, this Defacer does *seem like the sort of creature that would not want to leave any witnesses to its mission.*

Hal took a deep breath. He began walking toward the Defacer, each step quieter than the last. The Defacer did not seem to notice. It was too busy staring at the paintings on the wall, perhaps still trying to decide the best way to deface them. It almost seemed indecisive, though Hal didn't mind. It could spend as much time as it wanted sitting and thinking.

Dragon, Hal said in his mind, raising his sword above his head as silently as he could. *If I kill this thing, will you promise to help me find out who really killed my father?*

I swear on Salard's most holy name, Keershan said. *In return, however, I must only ask that you help* me *uncover the truth behind the Dragon Riders and bring this knowledge to the humans and dragons. Do you swear?*

Hal hesitated. Keershan had already sworn on the name of a god, which meant that Hal technically didn't have to himself. He could just as easily take Keershan's one-sided promise and not have to promise Keershan anything in return. He could even justify it, seeing as

Keershan was a dragon, and dragons were not known for keeping their promises. But something told him what he *had* to do.

Stopping right behind the Defacer—close enough now that he could smell its rotting stench worse than ever—Hal nodded. *I do.*

And then Hal raised his sword and plunged it into the back of the Defacer with all his strength.

Chapter Nine

FRALIA HAD BEEN STANDING OFF TO THE SIDE AND TRYING to reach Hal when she'd been attacked.

"Hal. Something's not right. I need you to—"

A cracking branch caught her attention.

Two of the soldiers snuck up on her and quickly subdued her. She'd tried to fight, but wasn't strong enough. They tied her up with thick, scratchy rope which was engraved with some sort of magical runes that Fralia did not recognize, though she didn't have much time to study them before she was shoved to the ground on her behind.

Looking up, Fralia found herself staring up into the face of Lieutenant Bana, who still sat on his horse. Surrels handed her necklace to Lieutenant Bana, who turned it over with disinterest.

"A communication necklace," said Lieutenant Bana. "One of the more useful tools developed by mages, this tool alone has saved the lives of countless humans in the wars against the dragons. But if you dare to use it in opposition of the queen's mandate …"

Lieutenant Bana dropped the communication necklace onto the ground. The second the necklace landed on the cold, hard earth, Bana's horse stomped on it with one hoof, smashing it beyond repair.

"Then it must be destroyed," Lieutenant Bana finished. His eyes focused on Fralia. "And perhaps its user ought to be destroyed with it."

Fralia gulped. "You can't kill me. That would be murder. You'd go to jail."

Lieutenant Bana chuckled, although unlike before, it now had a more sinister tone to it. "Assuming anyone finds out about it, and even then, Queen Bariwa would simply pardon us. We are, after all, her most important agents, working the quests that only those in the shadows know of. She would never truly punish her Black Soldiers, not when we are her most loyal subordinates."

Fralia's eyes widened. "Black Soldiers—? What does that mean?"

Lieutenant Bana shrugged. "Since you likely aren't going to live very long after that blatant display of treason, allow me to explain. Our job is to escort the hooded creature to wherever he needs to go. His mission is to destroy any and all evidence of the so-called 'Dragon Riders' of old, lest news of them gets out and people start getting ideas about the dragons that they shouldn't."

"Dragon Riders?" Fralia repeated. "Who were they?"

"Humans who rode dragons much in the same way we ride horses today," said Lieutenant Bana, patting the neck of his horse affectionately. "They were never real, of course. Just myths and legends that delusional people who believe in any sort of peace between humans and dragons told themselves to comfort themselves at night."

"If they are so fake, then why would the queen send you guys on missions around the kingdom, destroying any evidence of them?" said Fralia.

Lieutenant Bana glared at Fralia. "Because we cannot afford any sympathy toward the dragons to fester among the Malarsans. Already, many people question the wisdom of the current war due to the toll it has taken on the country's economy. If people began to believe that humans and dragons were once friends, well, then that would weaken us and make us easier targets for the dragons to destroy."

Fralia pursed her lips. Although she'd was as skeptical of any sort of peaceful coexistence between humanity and dragonkind as anyone else, she was equally skeptical of Lieutenant Bana's claims.

You don't try to stamp out stories that aren't true. They must see some truth in those old legends if the queen is sending these Black Soldiers around to try to destroy all evidence of them. But whether they're real or not, I need to escape.

Fralia was an air mage, which gave her many escape options. She wouldn't be able to do something as flashy as fire or light mages, perhaps, but she could still take these non-magical soldiers by surprise.

A powerful but brief tornado ought to do the trick. Fralia glanced at the sky overhead. *I'll have to be careful to avoid creating a massive storm, but I'm going to make these guys regret messing with a mage.*

Fralia focused her mind and will on the air around

her. She envisioned the spell that one of her advanced instructors had once taught her in an empty field of hay and his words of advice to take the wind around her and 'grab' it and make it do her bidding.

But even as Fralia felt the magical energy within her begin to stir, the ropes constricting her tightened and even burned. The burning sensation made Fralia gasp, shattering her concentration as well as her attempt to cast a spell.

Lieutenant Bana must have noticed, because he said, in a sneering voice, "Don't bother with your magic. That rope is enchanted to detect and suppress magic used by the person wearing it. Makes me glad I thought to bring it along, even though my commander thought it was useless."

The rope loosened slightly and began to cool down, but that did not make Fralia feel any better. She wondered how such a rope could even be possible. She'd never even heard of an anti-magic rope before.

Then again, I hadn't heard of the Dragon Riders or the Black Soldiers, either. Looks like I'm learning all sorts of new things today.

"Are you going to kill me?" asked Fralia, staring up at Lieutenant Bana again.

Lieutenant Bana shook his head. "Not yet. I want to wait until the Defacer returns and let him decide. Just to warn you, he isn't very merciful, especially toward humans."

Fralia grimaced. She looked toward the Forgotten Temple. "When will the Defacer return?"

Lieutenant Bana also looked toward the Temple,

though his expression was more expectant than fearful. "Once he is done defacing the paintings within. And whether your Relic Hunter friend gets in his way or not."

Fralia felt a single raindrop hit her head and looked up at the sky. The clouds overhead were dark and pregnant with rain. She suspected a storm was going to start very soon.

Although a storm, Fralia knew, was easily the *least* of their problems at the moment.

Fralia's arms were starting to go numb from the antimagic ropes wrapped around her body. Two of Lieutenant Bana's soldiers stood on either side of her, probably to make sure she didn't sneak away while Lieutenant Bana wasn't looking, although Fralia didn't see why. It wasn't like she'd get far in her current condition, even if she could move her legs. The old mountain path up to this point had been extremely treacherous even with Hal's help, and she suspected going down it would be even worse.

Especially once that storm starts in earnest. Fralia glanced up at the rumbling, dark storm clouds overhead, which stretched out like a blanket over the mountains for as far as the eye could see. *The rain will make the rocks slick. If I survive, I might not even be able to make it down the mountain. If we can escape, we could camp out in one of the ruined buildings until the storm passes and it's safe enough to go down again. That would make us late, but I think we were going to be late regardless.*

Fralia glanced at the shattered remains of her communication necklace on the ground a few feet away. She could hardly believe that Lieutenant Bana would destroy something so valuable. Created by magical crafters about ten years ago, the communication necklaces had become an instrumental weapon in the war against the dragons because they allowed Malarsan soldiers and mages to communicate over vast distances. Fralia had studied enough military history in school to know that the necklaces had become extremely helpful on big battlefields where soldiers might be too far apart to hear each other normally.

Lieutenant Bana sat on his horse, which stood about ten feet away from Fralia, along with the other soldiers who were not keeping an eye on her.

Fralia tested the ropes which bound her arms and legs. They were very tight, almost tight enough to make movement impossible. The anti-magic inscriptions engraved in the ropes were currently not glowing, but Fralia knew from experience that casting even one spell would cause them to activate and disrupt her magic.

And if I can't use my magic, I really am useless.

It was one of the hazards of being a mage in the Malarsan Army. On one hand, mages were the main reason the Malarsans had been able to fight against the dragons at all. It turned out that dragons did not do well against lightning bolts, tornadoes, earthquakes, and various other feats of magic that humans had discovered over the years.

On the other hand, magical education was highly specialized. Most mage students spent the bulk of their time learning the basics of magic, such as the six Affinities, before moving onto advanced applications. Mage students rarely got any combat classes unless they chose to go the war mage route, but those roles were even more specialized and difficult to master than normal magehood.

That was why Fralia was not a war mage. Unlike her father, who was a powerful war mage, Fralia didn't do well in combat and didn't even like fighting. It was part of the reason she signed up to escort Relic Hunters. Although Relic Hunters were no strangers to combat—most used to be normal soldiers, after all—they usually didn't get into fights as often as normal soldiers did, so Fralia expected to have to fight less than if she'd stayed in the army as a war mage.

Kind of regretting that now, though. A cold breeze passed through, making her shiver. *Otherwise, I'd probably be able to escape.*

She could hear her father's voice asking her what the hell she was thinking, that he hadn't raised a quitter, and that the Jeniqs were not quitters or losers. However much Fralia might have differed from her father personality-wise, she had inherited his stubbornness (or had it beaten into her, depending on your point of view).

In Fralia's mind's eye, she saw her father—an absolute titan of a man, with the same sleek dark hair as her, though his was significantly shorter—sitting across from her in their family dining room, his hands on their dining table, a questioning look on his face.

Well, girlie? Father asked, his voice sounding as clear as if he was actually sitting there in front of her this very moment. *What's the one thing you notice about your situation that you can use to your advantage? And don't whine to me about how there isn't any. There's* always *an advantage, even when you're alone, have a broken leg, and are dealing with a pissed-off dragon that you just poked out the eye of. Think.*

Having observed her situation carefully, Fralia replied, *None of the Black Soldiers are paying attention to me. Even the ones assigned to guard me and make sure I get away are chatting with each other about the weather or something silly like that.*

Father grinned, an expression Fralia had rarely seen but always treasured when she did. *Excellent. And what did I teach you and your siblings about not paying attention in combat situations?*

Clearing her throat, Fralia said, *You deserve whatever happens that you weren't paying attention to.*

Father nodded in satisfaction at Fralia's answer. *Exactly. Then you know what to do.*

Opening her eyes, Fralia straightened up a little.

With a gasp of air, she said, "Help! Something bit me. I … I think I'm going to die!"

To add to the effect, Fralia flopped onto the ground, rolling back and forth, her hair getting dirty and messy.

One of the two Black Soldiers protecting her hopped off his horse and knelt beside her. He was an ugly one, looking more like a toad in knight armor than a human, but the mere fact that he had jumped down at all—complete with a knife hanging from his belt.

"What is it, girl, girl?" said the Black Soldier. His rough words were almost tender.

"I got *bit* by something," Fralia yelled as dramatically as she could. "Maybe a mountain snake."

Surrels looked around in alarm. "A mountain snake?

I know we're in the mountains, but I didn't see any come up."

"Because mountain snakes are *really* good at sneaking up on people," Fralia snapped. "Or don't you Black Soldiers know that?"

The toad scowled, but said in a grudging tone, "Show us where you think the mountain snake bit you."

Fralia stopped rolling around and curled into a ball. "Ugh … I don't know if I want to show you. Maybe you should just get your med kit out first. That way, you'll be prepared to take care of it."

The toad scowled again, but turned his attention away from her briefly to grab his med kit hanging off a bag on his horse. Fralia spared a glance at Surrels, who was patting down the sides of his boots.

That was how Fralia was able to slip the toad's knife out of its holster and hide it down the folds of her robes without either of them noticing.

And she did it just in the nick of time, because the toad had turned back to her, his medical bag in one hand, and said, "Okay, girl, I've got my medical bag. Now, why don't you show me exactly where you were bit?"

Fralia stopped rolling on the dirt and sat up, smiling. "It's going to be hard for you to see it as it's been my toes."

The toad glared at her for a moment before shaking his head and muttering something about how mages were so overdramatic. Then he moved closer to Surrels, who immediately started rambling some long story about how he'd gotten bit by a mountain snake when he was a kid once and how it had made him deathly afraid of the creatures ever since.

After looking around to make sure that no one was looking at her, Fralia began cutting through the ropes around her ankles. The ropes were thick and it was tough to cut through them with her hands bound together, but she was pleased to see that she was making progress.

Just need a few more minutes and then I can escape into the mountains. With how rocky the ground is, I could easily lose these guys. Of course, I don't know *what I'd do after that, but—*

Fralia's thoughts were interrupted by Surrels suddenly pointing into the ruins and saying, "Hey, what's that?"

"What's what?" asked the toad. "Another scary mountain snake?"

Surrels scowled at his friend. "No, idiot. I saw a flash of light inside the temple."

"I didn't see noth—"

The toad was interrupted when a massive column of fire exploded from within the Temple, illuminating the entire ruins and capturing the attention of every single Black Soldier in the area.

Even Fralia paused to look at the fiery column, leaving her unsure if she should feel happy that the Black Soldiers were distracted … or afraid of whatever had created the fire.

Chapter Ten

Before the tip of Hal's blade could stab the Defacer's back, the Defacer whirled around and used its claw to hold back his sword, its green eyes glowing dangerously in the shadows of its hood.

"What is this?" said the Defacer in a hiss of a voice. "Have you decided to side with the dragon, after all? Pathetic."

The Defacer shoved Hal forward with surprising strength. Hal, who hadn't expected the bony Defacer to be that strong, was sent staggering backward from the blow. He fell over onto his back and accidentally dropped his sword, which clattered to the ground a few feet away. He tried to grab it, only for the Defacer to stab one of its claws into his right wrist and pin it to the floor.

Red-hot pain exploded in Hal's wrist where the Defacer's claw sank in. Hal cried out, feeling his blood leaking out.

The Defacer loomed over Hal.

A fireball launched out of nowhere and struck the Defacer in the face. The fireball hit the Defacer with enough force to send it flying backward, ripping its claw out of Hal's wrist at the same time. The Defacer slammed into the wall with a sickening *crack* and landed hard on the floor, its hood smoking from the flames.

Keershan was limping toward him. The runt dragon smelled heavily of blood.

"Keershan?" said Hal. He groaned and grabbed his bleeding wrist, holding it tightly against his chest. "You're still alive? I thought—"

"Barely," Keershan gasped. He looked at himself and Hal before shaking his head. "When we became bonded, I didn't imagine us looking quite so pitiful. I wonder if the original Dragon Riders ever looked like this after a battle with the demons."

A hissing sound that reminded Hal all too much of a rattlesnake's rattle filled the air. Fear shooting up his spine, Hal looked back toward the Defacer.

The Defacer was recovering from Keershan's fireball already. Pushing itself up onto its hands and knees, the Defacer continued to make that weird hissing sound, which Hal belatedly realized, through the haze created by the pain in his wrist, was the sound it made when it was breathing. Smoke continued to curl off what remained of its hood, while the stench of burned flesh and cloth wafted off its form.

"That thing survived a fireball to the face?" Hal asked in disbelief. "That would have *killed* a normal human."

The Defacer raised its head, allowing Hal to see its

face—no longer obscured by its hood—for the first time. It was an almost exact replica of the faces of the demons on the walls behind it. Long pig-like snout, bat-like fangs, and ears like a wolf's that stood up on top of its head. Its skin was badly burned and its features partially melted by the heat, but Hal felt like it would have looked as ugly as sin even before the fireball.

The Defacer launched forward, but Keershan fired another fireball, and it darted off to the side. It disappeared into the shadows of the Forgotten Temple, the slapping of its feet against the stone floor soon fading into silence.

"Did it run away?" asked Hal.

Keershan shook his head. "Demons usually dislike open fighting. They prefer to use the darkness around them to sneak around and hit when their target least expects it. We need to keep our eyes and ears open."

Hal nodded. "How did the Dragon Riders of old kill the demons?"

Keershan furrowed his brows or would have if he had them. He just seemed to be narrowing his eyes as a result. "Um … funny you should ask. None of the old legends I read said *how* they killed the demons. Only that demons could only be killed by a Dragon Rider and his Steed."

Hal looked at Keershan in annoyance. "I was hoping you were going to give me *specifics* on how to kill it."

Keershan scratched the top of his head. "Sorry, but it makes sense why that information would not be available. If these Defacers have been going around destroying all evidence of the ancient Dragon Riders, I assume that would include details on how to kill them."

And now he hid from them. Between the thick shadows and the remains of the toppled statues, the Defacer had plenty of places to hide in wait.

But what if it isn't hiding at all? Those paintings show that the demons have wings. What if—

"Keershan!" Hal snapped. "Move!"

Hal shoved the dragon to the side as quickly as he could.

The Defacer fell straight down from above as silently as a snake and slammed its claw into the floor. The Defacer had missed them by a few feet, which meant that its thick claw was now embedded in the stone floor. The Defacer struggled to rip itself free.

Hal turned toward Keershan, and something strange happened when he touched the dragon. He felt a warmth like fire shoot through the dragon's shoulders into his hand and up his arm. It was like getting injected with fire and made Hal gasp.

The fiery warmth snapped Hal to attention and made him forget about his broken wrist and exhaustion. He felt like he could fight for hours without rest, and he wasn't sure why.

The sound of bone being ripped out of stone behind Hal forced him to whirl around.

The Defacer had succeeded in ripping its claw out of the floor. It rushed toward Hal and Keershan with deadly speed. There wasn't enough time for Keershan to shoot a fireball. Hal didn't know how he knew that or how he knew that Keershan needed time to build up the fire in his throat necessary to make a fireball.

Hal, energized by the flames burning within him,

stepped forward and raised his sword to block the Defacer's claw.

The Defacer didn't slow down. Its green eyes glowed with triumph as it swung its claw at his metal blade, ready to cut through it and slash Hal's face off his body.

Hal's grip tightened on the handle of his blade. *I won't let this thing kill me. Kill* us. *I will* burn *it.*

The burning warmth inside Hal suddenly exploded. It went up his right arm, into his hand, and channeled into the blade of his sword, wrapping the blade in fire. The heat washed over Hal and it was almost too bright to see with, but Hal could still see the Defacer's claw coming toward him. The Defacer's eyes widened in surprise at his fire sword, but it was too late for it to stop.

The Defacer's claw slammed into Hal's fiery sword, which cut through the Defacer's claw easily.

The Defacer howled in pain, jerking its arm back. Its claw was now about half its normal length, leaving only a thick, bony stub from which dark smoke rose. The half that had been burned off clattered to the stone floor at Hal's feet, barely audible over the Defacer's agonized screams.

Gripping the flaming sword tightly with one hand, Hal rushed forward and slashed at it. The Defacer raised its clawed hand, only for Hal's sword to cut cleanly through its hand and send it flying away into the darkness beyond their view.

Hal didn't even give the Defacer time to scream. He slashed at it again and again, carving deep, burning wounds in the demon's chest and face. The Defacer kept screaming in some strange, unnatural-sounding language that Hal did not understand, too focused on killing the damn thing to care about what it was saying.

Hal had driven the Defacer back to the altar where the relic had once stood. The Defacer—its body now a bloody, smoking mess—slammed into the altar, allowing Hal to pull his burning sword back and impale it directly into the Defacer's chest.

And with a grunt, Hal raised the impaled Defacer into the air, using strength he did not even know he had, and glared up into its pained, terrified green eyes. A single word escaped his dry lips.

"Burn."

A huge column of red fire erupted from his sword and into the Defacer's body. The Defacer immediately vanished inside the column of flame, not even getting a chance to speak.

The fiery column went straight up into the air and through the ceiling overhead, the sound of burning rock echoing inside the Forgotten Temple, which shook under the impact of the blast, dust falling from overhead.

Then Hal, through a supreme force of will, snuffed out the fire column, and it disappeared from his sword.

All that remained of the Defacer was ash, which softly rained down on Hal like snow.

Chapter Eleven

THE EXPLOSION DISAPPEARED AS QUICKLY AS IT HAD appeared, almost making Fralia doubt she'd seen it. But the burning, smoking hole in the rooftop of the Temple, along with the neat hole in the clouds overhead, told her that she had definitely not been dreaming.

Lieutenant Bana was barking orders at his soldiers to get them into line, but there was a level of panic that she didn't understand. She used the distraction to cut through her ropes, worry for Hal creeping in.

Knowing him, it was probably an ancient magical trap that he'd accidentally set off. If he escapes with only his hair getting burned off his head, he'll be luckier than a three-footed rabbit.

Fralia did not make much progress before a large shadow fell over her. She looked up in time to see Lieutenant Bana, still sitting atop his horse, standing before her. The other Black Soldiers had surrounded Fralia, leaving her no room to escape even if she hadn't been tied up. The stench of unwashed horsehair and mud was especially strong with so many snorting horses around her.

"Did you honestly think we wouldn't notice your escape attempt, mage?" Lieutenant Bana said. "I thought mages were cleverer than that."

Fralia, knowing that further attempts to escape would be useless, instead flipped the knife in her hands and pointed it at Lieutenant Bana. "Stay back. I've got a knife and I'm not afraid to use—"

Fralia's knife was knocked out of her hands by Lieutenant Bana's sword, which he'd drawn so quickly Fralia hadn't even seen him do it. That was how Fralia found herself looking down the tip of Lieutenant Bana's sword, which was mere inches from her face.

Lieutenant Bana grinned. "Mine is bigger, mage. *Much* bigger."

Fralia gulped. "You said you weren't going to kill me until *he* returned, didn't you?"

Lieutenant Bana shrugged. "Change of plans. That blast looked far too much like dragonfire."

"Dragonfire?" Fralia repeated. "Dragons haven't been seen in the Desolate Tops in over two hundred years."

"I know dragonfire when I see it, mage," said Lieutenant Bana, his grip on his sword never wavering, though his face was pale. "If the Defacer was attacked by a dragon, then we need to help him. And unfortunately, I don't trust my men enough to leave even one of them with you, as evidenced by the knife I just knocked out of your hands."

Fralia trembled. "But I'm the daughter of General Jeniq. If you kill me—"

"Relic hunting is a very dangerous business," Lieutenant Bana mused. "Out of all of the branches of the Malarsan Army, it has the highest mortality rate, even higher than war mages who directly do battle with dragons. Even the mages who often escort their Relic Hunters to these remote, out-of-the-way places have higher odds of meeting unfortunate ends on these quests."

"Don't worry, mage," said the toad-like Black Soldier. "We'll make sure the search parties find your robes so they can at least return them to your dear old father."

Lieutenant Bana raised his sword above his head. "We just won't leave them any *hints* as to where your body might be."

Before Lieutenant Bana could bring his sword down on Fralia's head, an arrow came out of nowhere and struck his hand.

Lieutenant Bana stared at his bleeding hand. "Where did—"

Another arrow answered his unfinished question by embedding itself directly into his throat. As his body slumped, his horse spooked and bolted.

"Over there." The Black Soldier who Fralia had identified as Bana's second-in-command pointed toward a hill. "I saw someone with a bow!"

Fralia, peering through the legs of the horses surrounding her, looked toward the hill the soldier was pointing at. She caught a glimpse of brown robes disappearing behind the hill, robes which definitely did not belong to Hal.

Bana's surviving second-in-command pointed again at the hill. "Move!"

The Black Soldiers rushed toward that hill, forcing Fralia to cover her head with her hands to avoid the kicking horse hooves all around her.

"Over here, Black Soldiers," a slightly muffled, elderly voice called out from a completely different hill.

The Black Soldiers reined in their horses and looked in the direction from which the voice had called out. Fralia followed their gaze to a hill on the other side of the clearing, where she finally got a good look at her savior.

He was a man covered from head to toe in dirty, patched brown robes. A thick beige hood covered his head, while his nose and mouth were covered with a bandanna that made it impossible to identify him. Bright blue eyes peered out from within the hood, while an old-fashioned bow was clutched tightly in his right hand. A bundle of arrows poked out from his right shoulder, which he was already in the process of drawing from.

"Who is that?" asked Surrels in confusion.

"A mountain bandit, no doubt," the toad-like one said with a snarl. "I've heard of them. Ruthless lawbreakers who murder and steal from unwary travelers. I've never heard of one openly attacking a contingent of Black Soldiers, though."

"I am a hunter," said the old man, whose voice, despite the bandanna, sounded vaguely familiar to Fralia for some reason. "And your leader was the easiest prey I've ever hunted. Will you prove better prey? I think not, seeing the way you were planning to murder that innocent girl."

"That girl is *far* from innocent," the second-in-command snapped. He thrust his sword at the hunter. "But we're not in the business of talking with criminals. Now that you've shown yourself, it's time for you to die! Attack!"

As one, the Black Soldiers thundered across the clearing toward the hunter. The hunter, to his credit, didn't look even remotely afraid of the incoming mob. He merely raised his bow, took aim, and fired.

The single arrow split into three arrows. One of the arrows struck the toad-like soldier in the neck, sending his horse crashing into Surrels, and both sets of soldiers and horses went down. The other two arrows struck the horse of the second-in-command, hitting it in the head and bringing it down, causing the second-in-command to strike the ground headfirst and his head to crack open like an egg upon impact.

The remaining three Black Soldiers, without any sort of leadership or guidance, fell into chaos. One of them panicked and urged his horse toward the ruins, but as soon as the horse reached the rocky, uneven path at a fast pace, both soldier and horse went flying down the steep hill and disappeared from view.

The second remaining Black Soldier turned back the way they'd came and made a mad dash for freedom. Unfortunately for him, the hunter launched another arrow, which struck him in the back, sending him and his horse careening off course until they went over a cliff that Fralia hadn't noticed, vanishing over the side.

The final remaining Black Soldier somehow managed to keep running toward the hunter, screaming his head off the entire time. The hunter put his bow on his back, grabbed an arrow, and rushed toward the Black Soldier with surprising speed.

Once the hunter got close enough, he dodged the Black Soldier's panicked swings of his sword and leaped onto the back of the horse. Sitting behind the Black Soldier, the hunter stabbed the arrow into the Black Soldier's neck, causing a veritable sea of blood to rush down the soldier's neck and onto his armor. Then the hunter shoved the now-dead Black Soldier off his horse and, taking the reins, immediately began working on getting the frightened horse under his control.

Fralia blinked. In less than five minutes, the hunter had killed or defeated all six of the Black Soldiers. Without getting harmed himself.

Just who is *this guy and why does he seem so familiar?*

She'd been so distracted by the hunter killing the Black Soldiers that she had forgotten about freeing herself. She immediately spotted the fallen knife and, scooping it up, went back to work trying to cut through the ropes binding her.

But Fralia didn't make much progress before she heard a snort overhead and a shadow fell over her. Once again, Fralia looked up.

The hunter stood over her now, having apparently gotten the horse under control. Up close, his robes looked even more ragged and patched and even had some fresh bloodstains on them. The man's hands were thick and gnarled, wrapped in what looked like bandages, clutching the reins of his newly mastered horse tightly.

"Miss mage, are you all right?" said the hunter. "Do you need some help with those ropes?"

He jumped off the horse and, drawing his own knife from a holster hanging off his belt, cut through the thick ropes without any trouble. Fralia was actually amazed at how quickly and swiftly he did it. The ropes seemed to snap at the slightest touch of his curved, ragged blade, and in seconds, all of Fralia's ropes lay on the ground around her like so many dead snakes.

The hunter stood upright and held out a hand toward her. "There you go. You're free to move and use your magic."

Fralia took the hunter's rough, calloused hand and let him help her up. "How did you know the ropes were restricting my magic?"

Letting go of her hand, the hunter said, "I've been trailing those Black Soldiers since they entered the Tops. Overheard them explaining their dastardly plan to you. They talked too much."

Fralia nodded, trying not to show how worried she was at this man's nonchalant way of talking about the Black Soldiers as if he had not just killed them all. Although Fralia knew that killing other human beings was justified in some instances, she had never personally done it and she didn't understand how others could. "So you've been tracking them? Why?"

The hunter tilted his head to the side in confusion, his blue eyes blinking. "Isn't it obvious? I am the protector of the Forgotten Temple and all its secrets. And I have no intention of letting those Black Soldiers—much less their Defacer—destroy more of our history."

Fralia blinked. The hunter's words reminded her of someone she'd met not too long ago. "Our history? What do you mean? And who *are* you, anyway?"

The hunter's eyes smiled. He reached up and lowered his hood and bandanna at the same time, allowing Fralia to see his face clearly for the first time.

The hunter had a shock of snow-white hair, with a short, yet thick beard covering the lower half of his face. The skin of his face was rough, similar in color to the dirt and rocks of the Desolate Tops, but his blue eyes gleamed with a youthfulness that was different than the last time she'd seen him.

"Old Snow?" she whispered. "What? How?"

"Ah, my dear, because I am the last known descendant of the Dragon Riders."

Chapter Twelve

As the heat subsided, the pain and exhaustion from Hal's injuries came back in full force. His broken wrist especially burned. Keershan appeared behind him and let Hal lean against him. Normally, Hal would have recoiled at the mere touch of a dragon's scales, but then he felt the same heat as before filling him again, and he decided to just let the dragon help him for now. It did not entirely stop the pain, but it did dull it somewhat.

"Are you okay, Hal?" said Keershan. "How do you feel?"

Hal grunted. "Not as bad as someone with a broken wrist *should* feel, but hardly like a million coins, either."

Keershan sighed in relief. "Thank Dragos! When I saw that demon stab your wrist, I was really worried. But it looks like you powered through somehow, and I think I know how."

Hal looked at Keershan in confusion. "You do?"

For as long as Hal had lived, he'd heard that a dragon's smile was one of the scariest things a person could see. If a dragon was smiling at you, it meant that not only were you the target of its ire but that it would probably *enjoy* killing or maiming you. There was a reason the term 'dragon's smile' meant bad luck.

But none of the firsthand reports Hal had heard or read had ever described a *goofy* dragon's smile, which was exactly the best way to describe the smile that spread across Keershan's face.

"I do!" Keershan said. "Never did I ever think I would see it with my own eyes, but you used *my* dragonfire to kill that thing! You channeled it through your sword. Just like in the legends of old, which spoke of Dragon Riders channeling the flames of their Steeds through their weapons and hands. Some legends even say that certain Dragon Riders were able to *breathe* fire through their mouths like actual dragons."

Hal grimaced. "How did they do that without burning their throats?"

Keershan shrugged. "Not sure, and honestly, those legends seem more recent than the others, so I think they were just added later by people trying to spice up the original tales. But Riders using dragonfire was *definitely* something that happened, and flaming swords were the most common way they did it. Some legends even say that dragonfire used by humans is actually hotter than when dragons use it."

That explained how Hal was able to completely burn the Defacer to ash and even cut a hole through the roof of the Forgotten Temple.

But Hal, unlike Keershan, was not enthusiastic or

even happy about this development. He pushed himself off the dragon and staggered forward. As soon as Hal ceased making physical contact with Keershan, the warmth faded and the pain returned in full force, but Hal ignored it to pick up his sword and sheath it.

"Hal?" said Keershan in a hesitant voice. "What's the matter? Are you upset?"

Hal turned to face Keershan, whose expression now looked oddly worried. "Why wouldn't I be? I just used the same flames that killed my father and countless other innocent humans. Forgive me if I'm not singing praises to the gods for this curse."

"Curse?" Keershan repeated in disbelief. "What are you talking about? Didn't it feel good to use those flames? You saved our lives."

Hal scowled. "It *did* feel good. And that's the problem."

Keershan blinked. "It is?"

Hal wanted to scream at Keershan, but he didn't. "You wouldn't understand. How dragonfire looks from a human's point of view. How ash towns look to us."

Keershan licked his lips uncertainly. "Oh. Yes, I've heard of ash towns, but—"

"Yes, *heard* of," said Hal. His wrist pulsed angrily, but he ignored it. "But have you *seen* them? Or the devastation that your fires leave? Ash towns are never rebuilt because they *can't* be rebuilt. Once dragonfire scorches a village or town and kills everyone within it, that town is gone forever."

Keershan bit his lower lip. "I know, but—"

"And I just used it," Hal said. He looked at his sword,

which now felt less like a trusty weapon given to him at the end of his relic hunting training and more like a steel snake in his hands. "I feel like a monster. Humans aren't *supposed* to use dragonfire."

"But you're not *just* a human, Hal," said Keershan. "You're a Dragon Rider now. The relic on your head proves it."

Hal had forgotten about the dragon-shaped helmet on his head. He would have taken it off if his right hand hadn't been broken.

"And most of them were false," the voice of an old man rang out in the Forgotten Temple behind Hal, startling both him and Keershan. "Or exaggerated, at best."

Hal whirled around and saw two people walking across the broken stone floor of the Forgotten Temple, toward the altar upon which Hal and Keershan stood.

Fralia walked with her hands stuffed into the pockets of her robes, her eyes wide as she looked this way and that at the statues and carvings on the walls. She looked rougher than he remembered, with her dark hair messier and dirt on her face. Her green robes were a stark contrast to the earthy tones of the Temple's stone.

The other person was an elderly man in brown hunter's robes whom Hal did not recognize quite so quickly. He walked upright with his chest out and a bow and arrows slung over his right shoulder. His hair and beard were an equally white shade while his bright-blue eyes peered out with unusual vigor and youth.

"Fralia?" said Hal. "What are you doing here? I told you to stay put until I needed your help."

Fralia snapped her attention back to Hal and

scowled. "I'm still your bodyguard, Hal. And what's with the helmet, anyway? Looks tacky." Then Fralia stared at Keershan like a mouse that had just noticed a sleeping cat. "A dragon? Here?"

Keershan looked at Fralia and gave her what was probably supposed to be a friendly smile. "Hi there. My name is Keershan. Nice to meet you. Are you Hal's mage friend?"

Fralia took a *long* step backward. "Did that … did that thing just *talk* to me? With words?"

Keershan tilted his head to the side in genuine confusion. "How else am I supposed to talk to you? Humans don't have tails and wings like we dragons, so anytime we want to communicate with humans, we have to use your words. It would be kind of funny to see a human try to mimic dragon body language, though."

Although Hal still didn't exactly think of Keershan as a *friend*, he had to admit he found it privately amusing how scared out of her wits Fralia looked. He always thought that mages like her needed to be taken down a peg or two, and what better way to do that than to have her come face-to-face with a real dragon?

"Keershan will not hurt you, Fralia," said the old man standing next to her. "Isn't that right, youngling?"

Keershan looked at the old man in surprise. "Old Snow? Is that you? What are you doing here? I thought you said you'd wait at the foot of the Tops for me to return."

Keershan's words sparked a memory in Hal's mind, of an elderly man in a tiny hut at the foot of the Tops offering him some warm goat soup before they headed up into the mountains. Hal remembered denying the offer, saying they already had rations and were trying to make it up before the storm got bad and the man's even-tempered reply that they could just get some soup on their way down, then.

"I didn't think you'd make it," Old Snow said.

"You mean you know Old Snow, too?" said Keershan, looking at Hal in surprise.

"It's hard not to know him," said Hal, gesturing at the old man. "His hut is literally right at the start of the main road up into the mountains. He's almost like a gatekeeper, even though there isn't a gate."

"I prefer to think of myself as the ruins' caretaker," said Old Snow. His gaze became downcast suddenly. "And protector. Especially from threats."

Hal frowned. He looked at Fralia, who was still staring at Keershan as if he was going to eat her, and said, "What's he talking about? Did something happen outside?"

"I saved her from the Defacer's escort," said Old Snow, "otherwise known as the Black Soldiers. Have you heard of them?"

Hal frowned even deeper. "The Black Soldiers are a myth made up by old soldiers who've drunk a little too much cheap wine."

"Lieutenant Bana would disagree," said Fralia. "And his men who tied me up like cattle and were going to kill me because I was a threat."

"And they would have, if I hadn't stepped in and saved her," said Old Snow grimly. "Quite the charming lot, those ones were."

For what felt like the hundredth time in the past hour, Hal could not believe what he was hearing. The Black Soldiers of the Malarsan Army undertook quests from the queen not appropriate for normal soldiers. They were considered largely myth and legend among the normal ranks of the Malarsan Army and the Relic Hunters.

But I also always thought that demons were just a myth, too. And then I burned one to ash using dragonfire.

Shaking his head, Hal looked back at Old Snow. "Tell me, did the Black Soldiers escort the Defacer?"

"If you mean the creepy guy in the hood, then yes," said Fralia, drawing Hal's attention back to her. She rubbed her wrists anxiously and looked around. "He's not still around, is he?"

"Nope," said Keershan brightly. He nudged Hal with his head. "Hal here killed him with dragonfire. A huge column of flame that would have made Chief Dragos himself proud."

Fralia stared at Keershan again. "Am I the only one who is trying *not* to freak out at the talking baby dragon?"

"I am not a baby," Keershan said defensively. "I'm just small for my age, that's all."

"Don't worry," said Hal dryly, "I'm not very fond of him either, though he's not as scary as he looks."

Keershan fluttered his wings at Hal in a gesture that was clearly meant to convey confusion. "I … don't know if I should take that as an insult or as a compliment, but I'll take it, I guess."

Old Snow chuckled. "I forgot how energetic you young'uns are. Makes me feel young again just being in your presence."

Hal pointed at Old Snow. "Don't act like a kindly old man. If you knew Keershan, then you must have known he was here, but you didn't warn either of us. Plus, you seem to know an awful lot about the Black Soldiers and the Defacer for seemingly a simple mountain hermit."

"He told me that he's the last living descendant of the Dragon Riders," said Fralia. She pursed her lips. "But I don't know what that means."

"It means exactly what I said it means, my dear," said Old Snow. He patted his chest. "My lineage extends all the way back to the end of the Fall, shortly after the death of the Nameless One himself."

Keershan gasped. "Even I didn't know that. You must tell me more, elder."

Hal, however, shook his head. "You know what? I'm done listening to fables and myths. After everything that's happened today, I'm about ready to head back to the capital to report on the relic I retrieved."

Hal tried to walk past Old Snow, but the hermit stepped in his way and said, "You're assuming that the capital is a safe place for you to be right now, Relic Hunter."

Hal stopped and glared at Old Snow. "Why wouldn't it be? I'm a Relic Hunter. My captain is located there."

"That may be true," said Old Snow, speaking each word with an irritating slowness that Hal didn't appreciate, "but consider, if you will, that you played a role in destroying and killing a servant of the queen. You also may be viewed as an accomplice to the deaths of an entire contingent of Black Soldiers, a crime, I assure you, that Queen Bariwa takes with utmost seriousness."

Hal tried not to tremble, though it was difficult. He'd felt nothing but loyalty to the queen ever since she'd personally written him a letter after his father died and had even congratulated him on his graduation. "There's no proof that the Defacer worked for the queen other than its word, which is questionable."

Old Snow shrugged again. "Perhaps. But are you willing to risk walking into a potential death trap, especially knowing how harsh Queen Bariwa can be? I wouldn't, myself."

Hal scowled. "I'm not as much a coward as you are, old man. Move."

Old Snow did not. "And consider, too, that you are tired and injured from your fight. Your wrist looks especially bad. Do you think you'll be able to make it all the way down the Tops and back to the capital in that state?"

"Fralia will help me," said Hal. "Right, Fralia?"

Fralia looked hesitant. She folded her arms in front of her chest and glanced at the open doors of the Forgotten Temple as if she expected the Defacer to hop out and spook her at any moment. "I think we should listen to Old Snow. After what the Black Soldiers almost did to me, I think he might have a point."

Hal scowled deeper. "Come on, Fralia. He's clearly a crazy old man living by himself in the Desolate Tops. That hardly makes him a reliable source of information about—"

A *boom* outside the Forgotten Temple interrupted Hal and made Keershan jump. A second later, rain fell through the hole in the roof of the Forgotten Temple overhead, though surprisingly little of it given how big the hole was.

"The Desolate Tops are a difficult trek even on the best days," said Old Snow idly. "Even I, who have lived here my whole life, couldn't imagine making the trek down to the Outpost in this weather. You might slip and fall a very long way before you stop."

"And I'm not experienced enough to drive the storm away on my own with my magic yet," said Fralia with an apologetic shrug.

Hal's scowl deepened. "Fine. I'll stay. But only until the rain ends."

Old Snow nodded. "Fair enough. But first, let me go get someone else to join this little party of ours. It shouldn't take me long."

With that, Old Snow turned and disappeared into the shadows of the Forgotten Temple, moving surprisingly quick for a man of his age. Hal shot Fralia a questioning look, but Fralia just shrugged as if to say *Don't ask me.*

Almost as soon as Fralia finished shrugging her shoulders, Old Snow reappeared, pulling a long length of rope behind him. The rope extended into the darkness, making it impossible to see who—or what—it was attached to.

"What is that?" said Hal. "Another dragon?"

Old Snow flashed Hal a smile. "No. A myth."

With that, Old Snow yanked on the rope and a Black Soldier—bound from head to toe in thick rope—fell on the floor behind him into the light of the altar that they all stood in.

Chapter Thirteen

KEERSHAN HAD EXPERIENCED A LOT OF STRANGE THINGS in his short life. It was, he supposed, the hazards of the life of a scholar and researcher. He'd traveled to obscure and forgotten ruins, spoke with humans and dragons alike who had knowledge thought lost to time, and had spent countless hours poring over books and other ancient documents purporting to be from the time of the Dragon Riders. The human books, in particular, were difficult for a dragon to use without ripping or tearing them.

But bonding with a human and becoming said human's Steed—even if said human still didn't like or trust him much—put everything else to shame.

Keershan could not quite put it into words. In some ways, it felt like the reverse of being born. Whereas hatching from a dragon egg and into the world was when you were separated from your mother and became your own dragon, bonding with a human felt closer to being put back in his egg. He could feel much of what Hal did, even hear a lot of his thoughts, although much of them were very unclear to him even now.

Not that it surprised him. Keershan had heard legends that spoke of Rider and Steed needing time to deepen their bond and connection to one another. Some of the oldest myths even spoke of Rider and Steed becoming so close that they were practically a single being in all but physicality.

In any case, Keershan found that the bond was a double-edged sword. It was amazing to think that he and Hal were the first Dragon Rider pair in thousands of years, but it also meant he knew exactly what Hal was thinking and most of Hal's thoughts were not very nice toward either him, Old Snow, or the man lying on the floor before them at the moment. Only Fralia seemed to escape Hal's annoyance, and even then, Keershan suspected it was only because Hal had not yet figured out how Fralia had contributed to his current predicament.

Fralia had finally stopped staring at Keershan like he was a dangerous wild animal. She'd turned her attention to the man in black armor lying on the floor before them all, her eyes wide with surprise and even fear.

Keershan did not see what the big deal was. The man in black armor was thin and even frail-looking. His arms and legs were bound with thick ropes with odd engravings on them, and he seemed unarmed. His face was as thin and narrow as his body, and he smelled like blood and dirt. He also appeared to be unconscious. Not dead, but pretty close to it based on his injuries.

"What the …?" said Hal, staring at the man on the floor. "Who is that?"

"A Black Soldier," said Old Snow idly. "The men you said were a myth. Of course, you're free to disbelieve your own lying eyes, but I wouldn't recommend it unless you're as old as me."

"What are Black Soldiers?" asked Keershan curiously. "I've never heard of them before."

"Essentially covert troops of the Malarsan Army," said Old Snow. He tugged on the rope. "They do the quests that the normal troops aren't supposed to and answer directly to the queen herself. Such as escorting demons to forgotten ruins to destroy any trace of the Dragon Riders, for example."

Keershan nodded. He found the idea of a group of covert soldiers whose existence was apparently considered a myth by the other soldiers odd, but then, humans did a lot of odd things from a dragon's point of view.

That's why they're so fascinating to me. And why the other dragons think I'm a freak.

Old Snow tugged on the rope again. "I found him underneath his horse near the entrance to the ruins. I assumed he could be useful, seeing as he probably knows more about the queen's plans than any of us."

"He doesn't look very conscious," Keershan observed. He sniffed the air, taking in the Black Soldier's bloody stench. "Or alive."

"He'll come to eventually," said Old Snow, "but in the meantime, I'll be happy to answer your questions, children. I suspect this storm will last quite a while, so we have plenty of time to talk."

As if to emphasize Old Snow's point, the storm outside suddenly intensified. Lightning crackled overhead, briefly illuminating the dark night sky beyond the windows, while the rain fell harder than ever. The sudden snap of lightning made Keershan jump again. He hated thunder and lightning ever since he was a little hatchling, though he was grateful they were at least indoors.

That means we're safe in here. Or at least dry.

Fralia turned to Old Snow. "You said you are the last descendant of the Dragon Riders. What does that mean?"

Old Snow scratched his short white beard. "I am the direct descendant of Captain Domon Azertan himself."

Keershan gasped. "Captain Azertan? I've heard of him. My research says that Captain Azertan, along with his Steed Mathoh, was the leader of the Dragon Riders. Some legends even say he was the man who dealt the final blow to the Nameless One. That is so fascinat—"

A sharp stabbing pain interrupted Keershan. At first, he thought his *own* right front ankle was broken, but when he tested it, he found that it could move just fine without any pain.

Then he heard a groan to his right.

"Hal, are you all right?" asked Fralia. She swept over to Hal and studied his wound. "Ouch. What did you do to your wrist? It looks like someone stabbed it with a knife."

"Blame the Defacer," Hal grunted.

"I know just the spell to heal it, but we'll need to bandage it and you'll probably have to avoid using it too much for the next couple of days. At the very least, you'll need to avoid swinging your sword around like a mad man."

Keershan leaned toward Fralia with interest. "Are you going to use *human* magic to heal him? Can I watch?"

Fralia jerked back and pointed sharply at Keershan. "You keep your distance. And don't try anything while I'm healing Hal or else I'll show you why I'm the daughter of a war mage."

Keershan would have argued, but he found Fralia's gaze intimidating despite how small she was, so he took a couple of steps back. He watched as Fralia took Hal's wrist and started cleaning the blood off, using tools from a kit hanging off her waist to prepare the wound. Hal stood surprisingly still, though Keershan could sense that Hal didn't enjoy having to get doctored like this.

It looks like it's true. Humans really don't *have the same self-healing abilities that we dragons do. I wonder how they've survived this long without it.*

Keershan's own back injuries had largely healed by this point on their own, although a part of him was interested in experiencing human healing magic. He wondered if it felt nice.

"Anyway," Old Snow continued as if he had not been interrupted, "yes, I am Captain Azertan's last living descendant. This village was once known as the Birthplace of the Dragon Riders. Even after the Fall, when wars erupted between humans and dragons and knowledge became lost all throughout the world, we still remembered. We protected the relic which Hal is currently wearing and ensured it would not fall into the wrong hands."

"But it looks like a ghost town now. What happened to it?"

Old Snow sighed and suddenly looked as old as the Dragon Chief. "Over the years, people left or died. Some went to other towns and cities to seek a better life for their families while others died and left no descendants or people to replace them. Bit by bit, the village died over the years. My family was the very last family to remain here and, obviously, we couldn't take care of it ourselves. Besides, by the time my grandfather was born, the village's best days had been long behind it."

"So you were born and raised in this village your whole life?" asked Hal, who had apparently been listening as Old Snow spoke. He grimaced when Fralia started wrapping a bandage around his wrist; Keershan had missed his chance to see Fralia use her human magic (*Darn*).

Old Snow nodded. "Yes. It was my family who protected this place and its history from outsiders and threats like the Defacer. We did not precisely *maintain* these ruins—that would be too big a job for one family—but we at the very least kept them from being destroyed. We ensured that the ruins and their secrets would remain preserved for the day that someone would come and use them correctly."

"You mentioned that others came before us," Keershan said. "Do you mean other dragons? Or even Relic Hunters like Hal?"

Old Snow scratched his beard. "Treasure hunters, thieves, the occasional rogue soldier seeking to increase his own power and fortune by finding hidden or long-forgotten art to sell on the black market."

"What happened?"

"I gave them some unhelpful advice for getting to the ruins. You'd be surprised by the number of people willing to believe the ramblings of a crazy old hermit living by himself in the mountains."

Keershan shuddered at the thought. He hadn't realized that Old Snow had been deliberately misleading visitors to the Desolate Tops as to the location of the ruins. He wondered how many of those visitors gave up and went back home after failing to find the ruins and how many of them died.

"If you have been lying to people about the ruins' location this entire time, then why did you give *us* the proper location?" Hal asked. "And did you share that information with the Black Soldiers as well?"

"To answer your second question, the Black Soldiers didn't stop at my hut," Old Snow said, glancing at the unconscious and bound Black Soldier at his feet. "They marched straight past it on their way up the mountains. They might not have even noticed it. But I, of course, noticed, which is why I followed them."

Another *boom* of thunder overhead made Keershan shake where he stood. Irrationally, he almost wished he was a hatchling again, small enough to hide under his mother's wing during storms.

But my mother is gone. At least we're inside.

"As for the first," Old Snow glanced from Keershan to Hal like he was trying to find the words to describe something to them. "You two seem different."

Hal glanced at Keershan with a rather judgmental look. "You mean you gave this information to *both* of us?"

"Of course," said Keershan in surprise. "How else do you think I know him as well? I was actually surprised when Old Snow willingly sat down and spoke with me after I asked him my questions. Most humans are so afraid of dragons that they won't even talk to us."

Keershan did not look directly at Fralia when he said that, but he sensed her tense next to Hal. He wasn't sure how, though, other than his bond with Hal meant he could feel most of what Hal felt. He did notice Fralia draw a little closer to Hal, however, like she thought he would protect her.

Wish I could tell her that I'm not scary, Keershan thought wistfully. *Guess it's something she'll have to learn on her own.*

"That's because of my ancestry," said Old Snow. He gestured at the Dragon Rider carvings on the wall behind them. "I knew that humans and dragons were once kin. Although I must still exercise some caution when dealing with dragons—not all dragons are as friendly as Keershan—I like them more than most humans, so I didn't mind talking with young Keershan."

Keershan tried not to look too pleased with himself. He hoped that Fralia was listening when Old Snow said he was 'friendly,' but a glance at her showed him that Fralia viewed him with as much skepticism as ever.

"Anyway, I felt as if I could trust you two," Old Snow continued. "Neither of you struck me as particularly money-hungry or power-hungry. You clearly were not trying to destroy the ancient history of the Dragon Riders. And maybe you were..." Old Snow quickly moved onto the next subject. "Anyway, I am pleased to see that I was correct, although our situation is still quite grim."

"What do you mean?" asked Hal. "We killed the Defacer, and the Black Soldiers are gone. I'd say our situation is looking pretty good so far."

Old Snow looked at Hal like he was an idiot. "Did you already forget that the Defacer and his escort worked directly for the queen of Malarsan herself? Should they fail to return to the capital in time to report on their mission, Queen Bariwa *will* notice and she *will* send someone to check."

"We don't know that for sure," said Hal in a voice that didn't sound like he entirely believed his own words. "They might have been lying."

"I don't know, Hal," said Fralia. "They sounded very official to me."

"Anyone can claim to work for the queen, though," Hal said stubbornly. "And without proof, there's no reason to believe they really work for her."

Old Snow smiled sadly. "Proof, eh? You mean like this?"

Old Snow drew out some kind of metallic emblem from his robes and held it high for everyone to see.

The emblem was a necklace, ending in a small piece of metal shaped like a sword crossed with a bow and arrow.

"It's the symbol of the Malarsan Army," said Keershan in recognition. "I've seen it on the banners and armor of Malarsan soldiers."

"More than that, it's the official seal of the Malarsan

royal family," Old Snow said. He shook the emblem in his hand. "These can only be obtained from the queen herself, which she gives out only to those who serve her."

"Where did you find that?" asked Hal in a tight voice.

Old Snow gestured at the unconscious Black Soldier. "I found it on the body of his dead lieutenant. Which means only one thing: The Defacer and the Black Soldiers work for the queen, and killing them has effectively made us—*all* of us—the enemy of the throne."

Chapter Fourteen

"WHY? QUEEN BARIWA WANTS TO END THE WAR. Everyone does, in fact. And everyone knows the best way to end the war is for us to gather the relics and use them to control the dragons."

"*bond* with the dragons, you mean," Keershan corrected him. "No need to use a word like 'control' around here."

"Actually, 'control' is very appropriate when it comes to the queen's true intentions for the relics and the dragons," said Old Snow with a grim chuckle. "She isn't interested in ending the war for its own sake. Rather, she wishes to gather as many relics as possible to control the dragons, which she could then use to take over the world."

Old Snow stuffed the medallion back into a pocket of his robes. "Since the Fall, a small group of people—demons, mostly, though with some human sympathizers among them—have dedicated their lives to obscuring the true history of the Dragon Riders. Throughout history, these Defacers, as they came to call themselves, have weaseled their ways into the halls of power. They have directed kings and queens, started and stopped wars, and turned entire empires upside down to achieve their goals."

"You mean the queen might be a puppet of these Defacers?" said Fralia questioningly.

Old Snow sighed. "Or, more likely, she's fully aware of them and supports their mission. Especially if the Defacers promised her power through the relics. She seems like an ambitious woman from the rumors I've heard about her, so I would not be surprised if she willingly works with them to achieve *her* goals."

Hal shook his head. He couldn't believe what he was hearing, but at the same time, he couldn't deny it, either. That medallion was solid evidence, if not outright proof, that the Black Soldiers had been working directly for the queen herself. Hal had learned how to identify the queen's medallions during his Relic Hunter training and this was definitely one of them.

"There must be a mistake. The relics are supposed to help us end the war by subduing the dragons. The queen never said anything about using the dragons to start more wars, much less wars of conquest," Hal said.

"Queen Bariwa doesn't say a lot of things to the people of Malarsan," said Old Snow. "Sometimes, this is wise, other times … it makes you wonder what, exactly, she's hiding."

"I am sure that once I speak to the queen, I—"

"What makes you think you will get a chance to

explain yourself to the queen at all?" Old Snow said, cutting Hal off. "You are just a simple Relic Hunter, of which there are many. I doubt Queen Bariwa would honor a request for an audience with her from you."

Hal said nothing, mostly because he knew that Old Snow was correct and he could not think of a good reply. He just rubbed his bandaged wrist, which, thanks to Fralia's healing magic, did not hurt nearly as bad as it did before, though she had warned him not to put a lot of weight on it yet. Hal found it a bit annoying, but better than losing his right hand entirely, which was apparently a real possibility if Fralia had not healed it in time.

Old Snow pointed at Hal. "And you do realize that you just killed a personal servant of the queen herself, yes, even if that kill was justified? One thing I do know about Queen Bariwa is that she does not tolerate anyone who kills her servants. What do you think she will do once she learns of our actions?"

"Send someone to investigate."

Old Snow chuckled bitterly again. "Not merely to *investigate*, my young friend, but to eliminate whoever had killed her servants. She may even send another demon, probably worse than the one you fought, to kill us and finish the defacing job that the original demon failed to do. Given the absolute secrecy of the Black Soldiers, this won't become common knowledge, either, so we won't even get a trial."

"What *should* we do, then?" said Hal. "If the queen won't talk to us and the Black Soldiers and demons will simply kill us, what choice do we have? Should we simply flee the kingdom in search of safety elsewhere?"

Old Snow stroked his beard. "That might work for a little while. Every last one of us is a threat to Queen Bariwa's rule now that we know about the Dragon Riders. I wouldn't be surprised if she sent mercenaries after us even in other countries."

"We could go live among the dragons," Keershan offered. "The queen's reach ends at the entrance of Dragon Valley, or so my mother always used to say. I bet even the demons wouldn't follow us there."

"I don't think it would be practical for us," said Old Snow. He gestured at himself, Hal, and Fralia. "The three of us are humans, after all, and you are already considered an outcast among your kind, yes? Why would the dragons take us in, especially if taking us in would put their own lives in greater danger than they already are?"

Keershan's smile faded and he looked at his clawed feet in shame. "Oh. You're right. I guess I forgot."

Fralia breathed a sigh of relief. Hal understood. No human being had ever entered Dragon Valley—a large valley in the eastern half of the Malarsan Kingdom and home to multiple dragon Clans—and come out alive. Hell, few humans had even *seen* the Valley out of fear of getting too close to the nests of the dragons.

Yet Hal felt far less afraid of it than Fralia. He wasn't sure why, but then he remembered the bond he shared with Keershan and wondered if that had something to do with it. Were Keershan's feelings about Dragon Valley influencing his own? Hal didn't pretend to understand the whole 'bonded' thing that Keershan endlessly spoke of, but that seemed like a logical assumption to him.

Am I going to become *a dragon like Keershan before long? Or will I still remain human? I'm not sure I like this whole Dragon Rider thing. I wonder if I can get out of it.*

"So if fleeing the country isn't an option and going to Dragon Valley won't work, then what should we do?" Keershan looked around uncertainly at all of the humans. "It's only a matter of time before the queen finds out about what we did. She might even know already, thanks to the demons' black magic. We can't just hide inside the Forgotten Temple forever."

That was when Fralia, surprisingly enough, raised a hand and said, "Actually, I think I have an idea."

"We're all ears, my dear," said Old Snow with a gesture of his hand. "Please share your idea with us."

Fralia tugged at the sleeves of her robe uncertainly. "My father is General Kolass Jeniq of the four generals of the Malarsan Army. If we can reach the capital, then we might be able to get in contact with him, explain our situation, and convince him to persuade Queen Bariwa to spare us."

"Are you sure about that?" asked Keershan doubtfully. "Because if the queen is behind this conspiracy, then I doubt she'd be willing to listen to anyone, even one of her top generals."

"The queen *can* be rather stubborn," Old Snow acknowledged, "but I think Fralia's plan might work nonetheless. General Jeniq has a reputation for being one of the more reasonable generals and is fairly persuasive to boot. If anyone could convince Queen Bariwa to spare us, it would be him."

Fralia smiled. "My father is closer to the queen than

the other four generals. We even dined with the queen's family last month."

Hal shot Fralia a curious look. "I didn't realize you came from such a famous pedigree. It makes me wonder why you became a bodyguard for a Relic Hunter like me rather than do something more prestigious, like become a professor at the academy or even a front line war mage."

Fralia tugged at the ends of her sleeves. "That's irrelevant. What matters is that I am pretty sure I can get my dad to listen to us. And normally, I would just contact him through my communication necklace, but ..." Fralia gestured at her bare neck.

"My communication necklace is still intact. Perhaps we could use it to contact your father."

Fralia shook her head. "Not going to work. One of the drawbacks of communication necklaces is that they only work when the beads on them are mined from the same general area. Otherwise, a mage can only set up a two-way channel between necklaces like what I did. Your necklace was mined from a different part of the kingdom than my father's, hence why I don't think it will work."

"I could reach out to Captain Namko," said Hal. "He's a reasonable man. He might be willing to listen."

"Captain Namko?" said Keershan. "Who's that?"

"The captain of the Relic Hunters," Hal explained. "He's basically the head of all Relic Hunters in the Malarsan Army. He's the man who assigns quests to individual Relic Hunters and often speaks directly with the queen herself. He's a good, respectable man."

"Unfortunately, that is why we probably should not approach him," Old Snow said with a shake of his head.

"If he's as close to the queen as you say he is, then he might be a part of this conspiracy as well. We should head for the capital tomorrow morning as early as possible, contact General Jeniq, and explain our situation to him."

"Shouldn't someone stay to guard the paintings?" Keershan said.

"As far as the queen knows, the Defacer has done his job, right?" Fralia said.

"That buys us days at most," Old Snow said. "I'll seal the temple as best I can, but our focus now is Hal and Keershan's safety. She won't stop until they are destroyed, too."

Chapter Fifteen

The weather was clearer the next morning. The storm, as strong and wild as it had been, passed quickly, which Old Snow claimed was normal for the Desolate Tops. He did suggest that they move quickly, however, because the clouds in the early morning sky were still quite gray and there was a high chance the storm could start up again today.

After a quick breakfast of travel rations that Old Snow had procured from the corpses of the Black Soldiers, the unusual party of four headed out from the ruins. Hal made sure to grab one of the Black Soldiers' swords—a standard-issue short blade that all Malarsan Soldiers received when they completed their training—and a shield to go along with it. He was a bit disappointed to find out, however, that the Black Soldiers' weapons were not actually superior to the kind that normal soldiers like himself were issued.

What is the point in being a member of a secret group of elite soldiers if you don't even get nicer equipment to match? Hal thought with annoyance.

Perhaps Hal should have asked their prisoner, Surrels, who woke up the next morning complaining about a splitting headache. Aside from his name, Surrels refused to give them any more information. Hal thought they should have interrogated him, but Old Snow insisted that they didn't have time.

They did not take the main route down to the Outpost, however, where Hal and Fralia had spent the previous night before heading into the Tops. Old Snow said that that path was too obvious and that the soldiers at the Outpost would likely detain them if they arrived there. They certainly wouldn't tolerate Keershan's presence for obvious reasons.

Instead, Old Snow led them to an obscure path to a small town at the foot of the Tops that was supposedly less watched than the Outpost. The hidden path—like so much else in the ruins—clearly hadn't been used in years. It was rockier than the main path, for one, and steeper. More than once Hal found himself looking down a long fall that he doubted even a dragon would survive.

Having put Surrels on Old Snow's horse to make sure he didn't get away, Old Snow led the group, holding onto the horse's reins and making sure it did not miss a step. Walking immediately behind the horse was Fralia, who kept pulling her robes more tightly around her body. Bringing up the rear were Hal and Keershan.

"So," said Keershan when they were about halfway down the Desolate Tops, "what made you decide to become a Relic Hunter in the first place, Hal?"

"Surprised you felt the need to ask."

"I obviously can't read your mind when you're not wearing our relic."

Hal shot Keershan an annoyed look. "*Our* relic? I think you mean the *queen's* relic."

"Why would it be the queen's relic?" said Keershan with a blank stare. "I didn't see her travel all the way out to the Desolate Tops and explore the ruins of an ancient temple to find it."

Hal patted his shoulder bag, feeling the solid metal mass of the helmet beneath the rough, old leather. "Because that's what Relic Hunters *do*. We search the kingdom for old ruins or obscure, forgotten places in search of these old relics. It's not an easy job, nor a particularly successful one. Most Relic Hunter quests end in failure because either we can't find a relic at all or the ones we find are damaged or destroyed, if not stolen already. This relic is actually in very good condition, given its age."

"Fascinating," said Keershan with too much sincerity, in Hal's opinion. "Among the dragons, relics are considered dangerous weapons, at least when used by humans. Their ability to take away a dragon's free will means that most dragons try to avoid them or, if unable to do that, destroy them. Of course, I know what relics *really* do, so yours is safe around me."

Hal rolled his eyes. "Do any of those old fairy tales say anything about severing a bond between human and dragon, perchance?"

"Every source I've consulted makes it sound like a bond between a Rider and his Steed can only be severed by death. So if you or I were to die, our bond would break, but otherwise, it's a life-long bond that cannot be destroyed by any means, ordinary or magical."

Feeling the weight of the helmet in his shoulder bag, Hal said, "What if the relic that created the bond got destroyed? Wouldn't that sever the bond?"

A thoughtful expression crossed Keershan's face, his claws leaving deep grooves in the ground as they walked. "It shouldn't. Legend has it that, while relics are often necessary to *create* bonds, they are not necessary for *maintaining* said bonds. All relics do is act as a conduit between Rider and Steed, making it easier to form and strengthen bonds. Some legends talk of bonds that can be formed without relics, but I still wouldn't risk it if I were you."

Hal scowled. "So we're stuck together until we die. Wonderful."

"Don't sound so down," said Keershan in a voice he obviously thought was encouraging. "According to legend, the deeper a bond between a Rider and Steed, the longer a Rider lives. Riders are known to live hundreds of years longer than normal humans, sometimes even thousands of years, thanks to their bond letting them copy certain things we dragons can do. Like the dragonfire you used on the Defacer, for example."

Hal scowled even deeper. "So not only can I not break our bond, but I might live longer than the vast majority of other humans at the same time."

"Exactly," said Keershan brightly. "Isn't that exciting? You and I get to live out history. We are the first Dragon Rider pair in thousands of years. I feel like I'm living one of the old stories that my mother used to tell me when I was but a wee hatchling, only this time I'm the star."

A loud snort up ahead made Hal look up at Surrels. "Do you have a cold, Surrels?" asked Hal with a frown.

Surrels looked over his shoulder at Hal and Keershan, a sneer on his face. "No. I was just listening to your conversation and thought it very amusing how self-centered you dragons are. The star of your own story. What arrogance."

"Watch it, ferret," said Fralia sharply. "Remember who's still in charge here."

"Oh, I am fully aware of my current predicament, girl," Surrels replied without missing a beat. He tugged at the ropes binding his wrists together. "I would be a lot more polite if you traitors to the crown would get these awful ropes off my wrists and let me walk of my own free will. I might even be willing to tell you a few secrets about the queen's real plans for Malarsan."

"We can't trust you not to run away," said Old Snow without looking over his shoulder. "Until we're done with you, you're staying put."

Surrels chuckled. "See, that's your error. I *know* you traitors are only keeping me alive because of the information I have. Should I ever decide to share some of my information with you, you would kill me and abandon my body to be devoured by the stone wolves of the Tops. Hence why I am going to keep my mouth shut."

"Yes, please," said Fralia in a sardonic voice of her own. "Keeping your mouth shut not only will prolong your life a little, but will make you seem more attractive as a person in general. What was the old proverb about keeping your mouth shut so people will think you're wise and not a blathering fool?"

Surrels glared over his shoulder at Fralia. "Presumably related to the one which talks about honey gathering more flies than vinegar."

"Appropriate," said Hal, "given how you are as annoying as a fly, although I doubt you'd fly very well if you were to accidentally fall off this cliff."

Hal gestured at the steep cliff on the right-hand side of the path, which had to be at least a hundred feet tall, if not taller. It certainly looked like a long way down.

Surrels must have been thinking the same thing because his face turned pale, and he immediately shifted his attention away from the cliff. "You're bluffing," he said, his voice catching.

"Why the stuttering, then?" Hal asked.

Surrels huffed. "If you must know, it's because I *hate* heights. I don't even know how I got assigned to this mission, other than someone higher up probably thought it would be amusing. If nothing else, I look forward to getting back down to the plains, where I don't have to climb up and down tall, dangerous mountains that no sane human being would ever live—"

Without warning, Old Snow quite 'accidentally' tugged on the horse's reins, causing the horse to pick up the pace and almost 'stumble.'

But Hal could tell that Old Snow hadn't actually made the horse stumble. It was clearly a signal he gave his horse for when he wanted the beast to walk faster.

Surrels, on the other hand, didn't seem to notice that. He just clutched the front of the saddle tighter than ever and looked like he wanted to throw up. That was clearly Old Snow's way of getting the Black Soldier to shut up, which Hal appreciated.

"Old Snow, how long is it until we reach the town you were telling us about?" Fralia asked. She furrowed her brows. "What was it called? Giant's Toe or whatever?"

"Giant's Foot," Old Snow corrected. "And we should get there before the end of the day. In fact, we're making such good time that we might get there in time for dinner. We should be able to find a place to stay for the night."

Keershan glanced at Hal again. "Since it sounds like we still have some time according to Old Snow, I noticed you didn't answer my question about why you became a Relic Hunter."

Damn. Keershan was smarter than he looked.

Hal sighed and rubbed his forehead. "I originally became a Relic Hunter because I was told it would end the war. The relics, after all, can be used to control the dragons. The logic goes that if we can gather enough relics, we can control enough dragons to end the war forever. And given how I lost my father to your people, well, I hope you can see the appeal."

Keershan nodded. "I expected as much, although you are wrong about your father. He wasn't killed by dragons."

Hal glared at Keershan again. "You said that back in the Temple but didn't explain what you mean. Or how you could possibly know that."

Keershan shrugged his large dragon shoulders.

"When we first bonded and we got to see each other's most formative moments in our lives, I recognized the helmet your mother was given by the visiting soldier. I'd seen it once before myself. Your father was part of a group of soldiers who attacked my mother's nest on the outskirts of Dragon Valley ten years ago."

Hal eyed Keershan suspiciously. "That would be an almost divine coincidence."

"I know, but I've got a pretty good memory, especially when someone is trying to kill me," said Keershan. "I didn't see your dad get killed by anyone in my nest. He did attack us, but my mother drove him and the others off. He did get burned by my mother's fire, but he didn't die then. I'm sure of it."

Hal suddenly forgot all about Surrels or the strange conspiracy which seemed to tie the queen to the mysterious Defacers. He forgot about the Desolate Tops and the Dragon Riders. He forgot about everything except what Keershan was telling him.

That prompted a single question from Hal.

"If the dragons didn't kill my dad, then who did?"

"I don't know," said Keershan. "It may have been a demon."

Snapped out of his initial shock at Keershan's revelation, Hal kicked a rock out of his path off the cliff and said, "And how do you know that?"

Keershan licked his lips, an obvious nervous habit, and Hal only knew that because of their bond. "Because I saw *something* go after the soldiers shortly after my mother drove them away. A large, stalking shadow. And it wasn't a dragon from another nest, either."

"Assuming a demon killed my father, why?" said Hal.

Keershan made a sad growling noise with his throat. "I wish I knew the answer to those questions, Hal."

As they neared the foot of the Tops, Hal could not help but look over his shoulder one last time at them. The barren peaks of the Desolate Tops looked particularly foreboding in the early evening sunset, their tips like claws reaching toward the sky. Hal could not see the ruins of the Forgotten Temple from here, but he knew it was somewhere within those peaks, full of secrets that had been hidden for an untold number of years.

And I may just be in the middle of them, Hal thought, feeling the weight of the relic in the bag over his shoulder.

"Hey, is that the town?" Fralia asked, pointing down the slope.

It looked barely bigger than a village with houses and businesses clustered closely together, allowing only for narrow dirt streets between them. Candlelight could be seen glowing from within the windows of some of the buildings, though most were dark.

"That's the place," Old Snow said. He stood at the front of the party on top of a flat boulder, which elevated him slightly above the others. "The village of Giant's Foot. There are no soldiers here, barely even any law enforcement of any kind. The kingdom's laws only apply to places where the kingdom can actually enforce them."

Fralia gulped. "Maybe we should keep going until we reach the next kingdom city that actually has some sort of law and order."

"Agreed," Surrels said from atop his horse.

"Best to stay off the major roads and highways until we reach the capital," Old Snow said.

"That's why we're spending the night in a town full of lawbreakers?" Fralia said, sardonically.

"Given how we killed several servants of the queen, we technically *are* lawbreakers," Old Snow said. "The people who live here are largely quiet hunters and trappers who make an honest living hunting and selling meat and fur they get from the beasts around here. Some are also shepherds. So long as you guys stick close to me, you should be fine."

Hal eyed Old Snow skeptically. "Why? Forgive me for my bluntness, elder, but you're not a stone troll yourself."

Keershan flapped his wings excitedly and began walking toward the village. "Well, what are we waiting for? It's getting dark and I, for one, smell cooked lamb, which I haven't had in forev—"

Keershan was interrupted when Old Snow jumped down from the flat boulder and landed in his path, holding up a hand to stop him. Keershan came to an abrupt halt and looked up at the old man with a curious and surprised expression on his dragonic features.

"You can't come with us into the village," Old Snow said. "Humans do not take kindly to dragons, to put it mildly. I recommend retreating further up into the foothills where the hunters usually do not go. While I doubt any of the hunters who hunt in the area have the tools or skills needed to kill dragons, I wouldn't put it past them to try."

"Okay," Keershan said, who sounded and looked

disappointed. He licked his lips. "But get me some cooked lamb, will you? It smells heavenly."

"Yes, dragon, stay here," Surrels said with a smug expression. "We humans will get to sleep in nice warm beds while you have to stay out in the cold and rock."

"Most of us humans will get to sleep in warm beds tonight, that's true," Old Snow said. "Unfortunately, you will not be one of them."

Surrels whipped his head toward Old Snow so fast that Hal was surprised it didn't go flying off his shoulders. "What?"

"You heard me," Old Snow said. He pointed at himself, Hal, and Fralia. "The three of us will spend the night in the local inn, while you and Keershan will stay out here among the foothills until the morning, where we will meet back up to continue our journey to the capital."

"This is outrageous," Surrels said indignantly. He wriggled his tied hands toward Keershan awkwardly. "I am no mere dragon or horse, to have to sleep outside exposed to the elements."

"I agree," Keershan said with a nod. "Why do I have to be stuck with the stupid human?"

Old Snow held up two fingers. "Two reasons. One, if we brought Surrels into town with us, we'd be forced to constantly keep an eye on him and there's a good chance he'd escape. Two, it would be awkward, even for me, to explain to the townspeople that Surrels is in chains for good reason."

"So you want me to keep an eye on him and make sure he doesn't get away, then," Keershan said.

Old Snow nodded. "Exactly. You catch on quickly. Can you do it?"

Keershan pursed his lips before sighing. "All right. If Surrels tries to escape, I'll bite his head off. But you *must* get me some of that fried lamb, okay? I'll accept a fresh piece of fried lamb as payment for my services."

Old Snow grinned again. "Of course. Thank you."

"Plus, look at it this way," Fralia offered. She gestured at Hal and Keershan. "You two share a psychic link, yes? Then you two can simply communicate with each other mentally in case of emergency."

"Great idea," Keershan said. He gave Hal a toothy grin. "What do you think, partner?"

Hal nodded very grudgingly. "It makes sense on a practical level, yes. Without our communication necklaces, we have no other way of remaining in contact with each other over distances."

Privately, however, Hal loathed the idea of having to continue to use his and Keershan's psychic link. It meant getting closer to a dragon that he wasn't sure he wanted anything to do with, even now.

On the other hand, this is yet another reason to get to the capital quickly. The quicker we get to the capital, the quicker we can get our names cleared and our lives can go back to normal.

But as Hal watched Old Snow discuss with Keershan how best to secure their prisoner, he exchanged a look with Fralia and could tell she was thinking the same thing: Regardless of whether they reached the capital or not, their lives were likely not going back to normal anytime soon, if ever.

Chapter Sixteen

It took them a little more than an hour to reach Giant's Foot. Not because the town itself was particularly far, but rather because Old Snow insisted on having an agreed-upon rendezvous point for the party. They eventually picked a group of boulders down the main road leading away from Giant's Foot.

Fralia didn't care. She was so tired after walking down the steep, treacherous slopes of the Tops that she just wanted to sleep in a real bed as soon as possible. Being the bodyguard of a Relic Hunter often meant camping out or sleeping in odd places, but Fralia preferred to sleep in a real bed where possible. She didn't even care that the beds of the inn they were going to were probably not very nice.

I'm tired, dirty, and my feet are killing me. Fralia walked side by side with Hal, the two of them following Old Snow, who moved far too slowly for her liking. *Nothing that a good night's sleep couldn't cure, I hope.*

"So where are we going, exactly?" Hal asked Old Snow as they walked under the archway leading into the town. The signboard reading *WELCOME TO GIANT'S FOOT* hung overhead, though it looked like it'd seen better days. "This town doesn't look big enough to have multiple inns."

"You are correct," Old Snow said. He pointed ahead. "We are going to the town's only inn: The Giant's Toenail."

Her attention piqued by the strange name, Fralia looked in the direction that Old Snow was pointing.

A large wooden building that looked like it might have been a barn at one point towered over most of the nearby houses and buildings. Loud, riotous laughter and singing came from within, and about half a dozen horses were tied up to the posts outside. Bright lanterns were strung on strings across the entryway with a steady stream of drunk-looking hunters, trappers, and villagers moving in and out of the building. Even from here, the stench of alcohol, smoke, and overcooked meat was obvious.

Maybe the food tastes better than it smells. Fralia rubbed her growling stomach. *I'm so hungry that I'd eat pretty much anything at this point, even if it was served from a place called ...*

"The Giant's Toenail?" Hal repeated skeptically. "Did I hear that right?"

Old Snow nodded. "Agate has always had a strange sense of humor."

"Agate?" Fralia repeated. "Who's that?"

Old Snow simply marched up to the front door of the inn, pushed it open, and stepped inside. Hal went in next, albeit with a skeptical look on his face, and then Fralia entered last.

Fralia blinked through a thick layer of smoke. The stench of alcohol stung her throat.

About two dozen tables were scattered in a rather haphazard fashion across the open floor, each full of men and a few women regaling each other with stories of their hunts or paying attention to the band playing on the big stage on the far-left side of the bar. The band was made up of half a dozen musicians who *really* looked like they played music only in their spare time. Their instruments, in particular, looked positively ancient and they sounded like it, too, although it didn't help that many of the inn's patrons were currently doing an enthusiastic round of some folk song whose vulgar lyrics Fralia did not care for.

On the far-right side of the inn was a long bar which was only half-full in comparison to the tables. An elderly, heavyset woman with steel-gray hair done up in a faded red bandanna was busily preparing drinks for a couple of young men who couldn't have been older than eighteen, chatting animatedly among themselves while flirting with the young-looking waitresses who passed them by. The interior was quite warm, too, no doubt thanks to the oven burning in the kitchen behind the counter, though it was a nice change from the chilly mountain air.

Hal began to plonk down on a chair but a woman with a red ponytail snatched it from him, glaring. "Oh, sorry," he said.

"Let's head to the bar," Old Snow said.

"Friendly crowd," Hal muttered as they headed over. "Hey, Fralia, look. They have moth whisky."

"That's disgusting."

"Popular place for such a small village," Hal said, looking at the spacious interior. "More people than I would have expected."

"Well, this *is* the only inn for many miles," Old Snow said. "Anyway, let's go and get us our rooms."

Old Snow made his way toward the bar, walking with complete familiarity and security through the crowded bar. Fralia and Hal followed with Hal looking at everyone suspiciously while Fralia just kept thinking about if the food was any good and what kind of food they served. The way she saw it, if Old Snow felt comfortable here, then it was probably safer than it looked. She did notice some of the inn's patrons turning their heads to watch Old Snow pass, but no one got up to bother or intimidate him.

"Remember to use fake names," Fralia hissed.

"Like that's going to matter when your robes scream 'special air mage, look at me'." Hal said. "I thought Old Snow told you to keep that shawl on."

"Well it's stuffy in here. Anyway, no one's going to notice—"

"Hello there." A big man with an even bigger belly waved his hand in front of Fralia. "What's a genuine army-supported mage doing all the way out here in the Giant's Foot? You lost, maybe?"

Hal gave her a smug look before saying, "Not lost, just staying the night."

A short redhead man stepped in front of Hal. "No

one asked you. Hey, if she's a mage, what does that make you, pal? A jester?"

"Don't mind Amos, love," the first man said. "Why don't the two of us find a nice corner to sit in? Name's Bloka."

Amos was slowly pushing Hal toward the wall.

"Maybe another time, Bloka," Fralia said. "I really have to go."

"What's the matter, kid?" Amos prodded Hal's chest. "Dad didn't teach you manners?"

Something twisted in Fralia as she watched Hal flinch.

Before she knew what she was doing, a tunnel of icy air had broken through the rafters. Amos leaped back to avoid a tile smashing onto his head. Rain-drenched chunks of wood landed in Bloka's beer.

"This way, Oliver." Fralia grabbed Hal's hand and marched him to the bar.

Old Snow glared as he pulled up two stools for them.

"What?" she asked sweetly.

Bloka stormed over, but his anger was interrupted.

"They already have a date, Bloka," Old Snow's voice said from behind the big man suddenly. "With me."

Bloka and his friends jumped back as if in trouble with their teacher.

"They're with you, old man?" Bloka said. "Didn't realize you had friends."

Old Snow nodded. "They're my grandchildren, actually. Come to visit this old man for the first time in years."

Grandchildren? Fralia looked at herself and Hal.

Neither of them bore any real resemblance to Old Snow, so she assumed that Old Snow thought Bloka was dumb enough to fall for such an obvious lie.

And apparently he was, because he scratched the back of his head and said, “They’re your grandkids? I didn’t know you had ’em.”

“There are lots of things you don’t know about me, Bloka,” Old Snow said. He looked at Fralia and Hal and gestured with one hand. “Come along now, kids. This old man is getting hungry himself.”

With that, Old Snow turned and resumed his walk toward the bar. Fralia and Hal did not hesitate to follow. Although Fralia did not look over her shoulder at either Bloka or his friends, she thought she could feel their eyes on her back. Or possibly they were still looking at Old Snow, whom they seemed to consider more dangerous than either her or Hal.

“Grandkids?” Hal asked when they caught up with Old Snow, speaking in a low tone that only they could hear.

Old Snow cracked a grin. “How else am I going to explain traveling with a couple of youngsters like you two unless we’re related? Or would you rather I tell people you’re my personal servants who wait on my every need?”

“I would just like a little bit of a warning before you decide to adopt us,” Fralia said, brushing back her long hair. “That’s all.”

Old Snow shook his head. “Too late. Anyway, it’s a good thing I caught Bloka before he got you two.”

“Is this Bloka guy bad news?” asked Hal, glancing

over his shoulder distastefully at the giant man. "He seemed crude to me."

"Bloka isn't a bad man, necessarily," Old Snow said, shaking his head. "He's just very … territorial. He's lived in Giant's Foot his whole life and thinks he's its protector."

Fralia pursed her lips. "I don't know. He seemed to want to do a lot more than just 'protect' Giant's Foot from us."

Old Snow chuckled. "There aren't too many young women out here, much less pretty ones, so you do stand out rather like a sore thumb, granddaughter."

Fralia blushed again while Hal rolled his eyes, but neither of them got a chance to say anything else before they reached the bar.

Old Snow took a seat at the bar with Hal taking a seat on his right and Fralia on his left. The old barstools squeaked and shuddered slightly under Fralia's weight, but they didn't collapse, although the lack of padding made them uncomfortable to sit on.

But Fralia didn't care. She just rested her chin in her hands and her elbows on the wooden bar, taking in the smell of fried lamb that was being cooked somewhere in the back.

Almost as soon as they took their seats, the gray-haired, heavyset old lady who Fralia had noticed at the bar said, "What do you want?" She kept her back to them and didn't even glance their way.

"Just the usual, Agate," Old Snow said in a polite tone.

Agate paused and looked over her shoulder at them.

Her face was rough with age, but her dark eyes belied an intelligence that Fralia certainly hadn't been expecting to see in the face of a rural bar owner. "Is that you, Snow? Me vision isn't too good nowadays, but I'd recognize that voice anywhere."

"It is indeed, Agate," Old Snow said. He gestured at Fralia to his left and Hal to his right. "And these two youngsters are my grandkids."

Agate's eyes darted from Fralia to Hal and back again like she was reading their minds. Fralia could tell that Agate didn't believe Old Snow's story one bit, which worried her for a moment because she thought Agate might out them in front of everyone.

But then Agate nodded and cracked a friendly smile, showing her rather yellow, uneven teeth. "Why, hello there! Snow, I didn't know you had grandkids."

"That's because they rarely come to visit their poor old grandfather, no matter how often he sends them nice letters," Old Snow said with a sigh. "The perils of old age."

Fralia resisted the urge to roll her eyes. She didn't know why Agate was going along with Old Snow's story but decided it was better than her outing them in front of everyone, especially in front of Bloka and his friends.

"How nice of them to visit," Agate said, "although it seems strange to me, it does, that the first thing you'd do is go drinking with your grands. Not what most grandparents do."

"We're not here to get drunk," Old Snow said with a shake of his head. "We want to rent two rooms tonight.

One for my granddaughter, the other for me and my grandson."

Agate set down the dirty glass she'd been polishing. "You, want a room? I thought you preferred living in that old hut of yours on the other side of the Tops."

"We're going on a journey, Agate, and probably won't be back for a while," Old Snow said, stroking his short white beard. "We spent the whole day climbing down the Tops. That's enough of a workout to make anyone, young or old, want a nice pillow to rest their heads on during the night."

Fralia somehow understood that Old Snow was speaking to Agate in some kind of code. The old barlady certainly seemed to catch on to what he was saying, because she nodded once and said, "Of course, of course. Luckily for you and your grands, I've got exactly two rooms available tonight. Here. Take the keys. You can pay in the morning."

Agate picked up a couple of keys hanging off of a rack behind the bar and tossed them to Old Snow. The keys, old and slightly rusted, clattered on the surface of the bar, and Old Snow quickly snatched them up and hid them away in the folds of his hunter's robes.

"Thanks for the rooms, Agate," Old Snow said. He stood up and yawned. "I'd love to stay and chat, but—"

"Nonsense!" Agate declared. "I know how climbing down a mountain can make a big appetite. Let me get some of our famous fried lamb going for you and your grands. You'll sleep much better on a full stomach than on an empty one. Trust me on that."

That sounded like a good idea to Fralia, but she

noticed that Old Snow seemed a little annoyed. Even so, he did sit down and say, "All right. I suppose a bit of food wouldn't be amiss for this old man's belly right now."

Agate just flashed Old Snow another friendly, lopsided smile before she disappeared into the kitchen, where Fralia could hear her barking orders to the cooks.

Hal, resting his cheek on his hand and his elbow on the bar, looked at Old Snow questioningly. "I take it you and Agate know each other?"

"We've known each other for years," Old Snow replied without missing a beat. He took a sip of the water which Agate had placed in front of them. "Smart woman. We have an understanding."

"I figured as much," Fralia said, still rubbing her stomach. "Just the way you talked to her and the way she responded told me that you two have a history together."

Old Snow looked at Fralia in surprise. "You picked up on that quick."

"So you think it's safe for us to spend the night here, then?" Hal said in a skeptical voice. "She won't rat us out to the government if someone comes knocking?"

Old Snow laughed. "As I said, we're on the outskirts of the law. Agate has her own reasons to ignore or mislead the authorities should they come asking. Not that I expect they will, at least not for a few days, by which time we should be well on our way back to the capital."

Fralia frowned. "And Agate doesn't deserve an explanation of *why* we're on the run?"

"Trust me, she doesn't need or want one," Old Snow said in a confident voice. "She trusts me wholeheartedly.

If I say I need time away, she knows that I have good reason to do it."

Fralia looked at the kitchen doors again. She didn't quite know what to make of that.

On the other hand, she was glad Agate was apparently such a trustworthy person that they did not need to worry about her ratting them out to the authorities. On the other hand, Agate was also just an ordinary woman with no magical powers or influence of her own.

If the queen decides to send Black Soldiers—or even worse, another Defacer—to hunt us down, then I don't know how Agate will react. Or if she'll even survive.

Sighing, Fralia sipped her water, which felt cool and refreshing on her parched lips. She decided to focus on her hunger and how good the food would taste rather than worry about a future she had no control over. Father had taught her that lesson during her youth, and it was one she often reminded herself of.

After all, the more she thought about it, the more her own future looked even bleaker than Agate's.

Chapter Seventeen

A SOFT *THUMP* MADE HAL'S EYES FLY OPEN AND HE SAT UP abruptly, the coarse wool blanket of his bed falling off his shirtless, slightly sweaty body. Hal's fighting instincts had kicked in, and he instinctively reached for his sword, only to realize that he'd left it on top of the dresser on the other side of the room.

Do I really need *my sword?* Hal rubbed his eyes. *Think, Hal, and look. What do you see?*

The room in which Hal slept was dark, nearly pitch-black, save for the light from the moon and stars outside that streamed in between the curtains covering the window. The sky was unusually clear tonight, a sharp contrast to the thick clouds that had been there the night before.

The Desolate Tops are well-known for their unpredictable, constantly-changing weather. I guess the strange weather extends even to the foothills.

A loud snoring sound made Hal start again.

Old Snow lay on a second bed a few feet away from Hal's. He lay flat on his back, his blanket pulled all the way up to his beard, eyes closed as he snored. He grunted under his breath a time or two and muttered something Hal couldn't understand, before turning on his side, his back facing Hal.

Just the old man. Wondering what he's dreaming about.

Hal lay back down on his bed, but didn't close his eyes or try to go back to sleep just yet.

The rooms were almost directly above the stage where the local band played, and the floorboards and walls weren't exactly thick. As a result, Hal had spent the first hour or so lying in bed, listening to the increasingly loud music being played by the band and the bombastic singing from the increasingly drunk bar patrons, including all of their favorite dirty songs that made even Hal, who didn't consider himself a prude, blush.

But it was absolutely silent now, aside from Old Snow's snoring. Agate had probably closed up for the night at some point, which Hal considered something of a miracle. He certainly couldn't imagine an elderly woman like Agate forcing men the size of Bloka to leave, especially once they were drunk and not cooperative.

Before they went to bed, Old Snow had instructed Hal to communicate with Keershan and make sure he'd found a good place to spend the night. Hal had done so reluctantly, using their bond to telepathically communicate with Keershan over a distance. He was surprised to hear a quick response from Keershan, who gave a brief description of his and Surrels's current location, as well as directions on how to get there from the inn. Apparently, Surrels had stopped complaining by now and was just sulking, which didn't surprise Hal one bit.

But Hal was surprised at being able to communicate with Keershan over a distance. Granted, it wasn't a very far distance—probably less than a mile, based on Keershan's directions—but he heard Keershan's thoughts in his head as clearly as if Keershan was sitting right next to him, speaking in his ear. It reminded him of the communication necklace, only clearer, more convenient, and even more efficient.

Long-range telepathy would be useful in a battle. I wonder if the war mages know how to do that, too, or not.

But Hal had to remind himself that, however convenient the telepathy was, it was a strictly two-way communication method between him and a dragon. An oddly friendly, scholarly dragon who apparently had no friends, but a dragon nonetheless.

Hal rubbed his forehead as a thought occurred to him.

His psychic connection with Keershan was two-way. Thus far, Keershan had largely been the one to initiate it, and when he did, he'd shown a surprising aptitude for delving deeper into Hal's thoughts than Hal expected.

But couldn't Hal do the same thing, just in reverse?

Hal sat up again and, swinging his legs over the side of his bed, looked toward the corner of the room where he and Old Snow had dropped their bags.

A draft from an opened window fluttered the curtains, casting a ray of moonlight into the room. It fell upon a dark figure. They were clutching the relic.

Hal and the dark figure stared each other down for

what felt like an eternity, although it was probably less than five seconds. Hal instinctively reached for his sword, only for his hand to grab empty air rather than a solid metal handle, which was when he remembered that his sword was on the other side of the room.

The dark figure, apparently taking advantage of Hal's momentary distraction, shot toward the open window with surprising speed. Hal leaped and grabbed the edges of the thief's scarf flowing out behind him. The thief grunted and came to an abrupt halt, though he didn't let go of the relic.

"Huh?" Old Snow's voice from his bed came somewhere in the darkness of the room. "What's all this racket? Hal, are you all right?"

"I'm … fine, Snow," Hal said in a tight voice, straining to hold the thief back, "but the relic isn't. This thief—"

The thief slammed his back into Hal. The unexpected blow knocked him to the floor, and the thief rushed toward the window. The thief leaped onto the window sill and, without even a single glance, dropped down like a rock and disappeared from view.

"No!" Hal scrambled to his feet.

He noticed a thick rope trailing down to the ground below. The thief was climbing down it, moving as smoothly as a snake on a tree.

Desperate, Hal hoisted himself out the window and began climbing down after the thief. He got about halfway before he heard an odd snapping sound.

The thief seemed to be smirking at him from under his black face covering. Hal looked up. The rope was already half-broken, perhaps unable to hold Hal's weight.

And as Hal watched, the rest of the rope's strands snapped entirely and he fell like a rock.

Hal landed on top of some bushes at the base of the inn's wall. The bushes broke his fall slightly, but his head still bumped against the ground and he heard something in his back crack.

Hal forced his protesting body to his feet and rushed after the thief as fast as he could. The rocky, slightly muddy earth bit at and clung to the soles of Hal's bare feet as he ran.

Despite the pain, Hal was slowly but surely closing the distance between them.

Glancing behind, the thief picked up the pace.

This wasn't going to work. Hal needed some way to make the thief slow down, if not stop him entirely.

But how?

Desperate, Hal bent over and picked up a rock on the ground while still running. Taking as careful aim as he could, Hal threw it at the thief. The rock hurled through the air but missed the thief's head, which he'd been aiming for.

But it did hit the thief's back, causing him to cry out and stumble.

Putting his hands on the thief's shoulders, Hal gasped, "Don't move, thief, or I'll—"

The thief whirled around and struck Hal in the knees with a quick kick. Hal instantly collapsed onto the ground in a heap of pain.

Hal watched the thief dart into the shadows toward

the foothills of the Tops, the relic clutched tightly in his hands. In seconds, the thief would vanish. Hal steeled himself to crawl back to the inn.

That was when a roar split the air, and the large golden form of Keershan flew out of the sky and landed squarely in front of the thief.

The thief, apparently not expecting a dragon, skidded to a halt. To his credit, however, the thief tried to dart around Keershan, but Keershan spread his wings wide and snapped his jaws, forcing the thief to jump back to avoid getting his hands bitten off.

"Drop the relic or else I'll get *really* nasty," Keershan said in a growl of a voice that hardly sounded like the scholarly dragon Hal knew.

Hal was also surprised to see Keershan, but he didn't stop to question it.

Instead, Hal forced himself to his feet and staggered toward the thief, whose attention was still fixed on Keershan. Spreading his arms wide, Hal came up behind the thief and wrapped his arms around the thief's chest before lifting him up and slamming him to the ground. The relic bounced a few feet away until it stopped at Keershan's feet, who immediately inspected it for damage.

Hal would have inspected it as well, but right now he didn't want to risk letting the thief get away. He pinned the thief's back with one aching knee and spat in his ear, "Try anything, thief, and I'll show you what the Kingdom of Malarsan does to relic thieves like you."

The thief immediately went still underneath him.

That was when Hal noticed how small and thin the thief was.

"The relic is safe," Keershan said to Hal. He shoved it toward Hal with his nose. "The thief did not damage it."

"Good to know," Hal said. He looked down at the thief and scowled. "Now to decide what to do with this one."

"There aren't any prisons in Giant's Foot," came Old Snow's voice suddenly, "so if you are thinking we can just hand him over to the authorities, forget about it."

Startled, Hal looked up to see Old Snow and Fralia, both sensibly wearing their day clothes and their shoes.

"Where have you two been?" Hal demanded.

"Unlike you, we couldn't just jump out of our room windows and go on a marathon after a thief we could barely see," Old Snow said. "These old knees of mine wouldn't have survived the fall. Then I'd need one of you youngsters to carry me for the next few days."

"Plus, it was hard to follow you in the dark," Fralia said, rubbing her eyes. "We only found you because we heard Keershan's roar. It's pretty distinctive."

Hal looked over his shoulder at Keershan and said, "And how did you know that the relic had been stolen?"

Keershan gestured at his head with one of his claws. "Surrels talks in his sleep and I spotted the thief running. It meant having to leave Surrels, but I'm pretty sure he's not going anywhere. He was sleeping like a baby last I checked."

Hal nodded and looked down at the thief. "All right,

then. Thief, who are you and why did you steal the relic from me?"

The thief kept silent.

Scowling deeper, Hal said, "If you won't *tell* us who you are, then we'll have to find out on our own."

With that, Hal grabbed the thief's mask and ripped it off his head …

Revealing the annoyed face of a red-haired young woman, glaring up at him with hate in her eyes.

Chapter Eighteen

"Who is this?" Old Snow said with a frown. He tilted his head to the side. "I don't recognize her."

"I don't, either," Hal said. He scratched the back of his neck sheepishly. "To tell you the truth, I was expecting another Defacer or maybe a Black Soldier."

"I don't even know what those are, Relic Hunter," the woman spat, her voice slightly scratchy and high-pitched. "I'm just looking to make a quick buck off some small-town fools. Didn't realize you had a freaking dragon for a pet."

"Actually, I am Hal's steed, not his pet," Keershan corrected. "Steeds are more like partners than pets."

"Tell us how you knew I was a Relic Hunter."

The woman sneered. "The whole world knows you're a Relic Hunter—or at least the whole town does—after you stood up to that Bloka fellow and tried to intimidate 'im with your fancy title. I was planning to take that relic and sell it to my employer. In fact, that's the reason I came out to this little town in the middle of nowhere on the very edge of civilization in the first place."

Old Snow suddenly stepped forward, a very interested expression on his face. "You mean you knew about the relic in the Forgotten Temple?"

The woman turned her gaze to Old Snow defiantly. "I did, actually. Me boss told me, though I don't know where he learned of it from."

Old Snow nodded, a troubled expression on his face.

Hal looked at the woman again and said, "So who is your employer, if you don't mind us asking?"

"I *do* mind, actually," the woman said, "and if you think I'm just going to tell a couple of blokes like *you* who I work for, then you've got another think coming for ya."

Hal tapped his chin. "I suppose you don't *have* to tell us, but I think it would be in your best interest to do so. Right, Keershan?"

Keershan blinked, but then realization dawned in his eyes and he bared his teeth at the woman in the best dragon's smile Hal had ever seen. "Of course. I haven't had fresh human meat in a long time, and you, lady, look positively scrumptious."

Scrumptious? Hal asked telepathically.

What? Keershan replied.

Hal rolled his eyes, but he couldn't argue with the results. The woman's eyes widened in fear, and she started trembling as if an earthquake was rocking her body.

"Fine, fine," the woman said, holding up her hands. "I-I'll tell you whatever you want. Just keep Toothy there away from me and I'll answer all your questions."

Keershan frowned. "Toothy? I don't know if I like *that* nickname."

"I'll call you whatever you want," the woman said, who now sounded like she was on the verge of tears. "Just don't eat me. Please?"

Even Hal couldn't help but feel pity for the poor woman, even if she was a thief who had nearly stolen their relic. He waved a hand toward Keershan and said, "We promise not to set our dragon on you if you tell us who you are, who you work for, and why they want the relic."

The woman gulped audibly. She looked hesitantly at Keershan, as if he was a snake she was afraid would bite her if she looked away, before looking at Hal and the others again. "A-All right. My name is Anija Ti. I specialize in stealing relics."

"Who are you currently working for?"

Anija looked really hesitant. "I work for Shadow Mask."

Hal's eyes widened, and he leaned closer to her. "Shadow Mask? Did you say you work for *Shadow Mask*?"

"That's right," Anija said in annoyance, leaning away from Hal. "And not so loud, will ya? Shadow Mask doesn't like people knowing his secrets. Best if you keep this to yourselves."

"Who is Shadow Mask?" asked Fralia, brushing back a few stray strands of her dark hair. "I've never heard that name before."

Hal turned his attention from Anija to Fralia. "Shadow Mask is an infamous crime lord in the Malarsan criminal underground. He runs a large criminal empire called the Dark Tigers that does everything from blackmail to murder and everything in between. They've been a thorn in the side of the Malarsan government for decades now, but never would I have dreamed that Shadow Mask is a relic collector, of all things."

Keershan narrowed his eyes. "Why would this Shadow Mask person want a relic in the first place if he isn't planning to use it himself?"

"Because relics are rare, expensive, and generally only used by the government," Hal said.

"What will he do now that you've failed to retrieve the relic?" Fralia asked.

"Shadow Mask doesn't tolerate failure. If I don't bring him the relic back by next week, he'll send his men to kill me. And Shadow Mask's assassins are some of the most brutal bastards this side of the war. They make even the most vicious dragons look like fluffy bunnies."

"Perhaps you should try hiding out in the Desolate Tops. I doubt Shadow Mask has any people up there."

Anger flashed across Anija's face. She immediately jumped to her feet and, drawing a dagger from nowhere, slashed it at Hal's throat.

But Old Snow caught Anija's wrist before the knife landed. Old Snow then twisted Anija's wrist. She cried out in pain and dropped her knife onto the ground at Hal's feet. Hal himself took a couple of steps back, well aware that his delayed reaction would have gotten him killed if Old Snow hadn't been there.

"Young woman, I don't think that stabbing someone in the throat is terribly kind," Old Snow said, his voice polite yet firm as he continued to twist Anija's arm. "It's almost as unkind as breaking a person's wrist because they tried to kill one of your allies. Almost."

Anija gasped in pain and looked at Old Snow pleadingly. "Please. Let me go. I promise I'll leave you alone."

Old Snow suddenly let go of Anija's arm and then punched her in the face. The blow knocked Anija flat off her feet onto her back, groaning as she clutched her face where Old Snow had hit her.

Lowering his fist, Old Snow looked at Hal. "What do you think we should do with her?"

Hal bit his lower lip.

Right now, Hal was feeling very uncharitable toward Anija. Not only had she tried to steal his relic, but she'd also tried to steal his life. And if she was working for Shadow Mask, an infamous relic collector, then that made Hal like her even less.

Hal said, "We can bring her with us like Surrels."

Old Snow frowned, then winked at Hal. "I was thinking we could let Keershan have a nibble to slow her a bit and keep her from following us."

Anija, rubbing the nasty bruise on her cheek where Old Snow had hit her, sat up and said in a slightly trembling voice, "Hold on a minute, now, mate. Don't let that dragon have a bite out of me. Just let me go and you'll never, ever see me again. Ever."

Hal tilted his head to the side. "Weren't you just saying that you absolutely needed to get the relic to Shadow Mask by next week, otherwise he'll kill you?"

Anija gulped. The bruise on her cheek had gotten worse already, making Hal wonder how hard Old Snow must have hit her. "Shadow Mask is an idiot. He doesn't know what the relic looks like. I could easily give him a fake relic and he wouldn't know the difference. He doesn't even use them, so I wouldn't have to worry about him testing it out, either."

Old Snow, who had folded his arms behind his back now, said, "All right. We won't let the dragon have at you. Feel free to leave."

Hal pulled Old Snow off to the side. "Are you sure about that? I don't like the idea of killing her, but we could hobble her if we need to keep her from following."

"There's no need," Old Snow said. He looked at Hal, Fralia, and Keershan. "I understand your hesitancy in letting Anija go, but the truth is she did not get away with the relic, nor did she kill anyone."

Anija crawled over to Old Snow and, clasping his hand between hers, looked into his eyes and said, "Thank you, kind elder. No doubt you came upon this deliberation from your years of wisdom and cunning developed from a lifetime of lived experience. Truly, looking into your face is like looking into the face of the gods them—"

Hal sometimes forgot how quickly Old Snow could move, because even he was surprised when Old Snow grabbed the collar of Anija's shirt and lifted her up to eye level. Anija gasped in surprise, but did not try to free herself. She instead stared into Old Snow's eyes fearfully.

And Old Snow looked *scary*. Hal had never seen such anger in the old man's eyes before. He recalled Fralia describing to him how ruthlessly and mercilessly Old Snow had taken out the Black Soldiers, how most of them had died before they even knew it, how none of them had stood a chance even with all their weapons, armor, and training.

"Listen here, thief," Old Snow said, his voice dangerously low. "I am not sparing you because I think you are a decent person. No, I'm sparing you because I've met Shadow Mask and I know that whatever punishment he will see fit to inflict on you will be a thousand times worse than anything these kids could come up with."

With that, Old Snow threw Anija onto the hard-packed dirt. Anija slammed into the ground but immediately hopped to her feet and darted into the shadows. She moved even faster than when Hal had been pursuing her, almost flying rather than running, and soon disappeared into the shadows of the foothills of the Desolate Tops like a ghost in the wind.

Then Old Snow turned to face everyone else and, smiling like normal, yawned and said, "Who else is ready for a good night's sleep?"

Hal, Fralia, and Keershan nodded quickly. Keershan quickly left, likely to return to wherever he and Surrels were sleeping for the night, while Hal and Fralia fell in behind Old Snow, who walked without a care in the world before them.

Although neither Hal nor Fralia uttered a word, Hal could sense that she felt the same way he did: That they were glad they were on Old Snow's side.

Chapter Nineteen

The war camp was abuzz with activity, as it usually was in the aftermath of large battles. Though the battle had been a week ago, fighting a dragon left a mark on the camp. Soldiers ran to-and-fro, eating food, talking with one another, or polishing or cleaning their armor and equipment. Many, however, either laid on beds in the medical tents or sat outside, waiting to be healed while Kolass caught glimpses of the telltale flashes of blue light which indicated that the War Medics were still working their magic on the wounded.

Kolass stopped and spoke with some of the wounded, commending them on their bravery or asking them how they were doing. He even prayed over the recently deceased eighteen-year-old Magst Joss, a new recruit to the Slayer Squad. Someone in the army would contact poor Joss' parents and inform him. Kolass himself often wrote the letters that explained the deaths of his soldiers. He was too busy to deliver the letters to his soldiers' families and loved ones, but he remembered every letter he wrote.

The other generals, of course, never did anything like that. But Kolass believed that a General was not merely a military title, but a father to his men. He wanted each and every soldier, mage, medic, and everyone else under his command to know that he saw them and appreciated their sacrifice. It had the unintended side effect of making the Slayer Squad incredibly loyal to him, loyal to the death even.

Of course, speaking with the younger generation always reminded him of his kids. He wondered why he couldn't have the same relationship with them that he had with his men. He couldn't even remember the last time his kids had hugged him.

Regardless, Kolass did not get to spend as much time talking with his men as he'd liked. He made his way through the busy camp to his personal tent. The entrance bore his personal symbol—a drill piercing a dragon skull. Kolass entered the dark tent and let the flaps fall behind him.

"General Jeniq," a sharp, elderly female voice said in the shadows. "You are late."

Although the interior was almost pitch-black, there was faint light radiating off of the woman sitting in the center of the tent.

Even in her projected form—the way all of them would gather—the queen looked incredibly old and withered. Her throne, encrusted with gold and rubies, made her look taller than she was, but Kolass knew from experience that the woman seated before him didn't even go up to his chest.

Yet that did not mean that Queen Marial Bariwa was weak. On the contrary, the power she wielded dwarfed Kolass's own moulash reserves and she was never afraid to remind him of that when necessary.

Kolass knelt before her. *Was* he late? He'd followed the instruction on the summons. "Apologies, my queen. The battle has left wounded and I permitted myself a moment with the troops."

A snort came from Kolass's left. Kolass looked over. He hadn't noticed, but there were three other people, glowing the same color as the queen.

The first was a tall, muscular woman wearing light leather armor, her skin covered in tattoos. She was almost as tall as Kolass, if significantly thinner, and she wore a cruel, mocking smile on her face.

The second was a young man wearing black armor over his green robes. He leaned on his long staff lazily, his dark eyes twinkling with amusement. He winked at Kolass, although Kolass did not reciprocate.

And finally, there was a mountain of a man who made Kolass look tiny. His round form, covered in thick metal armor, looked almost like fat, until you looked closely and realized it was all muscle. The man had a short, dirty gray beard that covered some of the scars on his face. He merely gave Kolass a single nod in greeting.

"Do you have an issue with me," Kolass said, rising to his feet to face the woman. "I am on the front line, facing dragons directly. Not that you would understand, Mokoa."

General Mokoa shrugged. "My troops have been busy defending the southern border. If we were blessed with a dragon, we would handle it with minimal loss."

Kolass scowled at the slight. Out of all of the generals, she was the one he got along with the least, not in the least due to her sparkling personality and nonjudgmental attitude toward others.

The young-looking man, on the other hand, was rocking on the heels of his feet now and giggled. "Are we about to see a fight between the Dragonslayer and the Beautiful Death herself? Can't imagine it would be much interesting, since Mokoa is not physically there, but—"

"Take no pleasure in conflict among friends, Stayling," the huge man said. "Especially when these friends are fellow generals."

Kolass grunted but couldn't argue with the Grand General.

"Thank you, Tikos," Queen Bariwa said, inclining her head toward the Grand General. She cast her gaze over the four generals. "Unity is of utmost importance in our ongoing war with the dragons, but especially in these days."

"Forgive me for possible impudence, Your Majesty, but I don't see what there is to be concerned about," General Stayling said. "By all accounts, the war against the dragons has been going exceedingly well these past few months. More nests have been cleared out, more lands reclaimed, and a few dragons have even been killed outright."

Kolass nodded. He patted his own armor, which was still stained with the blood of the dragon he'd killed today. "General Stayling has a point. In fact, I just killed a dragon myself not more than half an hour ago, if that."

"Really?" Stayling tossed an amused glanced toward Tikos. "Sounds like you need to get to it, Grand General. How many dragons have you killed so far? One?"

"Eliminating the dragon menace is not a race," Tikos replied in his soft, rumbling voice. "Anytime a loyal soldier of the Malarsan Army slays one of the beasts, it is a victory for us all."

Mokoa smirked and looked up and down the line of generals. "But we don't want to kill *too* many dragons, right? Otherwise, it would make our *other* plan much more difficult to accomplish, wouldn't it?"

Kolass nodded. "It would, yes, but I had no choice this time. This particular dragon was stubborn as hell and wouldn't leave a nearby village alone. Had I been able to drive it off, I would have, although perhaps it would have been better if I'd had a relic on hand to subdue it instead."

Mokoa clapped her hands together. "Speaking of relics, my Hunters have all been reporting major success these past six months, recovering about thirty-seven active relics from various ruins across the kingdom. That brings our total relic count to about two hundred and thirty-four, with potentially hundreds more still out there to find."

Stayling stroked his chin. "Two hundred and thirty-four … that's a small army of dragons right there. Only the gods themselves, I imagine, would be able to stop such an army, although I suspect they won't care so long as we do not tread upon their domain."

"Do not congratulate yourselves too soon, my generals," Queen Bariwa said, her tone serious. "For it is due to the actions of one Relic Hunter in particular that I have called this meeting. One of my Defacers was killed, along with its Black Soldier escort squad, which was totally wiped out."

Shocked silence fell upon the four generals like a heavy blanket. "It was one of General Mokoa's Relic Hunters that did the deed."

All eyes turned on Mokoa now, who wore a shocked look on her face and put a hand on her chest. "One of mine? But I haven't heard anything about any Relic Hunters going rogue. And what was one of *my* Relic Hunters doing in the Tops, of all places?"

"It would seem that the Relic Hunters Corps received a report of a relic located in some ancient ruins located in the Tops," Queen Bariwa said. "The Corps then sent a young Halar Norath to retrieve said relic and bring it back safe and sound. At the same time, our own Defacers learned that these same ruins contained ancient murals and statues depicting the Dragon Riders, so I ordered them to send a Defacer with an escort of Black Soldiers out that way right away. The Relic Hunter and the Defacer ran into each other and fought, a struggle which ended with the death of the Defacer in question."

Mokoa's face turned paler than snow. "Captain Namko didn't report that to me."

"That's because Captain Namko still does not know about the actions of his Relic Hunter," said Queen

Bariwa with a slight shake of her head. "I only know because of a message I received from the Nameless One himself. I've sent some spies to corroborate his report, although I have no doubt that it is true."

"But *how* did this happen?" Stayling asked, looking around at the other generals, aghast. "Defacers and Relic Hunters are *never* supposed to overlap. In fact, the Corps and the Defacers regularly share schedules with each other precisely to avoid these kinds of situations, don't they?"

Mokoa pursed her lips. "Generally, yes, but it would seem there was some kind of miscommunication or something. I will have to ask Captain Namko for an explanation for this. He should know better."

"No need," Queen Bariwa said with a wave of her scepter. "The conflict happened because the Defacers learned only of these ruins a short time ago and were in a hurry to destroy them before anyone else found them. They simply had no time to check with Captain Namko to find out if any of your Hunters were there already."

Kolass frowned. "But even if that is the case, why did this Relic Hunter—Halar, I think you said his name was—kill the Defacer? I know the Defacers can be off-putting, but surely the Black Soldiers must have explained to Halar that the Defacers are on our side."

Queen Bariwa's expression became far more serious. "And that is why I called this meeting. Young Halar did not merely kill the Defacer. He stole the relic and used it to bond with a dragon he ran into up in the mountains."

"bond—?" Tikos said with a gasp. "You don't mean—?"

"I do, General Tikos," Queen Bariwa said. She looked at all four of the generals with a grave expression on her face. "The Dragon Riders have been reborn. Should this young Halar be allowed to live, his actions could spell the end of everything we have been working toward these past ten years."

"Impossible," Kolass said. "Forgive me for my outburst, Your Majesty, but how could a Relic Hunter bond with a dragon? All Relic Hunters are taught to hate and fear dragons and especially are taught to never use the relics they recover for themselves."

"Apparently, this one wasn't paying attention to *that* lesson," Stayling muttered under his breath.

Tikos stepped forward. Despite being a mere apparition with no physical presence, even Kolass felt uneasy at the bulk and mass of the Grand General. It probably had to do with the cold, focused anger in his eyes. "Where is this Halar? I will eliminate him and his dragon myself if they are nearby."

"Unfortunately, we lost track of the traitorous Relic Hunter shortly after that," Queen Bariwa said. "My spies indicate that Halar and his party have likely fled the Tops already, though where they may be headed next, we do not know."

"His party?" Kolass repeated. "Do you mean that Halar is not traveling alone?"

Queen Bariwa looked at Kolass, a displeased expression crossing her aged features. "Indeed I do. Aside from the dragon, Halar is currently traveling with a captured Black Soldier, an old mountain hermit who lives in the

Tops, and, perhaps the one most relevant to you, Kolass. Your daughter, Fralia."

Kolass's world seemed to shatter under his feet when Queen Bariwa said that. He now understood why Halar's name had sounded so familiar, because it was the name of the Relic Hunter that his daughter had told him she had been assigned to. Kolass had not actually met Halar himself, but at the time he'd assumed that Halar would be a normal, trustworthy young man, loyal to the kingdom, with a sense of bravery and daring that was expected of all Relic Hunters.

But if what Queen Bariwa said was true, the implications were so horrific that Kolass didn't even *want* to think about them.

Unfortunately, Mokoa apparently did, because she asked in a voice with barely disguised glee, "So General Jeniq's daughter has turned rogue as well? Did Halar charm her with his rugged good looks? I know that Relic Hunters tend to be considered attractive by the younger women, but I'd think that a mage like her would think more with her brain than with other parts."

"Fralia would *never* betray the kingdom," Kolass said swiftly. "Never. This must be a mistake, Your Majesty."

"Unfortunately, it is not, General Jeniq," Queen Bariwa said with a shake of her head. "Now, of course, we don't know for sure that Fralia is *willingly* aiding Halar. It's possible that he and the old man, who seems to be a prime conspirator, are holding her hostage or are in some way forcing her to travel with them. She did not participate in the killings of either the Black Soldiers or the Defacer, so she may be a victim in all of this herself."

The queen's words lifted a heavy burden off of Kolass's shoulders. "Yes. I hope you are—"

"But if not," the queen continued, "if she has truly voluntarily chosen to help Halar, then you know what must be done."

Kolass didn't move. He knew exactly what needed to be done to Fralia if she had indeed turned traitor, if Fralia had indeed become a threat not merely to the kingdom's security, but to the entire plan that the queen and the four generals had been working toward these last ten years.

Under normal circumstances, Kolass might have been able to use his sway in the army to pardon Fralia of her rebellion and save her life.

But the queen had made it abundantly clear some years ago that there was no forgiveness for those who betrayed the kingdom in *this* way. The plan to retrieve the relics and use them to win the war was unquestionable. Even if Kolass or one of the other generals tried to stop it, they would be put to death like any other foot soldier.

"What must we do about the traitorous Relic Hunter, my Queen?" Stayling asked in his usual smooth voice. "Do you want us to hunt them down?"

"No," Queen Bariwa said, shaking her head. "Each one of you is exactly where you are supposed to be for the plan. Instead, I am sending more Defacers after them. My spies are tracking the party as we speak, and I am confident they will catch them soon enough."

"Why, then, did you inform us of this, Your Majesty?" Tikos asked. "Knowing a Dragon Rider is out there somewhere makes it hard for even me to simply sit here and wait."

"Because you need to know in case the Dragon Rider and his party cross paths with any of you at some point," Queen Bariwa replied. "In any case, I will make sure to have one of my servants keep you four updated as this situation develops. But as I said, I am confident already that the Dragon Rider will be caught, executed, and burned before the end of this week."

The four generals nodded, including Kolass.

"Very well," Queen Bariwa said. "That is all for now. Return to your current stations and await further orders."

With that, Queen Bariwa waved her scepter and her glowing transparent form disappeared. The apparitions representing the other three Generals had also vanished, leaving Kolass alone.

Kolass stood a moment, reflecting on what Queen Bariwa had said. After a while, though, he walked over to his desk in the corner, sat down on the rickety wooden chair, and opened the top drawer. A single gold locket lay within the drawer, which Kolass opened.

The gold locket contained a painting of Fralia as a young girl, sitting in the lap of a painted version of himself while hugging him tightly. Clicking the button on the side of the locket let Kolass shift through painted images of his other children and, of course, his wife, but for the moment, Kolass just let his gaze linger on the image of the smiling, happy-looking girl in the locket.

And wonder if he might ever get to hug her again.

Chapter Twenty

"Trees, trees, trees," Fralia said as they walked. She bent underneath a particularly low-hanging branch, only to nearly stumble over thick tree roots poking out of the ground. "Remind me why we're going through this forest again?"

Old Snow, who walked at the head of the party seemingly without a care in the world, said, "Because the Dark Woods are less traveled than the main roads. The kingdom doesn't have any settlements here, so we are less likely to be caught."

Fralia frowned and looked down at her once beautiful green robes, which were now covered in leaves and debris from the tall long-needled pine trees around them. "Couldn't we have found a less … forested path to travel?"

Hal looked over his shoulder at her. His leather armor looked to be in better condition than her robes, although his hair was messy and had a couple of twigs in it. He stood on top of an ancient stump. "That's because you're wearing those fancy mage robes of yours, Fralia. They're not really good for traveling through thick forests."

"Tell me something I *don't* know," Fralia grumbled as she wrenched her robes free of the bush they got caught in before resuming walking after Hal and Old Snow.

"I actually agree with Fralia." Fralia glanced behind to watch Keershan stomping on a bush. "These trees are too tight and narrow for me to move very efficiently. I certainly couldn't fly here if I had to."

"You think *you're* suffering?" Surrels snorted. He wriggled on Keershan's back. "It feels like I'm riding a particularly pointy rock. I miss my horse."

Up ahead, Old Snow came to a stop and turned to face the party. "All right. We've been walking all day, so I suppose it wouldn't hurt to take a quick break. Plus, it's almost lunchtime and I am starving. We can camp here for the moment."

Grateful at Old Snow's decision, Fralia flopped down on the nearest stump while Keershan also laid down on the ground. Hal, meanwhile, jumped off his stump and walked toward the rest of the party, his sword and shield in hand. "This looks like a good spot to camp. It seems well-isolated and I don't see or hear anyone else around."

"Probably because we're in the middle of nowhere in one of the kingdom's most dangerous forests," Surrels said in a surly voice. "If we stuck to the main roads—"

"We'd get found, captured, and killed," Old Snow said, cutting him off.

"Why are we so worried about the capital anyway?" Surrels yawned. "Daddy's girl here will sort it."

"Shut up," Fralia snapped. "All I'm saying is that my dad is…formal. We need to think of a good way to approach this."

"I'm sure he'll understand." Hal said. "Especially when he hears you've been in danger."

"Hal," Fralia whispered. "The last time I saw my dad, he told me not to bother visiting again until I could fall three stories and not get injured."

"Look, my father could be strict too. It just means he cares about you."

"It was on my birthday, Hal. Two years ago. I still haven't mastered the damn air cushioning technique. Last summer I broke my wrist in three places after jumping off the astronomy building because I wanted him to come to my graduation." She sighed. "Just let me speak to him first when we get there, ok?"

Old Snow joined the rest of the party around the main stump and sat down, where he began digging through his bag. "Let's see … ah, here are the food rations I purchased back in the Giant's Foot."

Old Snow pulled out several tied paper packages, which he tossed to Fralia and Hal. Fralia caught hers and, opening it, found a dried and salted chunk of fried lamb in it. Keershan sniffed the air hopefully. Old Snow tossed him some fried lamb, which the dragon snapped up happily.

"What about me?" asked Surrels, looking enviously at the food everyone else was eating. "Even prisoners need to eat."

Old Snow rolled his eyes, but stood up and said, "All right. We're not going to untie you just to let you eat, but I can feed you like a baby if you like. Don't worry, I won't tell all your Black Soldier friends."

Surrels looked offended by Old Snow's joke, but he just grumbled under his breath as Old Snow walked over, another package of salted meat in hand, and began to unwrap it.

It had been a week since the thief Anija Ti had tried to steal the relic from Hal in the Giant's Toenail. The morning after Anija's theft, Old Snow had forced Fralia, Hal, and Keershan to go even further off the main roads. The Dark Woods was a thick forest essentially wrapped around the western edge of the Tops, forming a sort of ring that was too thick with undergrowth to travel effectively.

According to Old Snow, the Dark Woods was big enough to allow the party to bypass all of the main roads and major towns where they might run into government agents. That was probably true.

Even the dragons were said to avoid the forest. There were many reasons why, but the biggest came down to the fact that the Dark Woods was supposedly haunted by the spirits of dead humans and dragons alike. It was said that out of every hundred people that entered, only one might make it out alive.

Fralia had grown up hearing all sorts of scary stories about the Dark Woods. Granted, she'd mostly heard them from her older brother who had been trying to scare her, but everything Fralia had heard about the Dark Woods since her childhood had lined up with the ghost stories that her brother had frightened her with. Until a couple of days ago, however, Fralia had never set foot in the Woods herself.

That was why Fralia had strenuously objected to cutting through the Woods when Old Snow first brought up the idea. Unfortunately, Old Snow had shot down all her objections, explaining that the Dark Woods was not as dangerous as their reputation suggested and that, as long as they followed him, they should be okay.

And thus far, Old Snow was right. Aside from the stars obscured in the night sky, the Dark Woods was not scarier than any other forest she'd visited. True, they had run into a couple of bears and a pack of wolves, and even a fox, but even those animals had acted about the same as you'd expect wild animals to act. Actually, it was kind of strange how little wildlife they'd seen in the Woods since entering it a couple of days ago.

Although maybe not when you consider what one of our traveling companions is. Fralia glanced at Keershan, who munched happily on the fried lamb that Old Snow had gotten him.

That made sense. Dragons were considered the alpha predator. A single dragon of sufficient size could easily burn an entire forest down all by itself. Tree bears, blood wolves, and various other predators simply couldn't match the sheer power the average dragon wielded. Granted, Keershan was basically a runt and lacked the hyper-aggressive behavior that most dragons had.

Of course, the lack of dangerous wildlife did not mean that their trip had been entirely uneventful. The ground was uneven and muddy in places, not to mention it was getting colder and wetter. Though it hadn't rained nearly as hard as it had that first night at the Forgotten Temple, it had still drizzled a few times along the way south, and Fralia suspected, based on the glimpses of the sky she caught between the tree branches overhead, that it would rain at least a few more times before they reached the capital.

Not that Hal, Old Snow, or even Keershan seemed bothered. Hal teased her about her 'pretty' robes being rather impractical for wilderness travel while Old Snow seemed totally unperturbed by the weather and climate. Given how Old Snow had more or less lived among the elements for his whole life, that wasn't surprising.

What was surprising was Keershan, of all people, showing her a measure of sympathy. The runt dragon had admitted to Fralia that he didn't care much for the forest, either, primarily because as a dragon, the thickly gathered trees made it hard for him to fly or extend his wings. He also needed to be careful about his dragonfire due to all of the wood and leaves.

More than anything, Fralia was starting to like the little dragon somewhat. She still felt a little scared of his big, sharp teeth, his claws that looked like butcher knives, and his huge wings and ability to breath fire, but he'd shown himself to be a curious, thoughtful creature who reminded Fralia of herself when she first started attending the academy as a young teenager.

As if reading her thoughts, Keershan, who had plopped down on the ground nearby with his legs folded under his body, looked at Fralia and said, his mouth half-full of lamb, "Hey, Fralia, can you show me that neat magic trick again?"

Hal, who sat on a nearby log, took a swig of water from his canteen and looked at Fralia with a grin. "Neat magic trick? Is that what they're teaching you at the academy nowadays?"

Fralia rolled her eyes but decided to fulfill Keershan's request. She bent over, scooped up a handful of leaves and dirt, and then tossed the leaves into the air.

At the height of the toss, Fralia waved her hand again, drawing upon the moulash within her soul. A strong gust of wind blew gently through the area, striking the leaves, but rather than dispersing them, Fralia manipulated the air to make it look like the leaves were dancing.

It was, indeed, more of a 'trick' than anything. It was something her air teacher had taught her during the early days of her training, mostly for amusement but also to illustrate certain basic air magic principles. Granted, Fralia tended to use it to amuse or entertain others, especially children, but even she couldn't hide a smile when she performed it.

Keershan flapped his wings a little in excitement. "That is so amazing! I wish we dragons could use magic like that. I mean, we do have plenty of impressive abilities on our own, but human magic is just so different. I feel like I could watch you do that all day."

Fralia giggled slightly. "It's not that impressive, honestly. You should see the war mages who can summon tornadoes or even hurricanes. This is just a trick."

Hal, who was also watching the display, was clearly

trying to hide a smile. He snatched a nearby leaf out of the air and turned it over. "Aside from looking neat, does this particular trick of yours have any practical application or—"

"It's actually a beginner's exercise that is designed to help new air mages get the hang of using and manipulating air. You can use it with paper and similar light objects, but leaves are usually preferred due to how ubiquitous they are. It can be done pretty much anywhere, anytime."

"And yet it still looks entertaining as well," Keershan said with big eyes. He shook his head. "Humans are so fascinating."

"To a simpleminded *runt* of a dragon that has never left its nest before, perhaps," Surrels said atop Keershan's back. "But to sophisticated human adults like me, it's nothing more than a cheap display meant to amuse the simple. I've seen far more sophisticated displays of magical prowess from my own young children."

"You have children?" Hal asked, looking at Surrels with genuine surprise.

Surrels nodded. "I do, yes. Why do you ask?"

Hal finished his lamb and tossed the boned to Keershan, who snapped it up happily. "Because I honestly can't imagine any woman in the world wanting to get within five hundred feet of your sunny disposition."

Surrels's face went bright red at Hal's comment while Fralia and Keershan both snickered. "No one asked you, traitor. And you don't seem to have any children of your own. What does that say about *your* attractiveness to women?"

Hal shrugged. "Just because I'm not married yet doesn't mean I never will be. Besides, you're assuming I haven't already been with a woman. Or that that woman isn't your wife."

Surrels looked like he'd been slapped in the face with a wet fish. Rather than respond directly to Hal, however, Surrels dropped into angry, incoherent mumbling to himself.

Fralia did her best not to look too amused. She glanced to Old Snow. "Why are we still bringing Surrels with us? He's been nothing but a burden ever since we captured him."

"You make a good point, Fralia. We have been so busy moving that we have yet to actually interrogate our prisoner. We might as well start now."

"Interrogate me all you like, hermit, but it won't matter," Surrels said with a sneer. "We Black Soldiers are chosen for our ability to withstand the kind of pain that would make even the strongest of men faint with fear. In other words, do your worst."

Old Snow walked up to Surrels and stopped a few feet away, his arms folded behind his back. "You're assuming that I or anyone else will be using pain to make you speak. I don't recall any of us saying that. Instead, I'd like to point out that you have nothing to gain by *not* telling us about the queen's secrets."

Surrels looked even more confused than before. So did Fralia, in fact, who shared a puzzled glance with both Hal and Keershan. It was clear to her that they understood Old Snow's words about as well as she did, which was to say they didn't.

Old Snow shrugged. "I noticed you've spent more time complaining about your own personal discomfort and inconvenience on this journey than you've complained about how your capture might affect Queen Bariwa's plans. Such behavior doesn't make sense unless you had *some* self-interest." Old Snow stroked his white beard. "Perhaps that's why Queen Bariwa hasn't sent anyone to save you. She doesn't care about you or your loyalty and devotion. She sees you as expendable, a tool to use and discard as she sees fit. Should we kill you now and dump your body in the Dark Woods, I doubt she'd even care."

Fralia found Old Snow's words rather blunt. Granted, she agreed with pretty much all of it and it was perfectly within Old Snow's character to say things like that, but it still took even her by surprise. She was grateful that Old Snow was focusing on Surrels rather than her, as she didn't think she'd be able to stomach that kind of language spoken at her.

"What makes you think she hasn't sent anyone to find me? Even if not for me specifically, Her Majesty has undoubtedly sent people to locate us after you killed the Defacer and my brothers in arms."

"Undoubtedly," Old Snow agreed, "but I find myself asking, what is the point in devoting oneself to a leader who doesn't care about you and won't reward you even if you do come back alive and in one piece?"

"Once we reach the capital and I explain what happened to me to the queen, she will reward me for my loyalty and devotion to her. I am, after all, a loyal soldier to the crown first and foremost."

Old Snow nodded again. "I know another man similar to you who thinks the same thing. I just wish I could convince him of the foolishness of his desire."

Fralia almost gasped herself. She looked at Hal, realizing that Old Snow had not-so-subtly insulted Hal to his face. And based on Hal's expression, Fralia could tell that Hal had realized the same thing.

Surrels, however, seemed to miss the implication entirely. An ugly sneer appeared across his face as he said, "You know nothing, old man. I shall never, for as long as I continue to draw breath, tell you anything at all about the queen's—"

Twang.

An arrow came out of nowhere and lodged itself into Surrels's stomach. Surrels gasped and fell to the ground.

Chapter Twenty-One

Fralia screamed while Keershan jumped away from Surrels and Old Snow looked around wildly. Hal jumped up from his stump and looked up into the trees overhead. He had caught a glimpse of someone above them.

"What the hell?" Fralia threw her half-eaten lamb leg on the ground. "Who shot that arrow?"

Hal pointed up into the trees.

Old Snow tackled Hal off of his stump. The two of them hit the ground roughly, and an arrow whizzed by, embedding itself where Hal had been standing mere seconds ago.

"Everyone, find cover!" Old Snow snapped, rising off of Hal. "Quickly!"

Old Snow bounded off into the Woods while Hal scrambled to his feet and ran behind the nearest bush. He heard Fralia and Keershan running off as well. He dropped to the ground and became very still.

The archer was likely not going to risk climbing down

the trees to search for them himself, but Hal and his allies couldn't talk to each other without revealing their locations.

Keershan and I can speak telepathically. We might be able to coordinate something that way.

That was when Hal realized he'd left his relic in his bag. Crawling along his belly, Hal pushed apart a small portion of the bushes to get a glimpse at the clearing.

Sitting at the foot of the stump with the arrow in it was Hal's bag, right there in the open.

If I leave my cover, I risk getting hit. Hal glanced at the thick treetops overhead. *But if I stay here, then I won't be able to talk with anyone. I'm also risking the loss of the relic itself. What if the archer tries to steal it?*

For some reason, that bothered Hal on a deeper level than he expected it would.

Hal rose and dashed out of the bush as fast as he could.

A loud *thunk* indicated that Hal had been smart to use his shield. Even so, the impact of the arrow almost threw Hal off balance.

A sense of triumph filled Hal's body as his fingers tightened around the leather straps of his bag. Hurling it over his shoulder, Hal kept running, aiming to reach the other side of the clearing.

Another arrow fell, heavier this time. Hal hit the ground hard and lay there for a second, his senses slightly dazed from the impact of the fall.

Twang.

The second Hal heard that sound, he knew he was

dead. He couldn't raise his shield quickly enough. All he could do was watch the arrow fly toward him.

But then a golden creature appeared, and the arrow lodged itself firmly in its shoulder.

Keershan stood in front of Hal, his bulk blocking the archer's view of him.

"Keershan, are you all right?"

"It's not a problem. I've had worse injuries."

Hal grimaced and rubbed his own shoulder, even though it wasn't actually injured.

"You saved me from the Defacer in the Forgotten Temple, of course. Consider it a debt repaid."

Keershan grimaced and staggered slightly. Hal dropped his shield and bag and moved to hold the dragon, who leaned against Hal slightly.

"Sorry," said Keershan with a grunt. "I think the injury is worse than I thought."

Hal shook his head. "We'll get you healed, but first, we need to stop the archer." Hal tried desperately to think. Keershan hadn't been hit first, which meant he wasn't the main target. "Hey," he called. "I know you want the relic."

There was silence.

"I'll destroy it if you don't show yourself."

"Hal," Keershan began.

Something dark fell down from the trees on the other side of the clearing and rose to its full height.

"Stay there!" Hal shouted.

Keershan growled, and the figure stopped. It was a man in a hooded cloak.

"I mean it," Hal said. "I'll use dragonfire or get Keershan here to squash it. Whatever you need it for, it'll be no use broken."

The man began to laugh. "The relic isn't the only thing that can be broken."

Fralia and Old Snow were thrown into the clearing. They were tied up by what looked like the bodies of snakes reaching out from the shadows. "Call me the Archer. That's not my real name, of course, but it fits my position."

"The Archer," Hal said, eyeing the figure suspiciously. "I thought you Defacers all had the same name."

The Archer shook his head. "Unlike my Defacer brethren, my job has nothing to do with defacing art and statues. Instead, my job is to eliminate those who interfere with my brethren's holy mission. Especially Dragon Riders." The Archer gestured over his shoulder with his bow. "By killing my brother and his escort, you have made yourself an enemy of the crown you once served."

"It was an accident," said Hal desperately. "I can explain if the queen would just—"

"The queen understands enough, Relic Hunter," said the Archer. "Otherwise, why would I even be here?"

Hal could not argue the point, but he did notice some movement in the shadows of the trees around them.

The Archer chuckled. "Black Soldiers who fail to protect us demons are no more useful to the queen than a traitor like you. Had you managed to reach the capital with Surrels, he would have been put to death alongside you."

Hal had never liked Surrels much, if at all, but even he had to admit that he found it frightening how easily the Archer dismissed the life of the Black Soldier. It made him wonder just how cruel the queen was if she employed creatures like this to deal with her enemies.

"As for why we're talking, that's easy," said the Archer. His green eyes flashed from within his hood. "I didn't come alone."

Something emerged from the shadows nearby, although it didn't look like *human* movement to him. Something shaped vaguely like a cylinder moved among the trees of the Dark Woods, barely visible to the human eye, not helped by the thick treetops overhead blocking out most of the sun's light.

The creature must have been another demon, although it completely lacked the Archer and the Defacer's humanoid forms. It looked like a human-sized octopus with purplish-green skin and a disturbingly human-like face on its body. Its tentacles ended in eight serpentine heads, which hissed and snarled as the creature moved into the dim light of the Dark Woods. Beady red eyes peered out at Hal and Keershan while its beak opened and closed rapidly like it was hungry.

The Archer gestured at the octopus-like creature. "Behold, Rider, my other brother, whose real name cannot be spoken on the human tongue, so you may call him the Grappler. Although that may be the last thing you call him before he kills you and your friends."

Chapter Twenty-Two

UNDER ORDINARY CIRCUMSTANCES, KEERSHAN WOULD have been interested in seeing a real-life octopus. He'd never seen such a creature in person before, mostly because he had never ventured to the sea and the Kingdom of Malarsan was a landlocked nation. His mother, who had traveled much of the world in her younger days, had once described the creatures to Keershan and his siblings during storytime.

But Keershan could not recall his mother ever mentioning the tentacles ending in the heads of venomous snakes, nor could he recall her describing them as being bigger than humans.

She did tell me that they taste pretty good if cooked with dragonfire, though, but somehow I don't think I'm going to get to eat any seafood today.

Hot pain pulsed through Keershan's shoulder, reminding him that he was less than useful against the two demons.

"What in the world is that?" Hal asked, staring at the Grappler, his eyes big with horror.

"Were you not just listening?" the Archer said. "That is another demon. Admittedly, he doesn't usually see much action due to his strange appearance, but he's very good at crushing humans to death."

The Grappler grunted. It tightened its grasp on Fralia and Old Snow, forcing more breath out of them.

"What do you want?" said Hal. "Do you want me? Because if it's me you want, you can have me. Just … just leave my friends alone."

The Archer shook his head. "It's not you, specifically, I want. Rather, it's the relic in your bag. Give it to me. And in exchange, I will spare the lives of your friends."

Keershan didn't believe the Archer one bit.

Fortunately, Hal seemed to come to the same conclusion, because he said, "Liar. You just said that you were here to kill me and my friends. You don't just want the relic."

The Archer tilted his head to the side. "And? Can you or your pet dragon possibly stop us, even if that was the case? Between me and my brother, your options are limited, to put it nicely."

"Keershan," Hal whispered. "Don't look at me or move. On my command, I want you to breathe a stream of fire at both the Archer and the Grappler. Make sure it comes hot and fast so they don't have time to react. I'll follow up from there."

Keershan shifted his weight again, which Hal seemed to understand because he patted Keershan on the back approvingly.

"Well?" the Archer asked, prompting both Hal and Keershan to look at him. "What choice have you made? Have you decided to surrender, as would be most wise?"

Hal shook his head. His hand rested on his sword, which was still sheathed. "My choice, demon, is simple: Burn."

Without hesitation, Keershan opened his mouth and unleashed a continuous stream of fire at the Archer before shaking his head back and forth. Flame spread over the Archer and the Grappler, and they screeched in pain. The Archer fell backward, clutching at its burning robe while the Grappler's limbs started thrashing about as it tried to escape the burning flames. The stench of burning demon flesh soon filled the clearing, contrasting sharply with the damp smell of the wet leaves and grass around them.

"Kill the Grappler and save Fralia and Old Snow. I'll take care of the Archer."

Keershan rushed toward the Grappler, which was still thrashing its tentacles about. It didn't thrash Old Snow or Fralia, however, perhaps because of their weight, but Keershan opened his mouth and breathed more fire on those two tentacles. Hot flames scorched the Grappler's snake-like skin, forcing it to let go of Old Snow and Fralia. The two humans immediately crawled away from the fight.

Which was good, because Keershan charged straight into the Grappler.

The impact of Keershan's blow sent the Grappler rolling backward like a rock. The Grappler slammed into a tree hard enough to make leaves and a few loose branches fall. Keershan opened his mouth and launched a fireball at the stunned Grappler, the orange-red ball of flame hurtling through the air like an arrow.

But the Grappler held up its arms in front of its face and blocked the fireball, which exploded against its tentacles. That left black scorch marks on its limbs but did not seem to significantly harm the demon, which slowly lowered its tentacles and glared at Keershan.

Uh-oh, Keershan thought. *It doesn't look happy.*

With a roar like a bear, the Grappler got to its feet and rushed toward Keershan faster than he could follow. Its movement was halfway between the slither of a snake against the ground and the wriggling movement of an octopus, a strange sight that Keershan found somewhat mesmerizing.

At least until the Grappler crashed into Keershan and wrapped some of its tentacles around his body. The Grappler smelled even worse up close, like dead fish left to rot in the sun for too long. Keershan began biting and slashing into the Grappler's body and limbs, aiming for whatever his teeth and claws could reach.

The Grappler's snake heads snapped and bit at every available inch of Keershan's body. Its fangs were not long or sharp enough to pierce most of his scaly hide, but they still whipped his body hard, striking his scales hard enough that Keershan heard what sounded like cracking noises. Though, he couldn't be sure if it was his scales or the skulls of the Grappler's snake heads that was cracking. Keershan stretched out his claws, leaving deep grooves in the Grappler's flesh, causing black blood to flow out like water from a dam.

The Grappler slammed one of its heads into his wounded shoulder, creating an explosion of pain that made Keershan cry out. The Grappler slammed his face with two of its snake heads, knocking Keershan back. It started pummeling him over and over again, its tentacles whipping too fast for Keershan to follow or defend against.

Then, a powerful burst of wind came out of nowhere and struck both Keershan and the Grappler. Both were sent sprawling across the ground with the Grappler's tentacles coming off of Keershan's body with several soft pops.

Fralia's hands glowed softly with green energy, which reflected in her blue eyes.

The Grappler was already recovering from the blast.

Taking a deep breath, Keershan drew upon the fire inside his body. The flames built up hotter and hotter in his throat, but Keershan didn't unleash them just yet. He wanted to make sure that his next attack would be his last. That meant that Keershan couldn't move very much without destroying his own concentration.

An expression of realization crossed its disturbing features. Back on its tentacles, the Grappler rushed toward Keershan, snake tentacles flailing, its dark red eyes gleaming with hatred and hunger.

But then Old Snow dropped down from the trees overhead and, landing on the Grappler's head, drew a sharp, jagged, rusted-looking knife from his side and stabbed it directly into the Grappler's skull.

The Grappler came to an abrupt halt, hissing in pain. It immediately began snapping at Old Snow, but the hermit had drawn another even longer knife from within his cloak and was deftly deflecting the snake heads that came in from all directions while continuing to bury his blade deeper and deeper into its head. Black blood bubbled out from the space where Old Snow carved into it, though the injuries hardly seemed to slow the creature down.

Old Snow's attack did, however, slow down the creature just enough for Keershan to finish it off.

Unable to hold the burning fire in his throat anymore, Keershan opened his mouth and launched a column of fire at the Grappler. Old Snow jumped off its head. Keershan caught a glimpse of the Grappler's eyes widening in shock before the flames enveloped its entire form. The Grappler's death screams echoed throughout the Dark Woods, distorted among the flames.

Keershan didn't stop or hesitate. He just kept bathing the Grappler in flame until he could no longer feel the heat burning his throat, at which point Keershan closed his mouth and took a step back. He always felt a bit woozy after breathing so much fire, and today wasn't an exception.

Fralia used another burst of wind to carry the flames and sent them sweeping away.

As the flames died down, the Grappler was no longer there.

Where once had stood the demon was now a slowly growing pile of ash. Old Snow's knife that had been embedded in the Grappler's skull rested on the pile of ash, its blade twisted and melted from the heat, its wooden handle absolutely ruined. The stench of burned wood and scorched skin filled the air, though even as Keershan inhaled the scent, he could tell that it was dying off.

Good, Keershan thought with a sniffle. *It's an ugly smell, anyway.*

Keershan couldn't believe what he'd just done. He'd killed a literal demon. Granted, he did need help from Old Snow and Fralia, but that did not change the fact that Keershan had done what he'd only read about other dragons doing in the old legends.

Makes me feel like a real Steed. I bet Mother would be proud of me if she could only see—

Sharp pain—unlike anything Keershan had felt before—raced through his chest like lightning. In the back of his mind, he vaguely recalled myths speaking of 'death curses' that demons would sometimes cast upon their killers the moment before their death, but Keershan hadn't noticed anything as the Grappler was dying.

Fralia screamed, "Hal!" prompting Keershan to look across the clearing …

He turned to see Hal, standing before the Archer, a claw stabbed straight through his stomach.

Chapter Twenty-Three

Explosive hot pain spread through Hal's whole being from his stomach. The agony was so intense that Hal could barely even think. He dropped his sword on the ground and forgot about Keershan's amazing display of dragonfire and the Dark Woods around him.

Instead, Hal's focus solidified on the Archer, who stood before him, thick claw extended from his hand. The claw had pierced Hal's stomach, and, although Hal didn't—couldn't—spare a glance over his shoulder, he could sense that it had pierced all the way out the other side.

The Archer's face, once obscured by his hood, was easier to see now up close. It reminded Hal too much of the Defacer's visage, except thinner and clammier. The Archer still smelled of dried blood itself, but it did not seem to be in as much pain as one would expect from a creature that had been stabbed through once already.

"H-How …?" Hal gasped.

The Archer grinned, a distinctly snake-like expression. "Swords cannot kill a demon. Or have you never heard that only a Dragon Rider, wearing a relic, can truly kill one of my kind?"

Hal would have answered if not for the claw embedded in his stomach. Hal could barely even breathe. He just stared hopelessly into the Archer's eyes, feeling the life seep out of him.

Then the Archer abruptly ripped its claw out of his stomach, causing Hal to collapse onto the ground. He barely felt the impact of his head against the dirt and mud, however. All his attention was on his new stomach wound, from which blood gushed freely. He pressed his hands against it, but that did nothing to stop the flow, succeeding only in getting his hands bloody.

The Archer's foot appeared in front of his face and Hal looked up. The Archer looked down at him, an amused grin on its face.

"Where is the bravado and courage you were displaying so cavalierly earlier, Rider?" the Archer asked in a mocking tone. "Did I manage to kill it along with you? If so, then you are even weaker than I thought. Not that I am surprised. You are the son of a weak man."

"Son?" Hal repeated, practically spitting out the word. "My father …?"

The Archer grinned. "Oh, yes. I knew your father. He was even weaker than you."

Questions popped into Hal's mind, but he never got a chance to ask them because a fireball launched through the air toward the Archer.

The Archer did a backflip, neatly avoiding the fireball, which crashed into a nearby tree and set it ablaze. The light from the flames cast intense heat and strange shadows everywhere, although Hal barely noticed that. He only heard feet running to him and then felt two soft hands grab his shoulders and roll him onto his back.

It was Fralia. With her hair hanging down her head, her blue eyes were huge with worry and concern. Her face was dirtier than usual, although she looked mostly unharmed as far as Hal could tell.

"Hal, Hal, can you hear me?" Fralia said. She shook him gently. "Hal!"

Hal didn't understand why Fralia seemed so worried about him until his stomach burned again and he looked down.

His injury was even worse than he thought. His blood had a green tinge to it now, and some sort of infection seemed to be spreading. It was hard to tell, due to how much pain he was in.

"Fralia?" Hal said. He gripped his stomach wound tighter. "What happened?"

"Thank the gods," Fralia said with a sigh. "Don't move."

Fralia waved her hand over Hal's stomach. A soft white light glowed from her hand, and for a moment, Hal felt a warm, soothing sensation wash over his body. It managed to dull most of the pain, giving Hal a moment of clarity.

But it was a brief moment. In the next instant, the light faded, and Hal gasped in agony.

"What?" Fralia asked in surprise. She looked from

her hand to Hal's wound, furrowing her brows. "Why didn't the spell work? It doesn't make sense. I—"

Another loud roar interrupted Fralia, causing even Hal to forget about his pain just long enough to look toward the source of the sound.

Keershan and Old Snow were fighting the Archer. Keershan kept slashing at the Archer with surprising swiftness, while Old Snow would occasionally dart in to get in a few good blows here and there whenever the Archer left an opening to take advantage of.

But the Archer moved with unearthly speed, dodging or blocking their moves without much effort. Despite that, neither Keershan nor Old Snow gave the Archer any time to attack or respond. It seemed like they were putting their all into keeping the Archer off-balance and unable to react, although Hal had no idea how long they would be able to keep that up.

Why isn't Keershan using his dragonfire? His thoughts felt distant, as if he was listening to someone else's thoughts. *We know that dragonfire works. Use it.*

Keershan did not seem to hear Hal's thoughts because he kept using his teeth and claws to attack the Archer.

Granted, it seemed to be working. The Archer avoided another combined attack from Keershan and Old Snow, before jumping onto the branch of a nearby tree, well above both Keershan and Old Snow.

He readied another attack—this one targeting Old Snow—when Keershan breathed out a streamer of fire that Fralia redirected with her control over wind. She created a wall of flame, blocking the Archer from getting too close to them.

"We need to run," she said.

Old Snow glowered at the Archer through the tree, but pulled his gaze away. "Move. Quickly. There might be a place we can hide nearby. We've got him cut off. But we won't have much time."

Puzzled, Hal tried in his pain-filled haze to follow the hermit's finger and suddenly wished he couldn't.

Now half of the Dark Woods—or at least it looked like half—was on fire. Roaring flames ripped through the entangled trees and branches, casting an oppressive heat on the party that did away with the damp air that had previously filled the forest. Crackling wood popped and snapped as branches crashed down from the trees, including one that fell just a few feet from where Hal and Fralia lay.

"Did those demons set the whole forest on fire?" Fralia asked.

Hal blinked. No. He knew this was because of Keershan's dragonfire, which he'd used without worrying about their environment and what Fralia had done.

They staggered through the forest, Old Snow leading them quickly, gradually moving away from the heat and flame. When he stopped them near a small stream, Hal didn't know what Old Snow intended, but then he led them into a small cave.

"We can wait here," Old Snow said.

His voice sounded impossibly distant.

The pain from his infected wound suddenly became

too much for Hal to bear. Darkness rapidly gathered in the corners of his eyes as he heard someone—maybe Fralia—cry out his name.

And then shadows covered his vision, and Hal no longer thought anything at all.

Chapter Twenty-Four

THE ROAR OF THE FLAMES WAS GROWING LOUDER, AND the fire was spreading faster than ever. It consumed more trees, branches, bushes, and grass as it grew, pushing up toward the stream—which created a natural barricade from it—but they couldn't stay in the cave indefinitely. The heat combined with the humidity of the forest made Fralia break out into a heavy sweat.

Old Snow knelt beside Hal and touched his forehead. "Hmm. Not dead. Not yet." His eyes snapped open and he looked at Fralia. "Can you heal him?"

Fralia gestured at Hal's wound. "I tried, but my magic wouldn't work, and I don't know why."

"We'll figure that out later. For now, we need to get deeper into the cave to wait out the fire."

"Can't Fralia just use her magic to put it out?" Keershan asked, glancing over his shoulder at the burning flames behind him. "I understand that some of you human mages specialize in water magic."

Fralia shook her head. "Won't work. I specialize in air magic. While I do know a few basic water spells, none of them are powerful enough to put out a fire this big, at least not on their own."

Old Snow looked out of the cave. "I thought we had more time. Looks like the flames are pushing faster than I expected. Now we need to run," Old Snow said, sliding his arms underneath the unconscious Hal and lifting him up with surprising gentleness and strength. The hermit deposited Hal onto Keershan's back, setting him up in such a way that he wouldn't fall off.

Rising to her feet, Fralia said, "All right. We've got Hal, so let's—"

Old Snow, however, rushed back *toward* the flames. He ran too fast for Fralia to call him back, although she wanted to because as far as she could tell the old hermit was trying to get himself killed.

Old Snow disappeared among the flames briefly, his form obscured by the heat and smoke and fire, vanishing from view entirely.

"Old Snow!" Fralia called out in horror. "No!"

"What is he doing?" Keershan asked in disbelief. He shifted his weight, perhaps to make a more comfortable position for Hal. "Humans don't have natural fire resistance like we dragons do. Is he trying to kill himself?"

Fralia didn't have the answer to Keershan's question, but the answer presented itself soon enough. Old Snow suddenly burst out from the trees, carrying something large and black over his shoulder. He snapped, "What are you kids waiting for? Run!"

To Fralia, it seemed like they ran for hours through

the dark, dense woods. And the deeper they went, the thicker and denser the trees became until soon they could no longer see where they were going at all. Fralia kept tripping over her own robes until she got the bright idea to hike them up like she was wearing a very fancy long dress that went down to her feet.

But then Old Snow suddenly shouted, "Stop!"

Her stop was awkward. She skidded across the ground, which was even muddier than the rest of the forest, and would have fallen flat on her behind if she didn't lean against a nearby tree for support. Resting her back against the rough bark of the tree, Fralia looked back at her friends.

Keershan stood a few feet from her, panting hard, his golden scales scratched and covered in mud. Hal, fortunately, still lay on his back, although he looked even worse than before.

Old Snow, meanwhile, stood a little bit behind Keershan. Thanks to the darkness of the trees, it was hard to make out many of Old Snow's features, but she noticed he was still hauling the big object over his shoulder.

How can he run half a mile carrying something that looks even heavier than me?

At least this part of the Woods was cooler than the part that was on fire. In fact, now that Fralia thought about it, she couldn't even hear the flames anymore. It was eerily quiet here, which would normally bother her, but Fralia just wanted to relax and enjoy the relative silence for now.

"Did we do it?" asked Fralia in between pants.

"We outran them, yes," Old Snow said. He was panting, but not as much as Fralia. "I expect the flames will die out eventually, as the Dark Woods is rather green this time of year. If not, it will probably rain within the next day or so, which should put the fire out before it spreads too far."

Keershan grimaced. "Perhaps, but dragonfire is resilient. It would take a lot of rain to put it out."

Fralia looked at Keershan in confusion. "Isn't dragonfire just normal fire? It always seemed that way to me."

Keershan shook his head. "Common misconception among humans, but no, dragonfire is different from normal fire. It's even different from the magical fire that your fire mages can conjure. It burns hotter, longer, and deeper than normal fire. Water can put it out, but like I said, it takes a lot."

That explanation made no sense to Fralia, although that may have had more to do with her own exhaustion and pain than Keershan's words.

Old Snow seemed unperturbed. "The Dark Woods has survived worse than this."

Keershan knelt down and gently slid Hal off his back. The unconscious Relic Hunter didn't move at all when Keershan did that, nor did he make a sound.

Despite knowing how useless her magic was, Fralia walked over and knelt beside Hal. She brushed a finger across his right cheek, his skin cold and clammy to the touch. "He's still alive, I think, but barely."

Keershan growled under his breath.

Fralia noticed the arrow sticking out of Keershan's shoulder and asked, "Do you need my help with that arrow, Keershan? I might be able to heal you, at least."

Keershan shook his head and grunted. “No. I’ll be fine. It’s Hal who you should be worried about.”

“We have another person whose injuries likely *can* be healed by your skills,” said Old Snow.

Old Snow laid the burden on his shoulder on the ground, allowing Fralia to see the unconscious face of Surrels.

Fralia couldn’t decide who looked worse: Hal or Surrels. On one hand, Hal had a gaping, infected wound in his stomach. On the other hand, Surrels had an arrow sticking out of his stomach and was moving about as much as Hal. The two looked identical in their near-dead state and Fralia did not have high confidence for either of their rates of survival.

“What is this?” Fralia asked, looking up at Old Snow. “Why did you save this man’s life? He’s one of the bad guys.”

Old Snow, however, shook his head. “I didn’t save him because he’s good or nice. I saved him because I still think he could be an invaluable ally in our fight.”

“Fight?” Fralia repeated. “Who said anything about fighting?”

Old Snow smiled grimly. “Have we not been locked in battle after battle against the demons ever since Hal discovered and used the relic? What gives you any reason at all to think that we won’t keep fighting every step of the way to the capital?”

Fralia frowned. She had to admit Old Snow had a point, although she was loathed to give it to him. Not because he was wrong, but because Fralia still held out hope that somehow Father would be able to fix everything for them, and then life could go back to normal for everyone.

That was why Fralia tried desperately to avoid the voice in the back of her head that told her there were some things even her father couldn't fix.

"Fine," Fralia said with a shake of her head. She gestured at Hal and Surrels. "I *might* be able to heal Surrels, as his injury looks less severe than Hal's. But Hal is still the bigger priority, so how do you suggest we heal him?"

Old Snow scratched his chin in thought. "We can't save him ourselves, but I believe there may be someone living within the Dark Woods who can. An old friend of mine."

Fralia raised an eyebrow. "For a hermit who had supposedly spent his whole life in the Tops, you sure do have a lot of old friends around the kingdom."

Old Snow shrugged mysteriously. "I may not get out much, but you'd be surprised by how many visitors a silly old man like me gets. In any case, I think I may know of a way to slow the infection that's killing Hal. Do you have his relic?"

Fralia started and looked at the bag in her hands. She *had* picked up Hal's relic bag after the flames started. Oddly, she didn't even remember doing that, but she supposed there had been a lot going on at the time. "I do."

Old Snow pulled the relic out of the bag and put it on Hal's head. He tightened the straps as if to make sure that Hal wouldn't lose it. Hal's body glowed a faint golden color, the same shade of gold as Keershan's scales.

Although his stomach wound was still wide open, the green infection looked weaker. Fralia even thought she saw it contract angrily, almost like it was frustrated by this new roadblock in its progress.

I must be tired as hell if I'm anthropomorphizing an infection. Fralia rubbed her eyes.

Fralia turned her gaze to Old Snow. "What's happening? What did you do to Hal?"

Old Snow pointed at the relic. "I did nothing. It's the relic's doing. It is slowing down the rate of Hal's infection. Under other circumstances, it could potentially even cure him of the infection by itself, although I don't think it's strong enough to do that yet."

"How did you know the relic could do that?" Keershan asked in amazement. He yawned. "And why do I feel so tired?"

Old Snow pointed from the relic to Keershan and back again. "Technically speaking, it's the work of the bond between you and Hal. By putting the relic on Hal's head, I was able to create a conduit between the two of you. The relic is simply drawing upon your own natural strength and regenerative abilities, amplified through your bond with Hal, to fight off the infection. Many of the old legends of the Dragon Riders spoke of how the strong bond of a Rider and his Steed could save the Rider from injuries or illnesses that would kill any other man. A few legends even state that a Rider can come back from the dead if his bond is strong enough, although I sincerely hope we do not have to test out *that* legend anytime soon."

Keershan gazed upon Old Snow with respect shining

in his eyes. "I hadn't heard about that, and I've read or listened to *many* legends about the Dragon Riders. Admittedly, the parts about the bond have always been confusing for me, so I guess I shouldn't be surprised."

Fralia knew even less about the Dragon Rider myths than Keershan, but she couldn't deny that Old Snow's explanation had some merit. Although Hal still looked like a mess, his infection was already starting to look better and some of the color even seemed to be returning to his skin.

"Yes, I am glad it works," Old Snow agreed. He rose to his feet and stared off into the darkness. "Now, if you will excuse me, I need to seek out my old friend. She should be somewhere nearby, but it has been ages since I last saw her, so it may take me a while to find her. In the meantime, you two stay here and keep watch over Hal. Heal him and Keershan as best as you can. That arrow looks bad."

With that, Old Snow darted into the darkness. Fralia watched him go before turning her gaze back to Hal and Surrels. With a sigh, Fralia stepped around Hal and knelt beside Surrels. Inspecting his wound as closely as she could in the darkness of the trees, Fralia could not help but glance at Hal and his shining golden form.

I hope Old Snow can find his old friend, Hal. Because if he doesn't, then I don't know what we're going to do.

Chapter Twenty-Five

HAL BLINKED AND FOUND HIMSELF SITTING ON A HILL overlooking what he recognized as Lamb's Hand. The tiny farming village looked even tinier from up on this hill, which he realized was Manus Hill, named after one of the founders. It was the largest hill in the town and a popular spot for children to play or for couples to come together for some alone time. Hal himself had certainly spent a good chunk of his childhood up here whenever he wasn't working.

But I shouldn't be here, Hal thought. *I should be* dead.

That was what bothered Hal, he realized. He should have been dead.

That prompted another puzzled frown. *Wait.* Why *should I be dead?*

"Probably because you got ran through by a demon, son," an extremely familiar voice said behind Hal, a voice he had never thought he'd ever hear again.

Hal slowly turned around.

A man baring the tattered green-and-silver armor of the Malarsan Army stood just a few feet from Hal. He looked an awful lot like Hal, except older and with more gray in his hair. He also had several scars on his face that Hal lacked, scars gained from years of battle against the dragons. The only significant difference was the blackened spot on his chest.

It looked like the result of dragonfire.

But Hal didn't care too much about the tiny details. He was too busy trying to not believe what his own eyes were showing him.

"Father?" Hal asked, his voice breaking as he said that one word. "You're dead."

Father smiled that same warm expression that Hal had thought he'd never see again. "I am, son. I am."

Hal blinked. "But if you're dead, then how am I talking to you? What are we doing back in Lamb's Hand?"

Father glanced around Manus Hill, a frown on his face. "This isn't Lamb's Hand, and we aren't standing on Manus Hill. It looks—and even feels—just like it, but in the end, it only exists within your head."

A soft breeze blew through just then, a cooling sensation on Hal's skin, causing the necklace hanging from Father's neck to sway slightly. The grass under Hal's feet shifted under the wind.

Hal put a hand on his head. "In my head? What are you talking about? Where are we? What happened to me?"

Father walked over to the flat rock next to Hal and took a seat. He suddenly looked even older than before, his hair grayer, his skin a little tighter around his skull. His gaze went out over Lamb's Hand, although he seemed to be looking at something else.

"You were stabbed by a demon in the real world," Father said, putting his chin in his hand. "The demon didn't *just* stab you, however. It infected you with a demonic disease that will either kill you or turn you into a demon yourself."

Hal stiffened and looked at his body, which was whole and uninjured. "A demon? But I don't want to be a demon."

Father chuckled. "No one does, son, but sometimes we end up that way. One of the hard lessons of adulthood for sure."

Hal licked his lips uncertainly. He wasn't sure if he should be overjoyed to see his dad again or annoyed that this was apparently some kind of complex mental illusion. "That answers one question. What about the other?"

Father gestured widely with one hand. "This is essentially your body's way of protecting your mind from the infection. The infection is more spiritual than physical, so this illusion is protecting your mind from it. But the infection will reach you eventually, unless someone heals you first."

Hal rubbed a hand against his chest. "I didn't know my body could even do something like that."

"Not on its own." Father shook his head. "But you're special, Hal. Different. You're a Dragon Rider, the first in countless ages. There's a lot you don't know your body can do, especially with your bond with your dragon friend."

Hal stiffened. "Are you telling me that the only reason I'm not either dead or a demon right now is because of Keershan?"

"More or less," Father said. "It's strange, but life is often strange. And why the demons seek to destroy the relics. Should the Dragon Riders rise again, the demons would fail in their own quest, a quest that Queen Bariwa is happily helping them with. The old fool."

Hal blinked. He'd never heard Father speak so disrespectfully of the queen before. Anytime Queen Bariwa came up in conversation with Father in the past, Father would always speak of her with utmost respect and integrity. Sometimes he'd even go a little too far, treating the queen more like a deity in some respects than a mere human being.

What happened to sour him on Queen Bariwa like this?

Shaking his head, Hal said, "So you know what the demons are trying to do. Can you tell me?"

Father smiled sadly. "I would if I could, son, but unfortunately, I died before I found out."

Hal frowned. "But you seem so real."

Father chuckled again. "My knowledge is largely limited to what you know. Wish I could be of more help."

Hal nodded slowly. "That still doesn't make a whole lot of sense to me."

Father nodded. "Welcome to the club. I'm just happy I got to see my son again one last time before I need to move on. The gods are calling me."

"You're leaving?" said Hal, unable to hide the disappointment in his voice. "Already?"

"Soon," Father said. He tilted his head to the side, like he was listening to a voice only he could hear. "But not yet. I still have something to tell you. A message from those who came before you."

Hal scratched the back of his head. "Those who came before me? Do you mean our ancestors?"

Father smiled. "The others. The Dragon Riders of old. Not my ancestors, but yours."

"How can they be my ancestors but not yours?" Hal asked. "We are related, are we not?"

Father tapped Hal's chest with one finger. "Because, son, you are a Dragon Rider and I am not. I wish I was, though. Then I might still be alive. What matters is delivering the message that your ancestors asked me to give you before I fade away."

"Fade away?" Hal repeated. "What does that mean?"

Father shook his head. "No time to explain. Your ancestors told me to tell you that you must *avoid* the capital."

Hal frowned. "Avoid the capital? Why?"

Father leaned toward Hal, his expression far more serious than it had been even a few minutes ago. "Because it is the heart of evil, and you and Keershan are not ready to face that."

"Heart of evil?" Hal repeated. "But that's where the queen is."

A grim smile crossed Father's lips. "When did I ever say I was talking about the queen?"

Before Hal could ask Father to elaborate, another

gust of wind passed through. It was much stronger than the last, however, the sort of wind that would have knocked a hat off Hal's head if he had been wearing one.

Instead, the wind merely made Father's necklace sway again, prompting Father to look up at the sky. "Time for me to go, it seems."

"Go?" Hal asked, startled. "Go where?"

Father looked at Hal again, a peaceful expression on his face. "To the gods, Hal. To the gods."

Without warning, Father stood up and hugged Hal. Even though it was just a mental illusion, Hal was surprised by how *real* Father felt. It reminded him of all of the times that Father had hugged Hal when he was a kid, feeling his big, strong arms wrap around his body.

And then Father whispered in his ear, "There is something else you should know. Old Snow is not…"

He didn't finish before he vanished.

Hal just stood there for a moment, blinking. He looked around, but, of course, did not see Father anywhere. He even rotated on the spot, just to make sure.

That was when Hal saw it.

On the horizon, almost too far to see, was greenish-black darkness. It was slowly but surely growing, drawing closer and closer to Manus Hill.

The infection was coming.

Chapter Twenty-Six

Fralia was not expecting a walking tree that resembled a human woman to step out of the woods behind Old Snow, clad in a dark travel robe that partially covered her body.

Walking tree was the best way Fralia could describe the creature before her. She was tall and thin, with green, bark-like skin that covered her body from head to toe. Her 'hair' was mostly leaves and twigs, while intelligent yellow orbs glowed from within her simple face, which Fralia supposed were her eyes. A large, old-looking leather bag was slung over one shoulder, its contents clinking and clanking with every step she took.

Even Keershan's jaw dropped at the sight of the woman. "What is that?"

The tree woman looked at Keershan with obvious annoyance on her features. "A hallucination, clearly."

"Now, Tremas," Old Snow said in a patient tone that told Fralia he was used to the tree-woman's snide comments, "that's no way to respond to one of my friends."

Tremas, apparently the tree woman's name, glanced at Old Snow. "Apologies. I just didn't realize you were hanging out with runt dragons nowadays."

Fralia blinked. "Your name is Tremas?"

Tremas looked at Fralia like she might be a bit slow. "Snow, I am getting a bit concerned about the listening ability of your choice of traveling mates nowadays. Last time you were here, you had a much better choice of companions."

That snapped Fralia out of her shock at seeing the walking, talking tree person. She glanced at Old Snow, wondering what Tremas meant about the 'last time' Old Snow was here.

Old Snow shrugged. "What can I say? The youth of today are lacking in many ways, although courage is not one of them. Such as this young man here."

Old Snow gestured at Hal, who was surrounded by the mysterious glowing golden aura. In between healing Surrels's wounds, Fralia had spent a good amount of time studying the aura that covered Hal, trying to make sense of it and see what sort of magic it might be. She thought it might be some form of healing magic, which would make it a branch of water magic.

But to Fralia's puzzlement, the golden aura hadn't been like any magic she'd ever studied or practiced. It didn't obey the magical laws Fralia learned in school, nor did it seem to have any elemental basis. It would have been easier to study it, perhaps, if she had been the one directly experiencing the aura, but since that would require removing the aura from Hal's body and potentially killing him, she refrained from doing so. Even Keershan couldn't explain how it worked. He just sat by Hal's side, looking much like a dog lying loyally next to its owner, and didn't take his eyes off the Relic Hunter.

A snort behind Fralia reminded her that Hal was not the *only* person who'd needed medical attention. She looked over her shoulder to see Surrels sitting at the base of a nearby tree.

Surrels looked much better than he had even five minutes ago. His stomach wound was closed and bandaged as tightly as Fralia had been able to do, completely staunching the flow of blood. What little color his skin had managed to recover, however, vanished as he looked at Tremas with fear.

"Wonderful," Surrels said in a low voice that he clearly thought no one else could hear. "First talking dragon runts, then Dragon Riders, and now a talking tree. What other legends will just come waltzing up to us, acting like they've always existed, I wonder? The Rolling Golems?"

"I *have* always existed, thank you," Tremas replied to Surrels without turning to see him. "Or at least since I was a little sapling about five hundred years ago, which makes me far older than the rest of you put together."

Surrels bit his lower lip but did not respond. Fralia could guess why. Ever since she healed him, Surrels had been quieter than usual. Part of that was because he was still recovering from the wounds he'd received from the demons. The other part probably had to do with the fact that Surrels seemed incapable of saying anything nice to Fralia or the others.

Fralia still had her doubts about saving Surrels, but not about helping Keershan. Despite insisting that the arrow in his shoulder didn't hurt one bit, Keershan couldn't stop thanking Fralia after she removed the arrow and healed his shoulder. She had been surprised, but still appreciated it nonetheless, especially after dealing with Surrels's selfishness.

Old Snow waved his hands and said, "Enough bickering. Tremas, this young man here needs your help."

Tremas looked down at Hal, a frown crossing her wooden features. "What happened to him? And what is that aura around his body? It looks familiar."

"You should recognize it," Old Snow said in a softer voice than normal. "It's a Healing Aura."

Tremas whipped her head toward Old Snow fast enough to send several leaves and twigs flying into his face. In fact, she turned her whole body toward him in shock. "A Healing Aura? But that would mean that this young man… No, he can't be."

Old Snow nodded. "He is. The first, in fact, of a new generation of Dragon Riders."

Tremas wore a skeptical look on her face, but then she looked from Hal's relic on his head to the Healing Aura on his body to Keershan lying loyally by his side. Although Fralia didn't know enough about tree people facial expressions and body language to accurately say, she did think the gears in Tremas's mind seemed to be moving as she put all the puzzle pieces together.

Finally, Tremas's shoulders slumped. "What happened?"

"A demon stabbed him with its claw," Old Snow said without missing a beat. He gestured at the gaping hole in Hal's stomach. "We think the demon created an infection in his body that is likely killing him as we speak."

"A demon?" Tremas shook her head. "Never mind. I can deal with that."

With that, Tremas knelt beside Hal. As Tremas did so, Keershan actually glared at her as if he was worried she might harm Hal, but Tremas said, "Don't worry, dragon. I won't kill your Rider. I'm going to help him and you are going to help me help him."

Keershan blinked. "What do I do?"

As fascinating as it was to watch Tremas and Keershan work together to heal Hal, Fralia noticed Old Snow take a step back, perhaps to give his tree friend room to work.

Walking up to Old Snow, Fralia asked in a low voice to avoid bothering Tremas, "Who is Tremas? No, better question: *What* is she, and how do you know her?"

Old Snow glanced at Fralia, his usual friendly smile on his face. "Tremas is one of the tree spirits that inhabit the Dark Woods and an old friend of mine."

Fralia's eyes widened and she glanced at Tremas again. The tree person had extended her branch-like fingers and arms all across Hal's body, a strange green light emanating from her fingertips. Keershan, meanwhile, was staring intently at Hal, whose Healing Aura seemed to be growing thicker and brighter as time passed.

Fralia looked at Old Snow again. "The Woods Spirits are real? How come no one has ever seen them or confirmed their existence before?"

Old Snow clapped Fralia on the shoulder in a grandfatherly way. "Because they like to keep to themselves. So long as humans and dragons do not bring our war to their forests, they could care less if we kill each other in a brutal war or become best friends forever. They truly are apathetic in that way."

Fralia tilted her head to the side. "Yet they must care to some extent if Tremas here learned how to heal Dragon Riders from her parents."

Old Snow stroked his beard. "Not quite. Do trees teach saplings how to grow? No. Once a seed is in the ground, it need only be exposed to the right amount of sun and water for it to grow into a towering oak. In the same way, the Woods Spirits do not 'teach' their young in the way humans or even dragons do. Knowledge is passed down organically through the generations. Likely Tremas's ancestors healed a Dragon Rider in a situation similar to Hal's at one point and their knowledge eventually trickled down to Tremas herself."

Fralia pursed her lips together. "This is fascinating and all, but for a hermit who has supposedly spent his entire life in the Tops, you sure know a lot about a people that most people don't even know exists."

Old Snow did not look at Fralia, but he did shift slightly. "When one doesn't have the responsibilities of civilization to attend to, one finds that one has time to explore all sorts of interesting possibilities and ideas, to learn about the world in a way that you could never pick up from a school."

Fralia frowned. Old Snow was clearly trying to avoid answering her questions. She didn't know if Old Snow was simply a very private person or if he, having lived away from civilization for so long, didn't really know how to answer her questions in a way that made sense to her.

Or he's hiding something. *Something he doesn't want* any *of us to know.*

Before Fralia could question Old Snow further, Tremas suddenly called out, "It's finished."

Hal's body looked a thousand times better than it did before. The gaping hole had been closed, and the weird greenish-black infection had disappeared. Even the Healing Aura was slowly fading away, perhaps no longer necessary now that Tremas was done.

Hal groaned on the ground and his eyes fluttered open. He immediately sat up, panting and gasping for air hard, like he'd just been underwater for hours. Glistening sweat covered his skin, but he otherwise looked okay.

"Hal?" said Fralia, stepping forward next to Old Snow. "Are you all right?"

"What?" said Hal, looking toward Fralia, blinking his eyes rapidly. "Fralia, is that you? Am I dead? Where in the gods' name am I?" Hal's words trailed off as he took in the sight of Tremas, who stood before him, her hands on her hips.

"What?" Tremas said in a mocking tone. "Never seen a tree talk before?"

Hal looked like he had a million things he wanted to say, but then Keershan suddenly shoved his head against

Hal's face and said, "Hal! Thank Salard you're alive. I was worried you wouldn't make it. You looked so dead."

Hal, however, pushed Keershan away. "To be entirely honest, I'm not sure I *didn't* die at some point. The dreams I had…"

"How do you feel, Hal?" Old Snow asked, who Fralia hadn't even noticed walk over to the young man. He knelt beside Hal, putting a hand on his shoulder. "Do you still feel sick?"

Hal shook his head slowly. He rubbed his stomach. "No. Actually, I'm more hungry than anything."

Old Snow chuckled. "Good to hear. We'll make sure to get you a big meal. In the meantime, why don't you thank Tremas here for saving your life?"

Hal once again looked at Tremas as if he couldn't believe his eyes. "Wait, you mean you see it, too?"

Tremas rolled her eyes. "I'm a *she*, not an *it*. But you're welcome. Glad I could be of service to the first Dragon Rider in thousands of years."

Hal just blinked at her.

"In any case, it's getting late," Old Snow said. He stood up and dusted off his old pants. "It's dangerous to sleep in the Woods at night."

Tremas glared at Old Snow. "You know what I want."

Old Snow rubbed his forehead. "Fair enough, Tremas. I can give you that."

Tremas tilted her head to the side. "Are you sure? What I ask for is—"

"What I can give you," said Old Snow. He met

Tremas's eyes. "Will you or will you not give us a place to stay tonight?"

To Fralia's surprise, Tremas was the first to break from Old Snow's gaze. "Fine. You and your friends may stay the night with me. It is probably the safest place in this corner of the Dark Woods. The soulsuckers know better than to trouble me, so you all should be safe there."

With that, Tremas walked back into the trees. Old Snow gestured at the others to follow and went after her.

Fralia hesitated for only a second before helping Hal to his feet. The two of them, plus Keershan, followed Old Snow's retreating robes into the dark trees. Even Surrels got up and followed after them, looking around at the trees with a fearful expression on his face.

Fralia still had a million questions about Old Snow and Tremas, but she knew that she likely wouldn't be getting the answers to those questions anytime soon.

Chapter Twenty-Seven

Tremas's 'house' was located even deeper in the Dark Woods than Hal thought it would be. There weren't any established trails for them to follow, meaning they had to rely solely on Tremas's direction to get there.

Tremas somehow summoned a bright green light on her right hand that allowed them to follow her. She would even occasionally slow down and look back to make sure no one was lost. Even so, that did not make the trek through the tangled overgrowth much easier. Hal and Fralia stumbled every few steps, not helped by the fact that Hal was still trying to regain the ability to walk. Keershan had a little better luck—he was big enough to stomp through or on the limbs and growth that Hal and Fralia couldn't—but even he had to move slower than usual.

Only Old Snow moved with little effort. That made Hal think that Old Snow must have been here before, although at the moment he cared little about the hermit's mysterious relationship with the tree spirit. His mind was still back in the world of dreams that he'd emerged from, the dream where he'd spoken with his dad.

Hal still wasn't sure what had happened. Fralia and Keershan had helpfully filled Hal in on everything that had happened after he got stabbed by the Archer, but that wasn't what Hal meant. He meant that he didn't understand his dream and whether he really had been talking to his father or if that had just been an illusion crafted by his mind.

Father had seemed so real. *He looked and acted just like he always did in the real world. And I never did see his body after he died, so how could I possibly have dreamed up the his injuries like that?*

At the same time, however, Hal had good reason to be skeptical about his own dreams. If the Archer's infection was as powerful as Old Snow had claimed it was, then who was to say that the dream hadn't been an aspect of the infection? Perhaps Father had simply been an illusion crafted by the infection for some reason.

Yet if that was the case, then why did Father tell Hal *not* to go to the capital? It would have made far more sense for a demon-crafted illusion to tell him to go there, because then it would be easier for the demons to catch him and the others there.

Hal had no idea what to make of it. Nor was he entirely sure that he should share his dream with the others just yet. He suspected that Old Snow, who seemed to know a lot more than he let on, might be able to help him understand his dream, but again, Hal wasn't sure.

He needed time to think about it first before he shared it with other people.

"You okay there, Hal?" Keershan asked as they walked, his voice sounding loud in the quiet Dark Woods. The dragon walked on Hal's left, his large claws stomping through the bushes and undergrowth all around them.

"I'm fine, Keershan," said Hal, turning his attention back to the light from Tremas up ahead. "I'm still recovering from my infection."

"Not surprising," Fralia said, who was on Hal's right. Hal had to lean on her for support, which felt a bit like leaning on a twig. "You looked awful. Worse than awful, actually."

Hal shook his head. "Trust me, I felt a *lot* worse than I looked. I'm just glad to be back in the land of the living."

"I know," said Keershan. A big, goofy smile suddenly appeared on his lips. "But wasn't that Healing Aura just amazing? We'll have to practice our healing powers on each other. I'm sure the Healing Aura works the same on non-lethal injuries, too."

Hal, who still wasn't in the mood to 'practice' anything related to their Dragon Rider powers, fortunately didn't have to respond to Keershan's idea, because Tremas suddenly vanished into the trees up ahead, and Old Snow called back, "Everyone, we're here!"

They passed through the same grove that Tremas and Old Snow had disappeared into.

They had emerged into another clearing. The trees here were nearly two dozen paces across, much larger than the rest of the Dark Woods. Their tops disappeared into the shadows of the night overhead.

His eyes, however, were drawn to Tremas's light, which was bouncing down toward the base of a large tree at the bottom of the small hill they stood upon. Tremas's light was a lot smaller than the lights gathered at the base of the tree, although it looked to be of the same type of magic. Old Snow's black silhouette could be seen following Tremas, and Hal and the others continued to follow.

Then Hal saw Tremas's 'house.' It was small and box-shaped, built directly into the base of the largest tree. It had a simple wooden front door with a window in it, a sloped roof covered in leaves and mud, and even a tiny gate and surrounding fence. If Hal had not known that Tremas lived there, he would have assumed the house was just an abandoned structure that nature was slowly but surely reclaiming with each passing year.

"Thank you for letting us stay with you for the night, Tremas," Old Snow said. He stood a few feet away from Tremas, a faint green glow on his face thanks to the lights hanging from the roof. "We greatly appreciate it, all of us."

"Let me get the house in order. Stay here."

With that, Tremas pushed open the door to her house and stepped inside.

As soon as Tremas disappeared within, Hal looked at Old Snow. "Can we trust her?"

"Strange thing to say about the person who saved your life," Old Snow said.

Hal rubbed the back of his neck. "I'm just saying

there are many people who want us dead. What if she's—"

"She's not," Old Snow said. "Her kind are mostly neutral in the conflict between humans, dragons, and demons. She's mostly annoyed that she's having to host us for the night."

Hal nodded, but before he could say anything else, Tremas stepped out of her house again and, waving at them, said, "Come in. Everything is ready."

Keershan couldn't fit through the door, so he offered to stay outside and make sure no one could sneak up on them. "Don't worry about me. I'm going to think of ways to get others like me involved. Maybe we can find more riders."

Hal wasn't sure if that was the right strategy but wasn't in a mind to argue. The interior of Tremas's house was bigger than it looked. The foyer opened up into a hollowed-out living-room-type area that had moss carpeting and more of those strange shining plant lights hanging from the ceiling overhead.

Several rooms had been carved out of the walls while a short set of stairs went up to a second floor. It was a little warmer than outside and smelled of freshly-cut wood and grass. Hal's boots clunked against the wooden floor as they walked.

Tremas put a hand on Old Snow's shoulder and said, "Come with me."

Old Snow wore a strangely resigned expression on his face, but nodded and said, "All right."

"What do you think Old Snow is going to give her?" Fralia asked after Tremas led Old Snow away.

Surrels snorted. "Who knows what a tree spirit wants? So long as she doesn't attempt to eat us, I don't care."

Hal started and looked at Surrels in surprise. "Eat us? Why would she eat us?"

Surrels smirked. "Have neither of you heard the legends about the spirits of the Dark Woods? It is said that some will take the forms of attractive young women or men to lure weary travelers into their homes. Then, once their 'guests' are properly worn out, they eat them alive and use their blood to water the roots of their offspring, which will then grow up to do the same thing to future travelers."

Fralia gulped. "I don't think Old Snow would lead us to be eaten by some kind of tree spirit."

"Or maybe she likes them old," Surrels said. He shook his head. "In any case, I suppose I already almost died once today. What's another time, eh? I'm going to bed. Might even write a note for my family in case I don't make it."

With that, Surrels opened the door to his room, stepped inside, and closed it behind him.

"Rude," said Fralia.

"Isn't he always?" Hal said dryly.

"Let's get you to your bed and then we can both turn in for the night," Fralia said.

"I need to get water for Keershan."

Fralia glanced behind her. "I can do that. Then I'm going to sit with Old Snow and see if we can find another path to the capital and avoid the troops."

Hal nodded and they both went into his room. It had

no furniture aside from a bed made of giant leaves and branches, along with a simple wooden chest of drawers that looked like it hadn't been used in a while.

Hal dropped his bag on the floor next to the bed and sat down on it with help from Fralia, who sat down next to him.

"Thanks," Hal said, rubbing his newly healed but still tender stomach. "Hopefully tomorrow I will feel good enough to walk on my own."

Fralia frowned. "You seem worried about something. What is it?"

Hal grimaced. He had forgotten how perceptive Fralia could be sometimes. "It's nothing."

Fralia frowned even deeper. "If it's nothing, then why are you so worried about it?"

Hal bit his lower lip. He debated whether or not to tell her, but decided that he should. What Father had said in his dream, if true, wouldn't affect just him or Keershan, but all of them.

So, taking off his relic, Hal told Fralia all about the dream he'd had while he was unconscious. He spared no detail, doing his best to describe it exactly as he'd experienced it.

Once Hal finished, a thoughtful expression appeared on Fralia's face. "Interesting. It sounds like you experienced a precognitive dream to me."

"Precognitive what?"

"A vision of the future," Fralia explained. She ran a hand down the side of her neck. "Dream magic is an area I am not terribly familiar with and I don't have much experience, either, but when I was training, my roommate talked about how certain individuals have been found to have dreams foretelling certain future events. Sounds like that's what yours was."

Hal shook his head. "But Fath—I mean, my dream didn't tell me anything other than to avoid the capital. It's not like I was given a glimpse of what might happen there if we keep going."

"Perhaps not," Fralia acknowledged, "but sometimes precognitive dreams are like that. A vague premonition of something bad to come. It's why dream magic is considered one of the less reliable branches. Unlike summoning a fireball or a tornado, there's a lot of interpretation in trying to understand dreams. It's why I didn't specialize in it. That, and my dreams are usually boring, anyway. Besides, if it can't be used to either kill a dragon or help the army, then there's generally little interest in teaching it."

"So what do *you* think, then? Should we keep going to the capital regardless?"

"Where else are we supposed to go? Did your dream say that?"

Hal furrowed his brow. "No, it did not."

Fralia folded her arms in front of her chest. "Then we really have no choice but to keep going. Besides, my own father should be at the capital by now. Even if the queen is, in some way, responsible for some of this stuff, my father should still be able to advocate for us."

Hal nodded, although deep down, he didn't really believe Fralia's words, and he suspected that she didn't, either. If there was one thing Hal had learned from the past week and a half, it was that nowhere was safe.

Chapter Twenty-Eight

The next morning, Hal woke up bright and early to the smell of fried bacon. It was strong enough to make him crawl out of bed and throw on his clothes, though not without noticing that he felt a lot better than he did the day before. His stomach wound was clean and he felt energized.

Fralia was right, Hal thought, stretching his arms. *Sleep really is the best medicine.*

His stomach grumbling, Hal left his room and made his way across the living room to the exit.

Stepping out into the cold winter morning air, Hal immediately spotted Keershan and made his way over to him. The dragon radiated warmth and looked up at Hal. "Good. You're up. You know, I was thinking that you should practice something with me."

"I'm not sure I'm ready to do anything. I'm still feeling… weak, I guess."

"We're going to have to have you try riding sometime, Hal. It takes practice."

The idea of sitting on Keershan felt odd, but maybe the dragon was right.

He strode over and held out his hand. Keershan lowered himself to the ground, dipping his head. "You just swing over, and then you have to balance. It should be easy enough with our… are you feeling unwell?"

Hal wobbled. "I think I should eat first."

"Oh. Right. Old Snow can help with that."

Old Snow sat in a cleared-away portion of the front lawn, a small fire pit ringed with stones blazing before him. Set atop the fire pit was an old cast iron pan with three sizzling strips of bacon. Several strips of raw bacon sat beside the pit on a metal table.

Old Snow wasn't the only one up. Fralia stood off to the side, working with her magic, and seemed to be sparring with Surrels, of all people.

"The legendary Dragon Rider awakens," Old Snow called out, causing Hal to turn his attention to him. A big smile poked through Old Snow's beard and he waved his spatula at Hal before turning the bacon over again. "Come and eat. We have plenty of bacon for everyone."

"Old Snow and I hunted down a couple of wild boars earlier this morning," Keershan said.

"It's pretty good," Fralia said, stepping over to them and grabbing a few pieces of bacon. "Better than the stuff we were served in the academy dining halls, at any rate, which isn't a high bar."

"And freshly-ground coffee, too," Surrels added, lifting his cup in the air briefly. He sipped it. "Better than

I expected, honestly. Turns out the old man was carrying coffee beans with him the whole time and didn't tell anyone." Hal gave Surrels an odd look, to which Surrels snapped, "What? Can't a man show his appreciation for a decent cup of coffee around here without getting weird looks?"

Hal shook his head and, walking over to the fire pit, took a plate of bacon from Old Snow and a steaming cup of coffee before walking over to join Fralia and Keershan. Sitting down on the same stump as Fralia, Hal said, "Where's Tremas? Is she going to join us for breakfast?"

"Tree spirits don't eat like we do," Old Snow replied. "Plus, even if she could eat like a human, she most certainly wouldn't eat meat. Tree spirits rely on water and sunshine like plants."

Hal nodded as he sipped his coffee, which was very bitter but relaxing nonetheless.

That was when he noticed how tired Old Snow looked.

What did Tremas take from him last night? Or was he up late last night for another reason?

"What's the itinerary for today?" Surrels asked the group at large, looking around at everyone.

Everyone instinctively looked toward Old Snow.

"The capital is about a two days' journey from here on foot," Old Snow said. "Once we're done with breakfast and pack everything back up, that's where we're headed next."

Hal expected Surrels to be happy with that, but then Surrels shook his head and said, "Stupid idea, or do you want us all to die horrible deaths?"

Fralia looked at Surrels in surprise. "Why are you so against going to the capital? I thought you couldn't wait to get there so you could show the queen how loyal and humble a servant you have been to her."

"Yeah," Hal chimed in. "I thought you were expecting the queen would ask you to marry her and you'd become the new king of Malarsan, thanks to your undying loyalty to the crown."

Surrels rolled his eyes. "I've had plenty of time to think since the demon attack yesterday, and I've decided that I can't go back to the capital. The queen would be as likely to kill me as she is to kill you traitors. At the very least, she would treat me as collateral and wouldn't care if I got killed along with you."

Old Snow did not say anything to that, but Hal noticed a soft smile creep along the hermit's lips.

"But my father is probably at the capital," Fralia said. "Whatever is going on with the queen and the demons, surely we can at least try to reach out to my father. He's a reasonable man. He'll listen to us."

Surrels snorted. "I sincerely doubt that one of the four generals would ever go against the queen. Or did I forget to mention that the four generals are *also* in on the plan?"

That caused everyone to pause, save for Old Snow, who continued to quietly cook his bacon as if Surrels had not just dropped a huge revelation on them like a bomb. Fralia had even paused mid-bite, her half-eaten strip of bacon held halfway between her plate and her mouth.

"What?" Fralia asked. "You mean *all* of the generals are in on the plan?"

Surrels nodded. "That's right. Including General Jeniq."

"No. That can't be right. My father would never support the queen if he knew she was working with demons."

Surrels laughed. "The four generals spend a lot of time with the queen, both individually and collectively. Sooner or later, all of them would notice if Queen Bariwa was up to something fishy. They aren't idiots, you know."

"Actually, I agree with Surrels on this," said Keershan quietly. "I'm not sure going to the capital is such a great idea. I'm a dragon, and the capital is a human city. You four might be able to sneak in, but I couldn't. I'd just be a liability more than anything."

Hal bit his lower lip. He couldn't deny that Keershan had some fair points. Dragons were expressly *not* allowed inside the capital alive because it was considered unsafe.

"And anyway, I never went on this quest because I wanted to fight anyone," Keershan continued. "We should spend our time locating and saving ancient knowledge we ourselves could use instead."

Surrels gestured with his half-drunk cup of coffee at Keershan. "See? Even the dragon agrees with me."

"But I don't," Fralia said quietly with a slight shake of her head. "I think going to the capital and talking to Father is still our best bet."

Old Snow nodded. He took the pan off the fire pit and, sliding the newly cooked bacon onto the big plate next to him, said, "I agree, but for different reasons. If we keep running, the queen won't simply leave us alone to search out and preserve ancient knowledge. Better to deal with the problem directly while we can, rather than run away and let it grow worse."

Surrels scowled. "Or we could flee. I hear the Solitary Isles are nice this time of year."

"What do you think, Hal?" said Keershan,

"We need to be *smart* about it. We can't just go waltzing in through the front gates, especially not with Keershan, but surely we can come up with some way for us to get in without being seen."

"I have an idea," Old Snow said, "But it would be messy."

Hal decided to skim over whatever 'messy' meant. "Fralia, are you sure your father won't still be in the Southern Plains? This would be a whole lot easier if we could intercept him outside the capital."

She shook her head. "Due back this week. He never goes off-schedule."

"What about getting him to meet us at a nearby village?" Surrels said. "You can borrow some of my writing paper if you like. Won't even charge you once all this is over."

"That's sweet," Fralia said, "But lots of his correspondence is opened by his assistant Shalla. Only officially sealed letters are saved for him."

"It's fancy paper," Surrels insisted. "Just put a note on the envelope saying it's from one of the Glaci cousins. They won't know the difference."

"We can't risk it," Old Snow said. "So here's my plan for getting in. And Keershan here will play the most important role."

Keershan cocked his head to the side in confusion. "I will? But I'm a dragon. How am I supposed to get into the capital without being seen?"

Old Snow's grin grew even larger. "Oh, *you* won't be getting into the capital, at least not right away. You're going to help *us* get in."

Chapter Twenty-Nine

It took a week, but the journey to the capital had gone relatively quietly. The capital of the Kingdom of Malarsan looked impressive at night. Contrasting the surrounding countryside, an abundance of lamps adorned its fifteen-foot exterior walls, flickering against the darkness. The city covered about two or three square miles, with the mighty Blue River passing under its walls, flowing through the city's heart and on to the distant southern regions. Soldiers clad in the green-and-gold armor of the Malarsan Army stood watch while mages clad in yellow for light and black for shadow were scattered among them to provide magical support.

The capital had four gateway entrances in each cardinal direction: North, South, East, and West. Most of the gates were closed for tonight, as usual, because the capital guards did not allow anyone inside the city after midnight.

The gates would also close in times of war in case of

a dragon attack, although the capital had not suffered a dragon attack in approximately a hundred years.

Until tonight, that is. Hal crouched low among the bushes and trees lining the sides of the north road that led to the north gate. *And even then, it won't be a serious attack. Just a distraction.*

Not a serious attack? Keershan's voice suddenly blurted out in his head. *I may be small for my age, but I'll have you know that I can be a very convincing scary dragon when I need to. You just watch. I'll be fiercer than Grabtha the Devourer.*

Hal sighed. He'd forgotten that wearing his relic made their telepathy two-way. *Are you in place, at least?*

Yes, Keershan's cheery voice said. *I'm right where Old Snow told me to be. Waiting for the signal to act.*

Hal sent an affirmative thought to Keershan before turning his gaze to his right. "Keershan says he's in place and ready for the signal."

Old Snow knelt next to Hal in the bushes. Unlike Hal, he looked perfectly at ease, as he always did, despite how risky their plan was. "Excellent. Tell Keershan that we'll move in on the north gate in five minutes."

Hal nodded.

"I still think this is a terrible plan that is as likely to fail as it is to succeed," Surrels grumbled behind Hal.

Hal looked over his shoulder. Surrels knelt behind him, his surly expression obvious even in the darkness of the night. "You can still leave anytime you want."

Surrels opened his mouth to reply, but then Fralia hissed in a low voice, "Guys, can you two bicker like a couple of schoolboys later? Remember the plan. We need to be as quiet as possible if we're going to pull this off."

Again, Surrels looked like he wanted to argue, but Fralia's point was hard to argue with, so he settled for rolling his eyes and shaking his head.

Hal, too, became quiet, keeping his focus on the north gate that was just visible through the bushes he hid behind. He could see a couple of guards chatting with each other, though they were too far away to hear clearly.

Old Snow's hand rested on Hal's shoulder. "It's time. Go!"

Hal didn't hesitate. He jumped out of the bushes, along with Old Snow, Fralia, and Surrels, and started screaming. They rushed toward the north gate as fast as they could, shouting at the top of their lungs.

The guards noticed them immediately. But they *did not* raise or draw their weapons.

Fralia was in the lead, tears streaming down her face as she screamed, "Help! Someone help us! We're going to die if someone doesn't help!"

The guard on the left stepped forward and said, "What is the matter?"

"Are you being chased by bandits?" asked the guard on the right. His eyes scanned the road behind Hal and the others through the visor of his helmet.

Skidding to a halt before the guards, Fralia said in a shaking, trembling voice, "Even worse, we're being chased by a *dragon*."

The two guards exchanged puzzled looks, and the left guard asked in a skeptical tone, "As in, a real one?"

"For the gods' sake, man, what other kinds *are* there?"

Old Snow asked, anger and fear mixing together in his voice perfectly. "Damn beast just came out of nowhere and started breathing fire and snapping at us like a hungry bear!"

The guards again exchanged a glance. "A dragon hasn't been seen around the capital in over a hundred years. Perhaps a bear or night cat attacked you. They can look a lot like dragons in the darkness, after all."

"You *idiot*," Surrels snapped in what Hal considered to be their best performance. He pointed at the sky. "If that's not a dragon, then I'm not a human being!"

The guards looked up in the direction that Surrels pointed …

At empty sky.

Puzzled, Hal looked again but did not see Keershan anywhere in the sky overhead. Old Snow and Fralia were also looking up, their faces going from afraid to confused very quickly.

"Hal?" Old Snow whispered to Hal. "Where is Keershan?"

Hal bit his lower lip. "Don't know. Without my relic, I can't talk to him telepathically."

The left guard, meanwhile, looked at Surrels with a deadpan expression. "Yes, sir, that *is* the sky. And it looks beautiful tonight, aside from the clouds."

Surrels blinked and looked at the sky again. "It's not there? Where did it—"

The Right guard stepped forward and held out his hand toward Fralia. "I don't know what may have been chasing you, but it's obvious at this point that it was not a dragon. Even so, my compatriot and I would be happy to let you four into the city after you provide us with some identification."

Fralia brushed her hair back out of her face. "Identification?"

The left guard nodded once. "Mage badges, Relic Hunter merits, the Malarsan royal family seal. Any sort of document or symbol that would identify you as citizens of the kingdom."

Hal rubbed the right pocket of his pants uncertainly. He did indeed have his Relic Hunter merit, a badge that all Relic Hunters of the kingdom were given to act as their official form of identification, but he couldn't show it to them unless he wanted to get arrested. Likely Fralia couldn't show her mage badge either.

Looks like we can't avoid a fight. Hal's hand slowly and subtly moved toward his sword. *Damn it, Keershan.*

At that moment, an earsplitting roar—more like a thunder cloud than a living creature—split the silent night air.

The guards drew their swords and raised their shields. It was actually impressive how quick their reflexes were, and it made Hal happy that they would not have to fight them.

"What in the gods' names was that?" the left guard asked. "Thunder?"

"Can't be," the right guard said, scanning the clouds. "The weather mages did not predict any rain tonight."

Hal wondered if the weather mages predicted the burst of white-hot flame that ripped through the clouds overhead, the fire briefly bright enough to illuminate the fields in front of the north gate. Fralia and Surrels gave convincing yelps of fear while even Hal and Old Snow jerked their heads up in surprise.

Keershan swooped out of the clouds, visible thanks to the glowing flames in his throat. His wings flapping quickly, his eyes glowing with flame and hate, Keershan let loose another roar even louder than the first before spitting some fire into the bushes on the side of the road, instantly setting them aflame.

"That's the one!" Surrels pointed dramatically at Keershan. "That's the ugly, evil, no-good, and very smelly beast that tried to kill us."

Somewhere in the back of his mind, Hal could sense Keershan's annoyance at Surrels's rather insulting description of the dragon.

It seemed to work because the right guard shouted up at the walls, "Dragon! Dragon attack on the capital! All available mages, guards, and soldiers to the north gate *now*!"

Keershan wasn't supposed to actually attack the place, but the mages, soldiers, and guards didn't know that.

And won't until it's too late for them to do anything about it. Hal tried to suppress a triumphant grin.

Fralia practically threw herself at the left guard and, looking up into his eyes, said, "Please, will you let me and my family into the city, now that you've seen this evil dragon yourself?"

"This is your family?" the left guard asked, glancing at Hal, Old Snow, and Surrels in surprise.

Fralia nodded. "Yes. The younger man is my

husband, the older man is my dear grandpa, and the other guy is our old uncle."

"Does it matter how we're related?" Old Snow snapped with very convincing anger. "Let us in now, or do you want to get in trouble for letting four innocent, law-abiding kingdom citizens die in the first dragon attack on the capital in over a century?"

The left guard hesitated then turned and ran over to the north gate. He pushed open a small door built into the base and stepped aside. "In here. Go to the nearest dragon shelter and stay there until the Captain of the Guard announces that it is safe to come out."

Fralia wiped fake tears from her eyes. "Oh, *thank* you, dear guard. You truly are our hero."

The left guard seemed to stand up a little straighter at Fralia's praise.

Fralia went in first, shooting the left guard a winning smile. Next was Surrels, who scampered like a dog, and then Old Snow, and finally Hal, who looked over his shoulder out the door one last time.

He caught a glimpse of Keershan launching a fireball near the guards, only for him to duck out of the way to avoid a sphere of water sent hurtling at him from one of the mages standing atop the walls.

And then the left guard closed the door.

Surrels wiped his forehead. "I honestly can't believe that plan worked."

"Will Keershan be okay?" Fralia asked, tugging on her hair nervously. "I noticed the mages were starting to attack."

Hal felt Keershan's emotions in the back of his head. "I don't sense any fear or pain yet."

"Good," Old Snow said. "In any case, Keershan knows he can flee if necessary. Our options are much more limited if we fail our mission."

Surrels looked at Fralia in annoyance. "Then lead the way, my dear 'niece,' to General Jeniq's mansion."

Fralia wrinkled her nose. "What? I thought it was a believable lie. How else could you explain our group?"

"You could have at least described me as something other than your 'old' uncle, you know," Surrels said.

"The longer we stand here, the more suspicious we look to the guards," Hal said. "We'd better start moving so they think we're going to one of the dragon shelters."

Fralia nodded and turned away from the group. "All right. Everyone, follow me. I know a shortcut."

With that, Fralia rushed over to a gap between a couple of nearby buildings, and Hal and the others followed, doing their best to ignore the sounds of battle raging on the other side of the walls.

Chapter Thirty

HAL WAS GLAD FRALIA KNEW THE CAPITAL AS WELL AS SHE did because otherwise he was sure they would have been caught less than five minutes into their plan.

As it turned out, their plan to use Keershan to stage a fake dragon attack worked out a little *too* well. News of Keershan's attack on the capital had spread like wildfire throughout the city. Every street they passed was full of soldiers and mages either heading toward the north gate to provide backup for their fellow defenders or barking orders at citizens to head to shelter.

That was probably the worst part. The streets became positively packed with scared, confused, and sleepy citizens, woken up by the trumpet blasts from the army band.

Dragon shelters were what the name implied: Underground bunkers and buildings designated by the city government as places where citizens could hide in the event of a dragon attack. Before tonight, Hal recalled how dragon shelters were regularly mocked for never being used or for only being used by homeless people and criminals who didn't have anywhere else to go.

Now look who's laughing, Hal thought, pressing his back against the wall of an alleyway, watching—and smelling—the half-dressed, frightened citizens stream down the street. *Not me, that's for sure.*

"Wonderful," Surrels said in a sarcastic voice, standing on the other side of the alley opposite Hal, partially crouching behind a trash can. "At this rate, we'll reach General Jeniq's mansion in a couple of weeks."

Fralia, who stood next to Hal and was looking around him at the street beyond, was frowning deeply and in frustration. "I didn't realize they would take a dragon attack so seriously."

Hal looked at her with a deadpan expression. "This is the first dragon attack on the capital in a century, and we are currently in the middle of a life-and-death war against the dragons. We probably should have expected this."

"Fralia, couldn't you use your air magic to give us a lift through the air?" Surrels suggested. "Perhaps even fly us to your father's mansion?"

Old Snow shook his head. "Every eye will be on the sky tonight. Even simply jumping from rooftop to rooftop will attract unwanted attention. Why don't we take *another* route?"

Hal frowned. "Another route? Such as?"

"That route." Old Snow was pointing at a manhole cover, which sat, unassuming and silent, between Fralia's feet.

"The sewers?" Surrels grimaced. "I'd rather be trampled to death by the crowds than have to experience *that.*"

Old Snow chuckled. "Never said it was a *pleasant* route. Just an alternate one."

Fralia frowned. "I'm not sure. I don't know the sewers nearly as well as the city itself and—"

Fralia was interrupted when a woman burst out of the crowd and into their alleyway so abruptly that she slammed into the mage. The two women fell onto the street, with Fralia groaning in pain while the other woman rubbed her forehead, dropping a cloth bag that *clinked* where it fell. The woman herself wore a hood over her head that hid much of her features, though tips of red hair poked out from underneath.

"Ouch," the woman said, still rubbing her forehead. She glared at Fralia. "Watch where you're going, lady."

"Watch where *I'm* going?" asked Fralia incredulously, staring at the woman in disbelief. "I was just standing here when you jumped me like that."

The woman snatched the bag from Hal's hand and stood up without even thanking him, dusting off the bottom of her pants. "Never mind that."

The woman's voice trailed off as she laid eyes on Old Snow, who was still crouched beside Surrels on the other side of the alley. He was looking right back at her, too, and even smiling, which Hal thought seemed inappropriate, given the situation.

Then Old Snow raised a hand and waved at her. "Hi, Anija. Long time, no see."

Anija turned to flee, but Hal reached out and

grabbed her arm. She pulled a knife out of her robes and tried to stab Hal, only for Fralia to flick her finger and send a gust of air that knocked the blade out of the woman's hand.

"Hey!" Anija glared at Fralia. "That was my favorite knife!"

"And this is my favorite life," Hal replied.

Anija glared at Hal.

Rising to his feet, Old Snow walked over to Anija and said, "You look rather good for a woman who was supposedly on Shadow Mask's hit list."

Anija cringed but did not look directly at Old Snow. "Shadow Mask *did* send some assassins to kill me, but I managed to ditch 'em. Figured I would lay low for a while."

Hal glanced at the clinking cloth bag in Anija's hands. "Stealing money from someone is what you call *laying low*?"

Anija snorted. "You wouldn't understand. There's this real asshole of a noble here in the capital who wouldn't pay his workers their due. So I decided to steal a small portion of his vast fortune to share with the unfortunate."

Old Snow tilted his head to the side. "Which is why you were complaining to us about not getting to leave the city with your spoils tonight, yes?"

Anija cringed again but did not respond right away. "My business is none of *your* business. Anyway, should've expected you blokes would be behind the dragon attack. Is that why your little pet isn't here?"

"Keershan isn't my 'pet,'" Hal said, "and we're not

attacking the city. We're trying to meet up with someone who can help us and the only way to do that is by distracting the city guard."

Anija smirked. "Then you blokes must be criminals just like me. How ironic."

Old Snow clamped a hand on Anija's shoulder, prompting her to look at him in surprise. "Exactly. Which is why you, a criminal, will happily help your fellow criminals get to where we're going."

Anija gulped. "Hold on there. I never volunteered to do nothin', old man. We're not even friends."

Old Snow smiled. "True, but we are both stuck here in the capital until the guards open the gates again, yes? I imagine they'll stay closed all night, even if Keershan flees."

Anija shook her head. "I'd be a poor thief if I used the front door to get into every house I've stolen from. Always use the sewers to get in and out."

"Then you must be very knowledgeable about the sewers's layout," Old Snow said, "yes?"

Anija shifted uncomfortably. "Where are you going with this?"

Old Snow gestured at the sewer lid again. "We need a guide to help us get through the sewers. And based on your extensive experience using them, you are the perfect candidate for the job."

"What if I don't *want* to?" Anija asked. "You blokes can't make me do a damn thing I don't want to. You're not my boss or me mommy."

"True," Old Snow said, "but we *can* hand you over to the authorities and return the wrongfully stolen money that you tried to get away with. I'm sure the corrupt noble who you stole from would be happy to see his money returned and you thrown in jail."

Anija's face became paler than the full moon. "No one is going to care about a few stolen coins when a dragon is attacking the freaking city."

Old Snow glanced at the money bag in Anija's hands. "A few coins? If I had to estimate, that looks like you've got about a year and a half's worth of wages in that bag alone. If this noble is as corrupt as you say he is, then don't you consider it very likely that he will want that money back, even if it's just a portion of his overall wealth?"

"He won't miss it."

"Even if that is true, that doesn't change the fact that this money is stolen," Old Snow said. "And theft is illegal in the capital, whether it's a lot or a little. But it's your choice."

Anija bit her lower lip. "Fine. I'll help you blokes navigate the sewers, but then after that I'm leaving this city and we'll never see each other again for the rest of our lives. Got it?"

"Perfectly," Old Snow said without missing a beat. He gestured at the manhole cover. "Now if you will be so kind, please show us the way to General Jeniq's mansion."

"General Jeniq?" Anija repeated in confusion. "You mean of the four generals? Why are you blokes trying to see him?"

Old Snow's grin grew bigger. "None of your business."

Anija frowned in annoyance, but she did bend over and lift the manhole cover open. A blast of hot, stinky air erupted from within the open sewer but Anija apparently didn't mind because she immediately grabbed onto the ladder leading down into it and said, "What are you lot standing around for? Let's go before someone sees us going somewhere we shouldn't."

With that, Anija began descending into the sewer, followed by Old Snow, Surrels, Fralia, and finally Hal, who made sure to pull the sewer lid back over the entrance to make sure no one would notice.

Here we go. Hal followed Fralia down the ladder. *One way or another, all of this will end tonight.*

Chapter Thirty-One

Hal had never been inside the sewers of the capital before and decided that he never would again after this experience. The worst stenches in the world combined to create a foul stink that would have made Hal lose consciousness, or possibly just his sense of smell, if not for Fralia, who used her air magic to create a soft air bubble around the group.

Still, the air bubble made the air breathable, although it didn't make the sewers themselves any cleaner. The arching brick walls were covered in sludge, mold, and only the gods knew what else, and a flood of disgusting crap flowed right down the middle, forcing Hal's party to travel single file on the narrow ledges on either side of the river.

Anija's torch did not extend very deeply, and Hal felt like he was in constant danger of being eaten up by the darkness that surrounded them.

If a demon chose to attack us down here, we wouldn't survive very long. Then again, could even the demons *tolerate this stink?*

Regardless, Hal kept his hand on his sheathed sword.

Not that they had run into much so far. They'd already been walking through the sewer for about half an hour, which seemed very slow to Hal, but Anija insisted that it was faster than trying to get through the crowds on the surface.

"Looking forward to meeting my dad, Hal?" Fralia called back.

"Pah. Parents like me. I'll crack out my father's jokes about Zaviero the Wise."

Fralia began to slip. Hal grabbed her arm and hauled her back onto the ledge.

"Eww," Fralia peered into the sludge. "Close one. Thanks, Zaviero."

"Oy!" Anija's voice suddenly called from up ahead. "What are you two doin' back there? Thought we had a deadline to keep!"

Hal and Fralia looked ahead to see Anija had come to a stop not far down from them, along with Old Snow and Surrels. Everyone was looking back at them with a mixture of impatience and confusion on their features.

Old Snow and Surrels resumed following Anija, forcing Hal and Fralia to start walking again to make sure they were not left behind. Hal doubted that Old Snow would let Anija abandon anyone, but Anija clearly didn't care about anyone else except for herself.

A splitting headache suddenly hit Hal like a bomb. His scream echoed off the walls of the sewers as he fell onto his knees. He clutched his head with both hands, trying to keep his skull from exploding.

"Hal?" Fralia knelt beside him. "Are you okay?"

"What's the matter now?" Anija asked up ahead in annoyance. "Did your boyfriend see a spider or something?"

Hal gritted his teeth.

But then Hal caught a glimpse of another mental image, that of Keershan flying through the sky with blood flowing freely from his chest.

"Fralia," Hal said through gritted teeth. "Get me my relic and put it on my head."

Hal felt her dig through the bag and place the relic on his head. Tying the strap securely around his chin, he took a deep breath and forced himself to focus on his and Keershan's connection.

Keershan! Hal turned his focus on their connection. *Keershan, what happened? Are you all right?*

There was no answer at first, but then Keershan's voice came through. It sounded distant and tinny as if Keershan was talking through a helmet, forcing Hal to strain his mental ears just to make out what Keershan was saying.

Help me, Keershan thought. *A war mage I hadn't seen before. They brought him out and he launched a huge boulder at me. I tried to dodge it, but it came too fast.*

Where are you now, Keershan? Hal asked desperately. *Are you still near the capital?*

I think so, Keershan said. *Please help.*

With that, Keershan's voice cut off entirely, causing

Hal to shout, *Keershan! Keershan! Keershan, are you there? Keershan!*

But there was no response from the dragon. Hal could still feel their connection, but it was as if something was blocking it.

"What's going on?" Old Snow asked.

"He's in danger. He might even be close to dying." Hal couldn't stop a single tear from running down the side of his face as he spoke.

"Can you locate him with your bond?" asked Fralia in a low, gentle voice.

Hal shook his head. "I can't even hear his thoughts anymore, either."

Fralia looked up at Old Snow. "Do you know about any magic that might be able to interfere with a Rider's bond with his Steed?"

Old Snow pursed his lips and rubbed his beard. "Only by dark magic from a—"

There was a sound of claws against stone.

"What in the gods' name was that?" Surrels asked. "Please tell me it was a mouse. Even if it's a really, really *big* mouse."

"Mice sound nothing like that," Old Snow said. He drew his bow off his back and nocked an arrow. "We have some visitors. Everyone, prepare to fight."

"Fight?" Surrels repeated. He gestured wildly. "In here? We should head for the nearest manhole cover and then get the hell out of this city before—"

A long, slimy tendril, covered in barbs, reached out of the shadows before them and snatched Surrels. The ex-

Black Soldier didn't even get a chance to scream before the tentacle yanked him into the darkness.

"What the *fuck* was that?" Anija asked.

"A demon," Old Snow said. "I should have realized they would have been watching the sewers. Darkness is a demons' best friend."

"Demon?" Anija asked, staring at Old Snow with a dumbfounded expression. "You mean an honest-to-god, child of the night *demon*? Like what me old gran used to tell me scary stories about when I was little?"

"Demons aren't just stories meant to frighten little children," Old Snow said in a harsh voice. "They're real and deadly and will kill you if you show even the slightest hint of fear."

Anija shook her head. "You blokes can play with the demons if you want, but I'm getting the hell out of here. You can even take my money. No amount of money is worth getting killed like a pig."

Anija tossed the money bag onto the floor, but before she could run, Hal heard a rumbling sound behind him and looked over his shoulder in time to see another tentacle lash out toward him.

But Fralia shoved Hal out of the way at the last second, and the tentacle wrapped around her. Fralia had just enough time to scream before she was yanked into the shadows.

"No!" Hal shouted, reaching out into the darkness. "Fralia!"

Fralia's disappearance caused the air bubble protecting them to vanish. His nostrils burned from the stink, but he didn't have time to worry about that. He scrambled to his feet, drew his sword and held his shield before him.

"What was that?" Anija asked. "Another demon? How many are there?"

"We'd like to know that as well," Old Snow said, who stood back-to-back with Hal now, aiming his bow into the darkness. "Keep your eyes and ears open. One never knows when a demon will—"

Another tentacle lashed out from the shadows ahead of them. Old Snow launched an arrow which landed in the tentacle's skin, but it wrapped around Old Snow's body and pulled him into the shadows as well.

"Snow!" Hal called out in horror.

Anija shook her head and said, "Fuck this. I'm out of here. Even if demons are crawling all over the place, that don't mean I should sit around and let 'em pick me off like a mouse in a box!"

Anija turned and rushed into the darkness, though she didn't get very far before another tentacle wrapped itself around her waist and yanked her into the shadows. The last thing Hal saw of Anija was her torch falling into the water below, where it landed with a hiss and a splash before going out, plunging the whole sewer into complete darkness.

Hal couldn't even see his hands in front of his face. He could only smell the eternal stench of the old sewers, feel the oppressive humidity from the lack of clear air to breathe, the mud squelching under his boots.

Intense fear threatened to overtake him. His grip tightening on his sword, Hal realized he had two options: Run or fight.

And Father didn't raise a runner, Hal thought.

That was when Hal heard something slithering through the shadows behind him. Without hesitation, Hal whirled around and slashed at the air, feeling the blade of his sword cut through some kind of flesh. An inhuman scream of pain echoed through the tunnels loudly enough to leave Hal deaf.

Which was perhaps why he didn't hear or even anticipate the solid blow to the back of his head.

Chapter Thirty-Two

HAL WAS ALMOST CERTAIN HE WAS DEAD THIS TIME. He saw nothing, felt nothing, tasted nothing, heard nothing, and smelled nothing. He could only imagine he had been killed by his mysterious assailant and his body likely abandoned in the sewers of the capital to become rat food.

All because I didn't listen to Father's warning. If only I'd listened and stayed away, all of this could have been averted. I could have survived. My friends *could have survived.*

That was why he was surprised when someone slapped him in the face, and slapped him *hard*. Hal realized he *wasn't* dead. Not yet, at least. He could feel the cool stone floor under his cheek, feel his body being constricted by some sort of chain, feel the warmth of nearby torches that blazed on the walls. He breathed in and out hard several times, each breath coming quicker than the last.

Then Hal felt someone—or perhaps some*thing*—pick him up and set him upright. He opened his eyes.

Hal did not immediately recognize the room in which he found himself kneeling. It was a large, ornately decorated stone chamber, the ceiling supported by multiple marble pillars carved with images of humans fighting dragons. Red torches burned on the walls at regular one-foot intervals. The room was rather warm. It smelled of roses and some kind of expensive perfume or incense, which was a welcome change from the stench of the sewers.

But Hal's eyes were ultimately drawn to the figure seated in the gold-and-ruby-encrusted throne before him. She was easily old enough to be his grandmother, dressed in purple and gold robes. Her gold crown, set with glowing diamonds, sat upon her head like it had been made for her. In truth, it probably had. She wielded a scepter topped with a half-emerald, half-ruby jewel that Hal had never seen before.

But Hal knew who the woman was. He'd seen her only once before, from a distance as she gave her blessing to his graduating class of Relic Hunters five years ago. Despite her small stature, her voice had boomed with such authority that even Hal's snarkiest classmates had felt compelled to listen.

Queen Bariwa was not alone. The four generals flanked her throne. Three of them were glowing and transparent, while the fourth looked as solid and physical as the queen.

But Hal almost wished that the other three had been here and not the fourth. Because the fourth was General

Kolass Jeniq, and he was scarier, in Hal's opinion, than the rest of the four generals put together. Despite that, he felt a measure of relief that they'd reached him.

"The Dragon Rider finally awakens, my Queen," said a hissing, snake-like voice.

Hal jerked his head over his shoulder. He almost wished he hadn't.

A demon stood behind Hal that he did not recognize. It was a tall, thin humanoid creature with a snake-like face and head. In its hands was a thick metal chain, the cold iron wrapped tightly around Hal's shirtless torso.

"Indeed he has, Snakeling," Queen Bariwa said. "It would appear that slapping him worked. I wonder when the others will join him."

Others?

Hal scanned the room. Fralia sat to his right, her head bowed, supported by a demon that looked like a wolfman, her robes torn in several places. To Fralia's right was Surrels, whose head lolled on his right shoulder while a demon that resembled a chicken held him, and Anija was on his right, held upright by a bear-like demon.

And finally, there was Old Snow, who looked like he had taken the worst beating of them all. His face was bruised and bleeding, while his robes were torn and ripped apart entirely in several places. He wasn't chained up, but was lying on the floor of a glowing gold cage that seemed to be made out of some kind of magical energy.

"Do you wish us to sing the song of the walking dead, my Queen?" asked Snakeling behind Hal, its hiss sending shivers down his spine.

Queen Bariwa nodded. "With my blessing."

Snakeling nodded. It opened its mouth, and a noise escaped from its lipless maw.

That was the best word to describe the 'song' that Snakeling and the other demons sang. It was like listening to the screams of the dead mixed in with the bestial roars of predators as they tore into their prey. The song not only was an assault on Hal's ears, but it even scraped the inside of his mind, making him feel like his very soul was under attack.

Whatever the 'song' was, it must have worked because Hal soon noticed his friends beginning to stir.

Fralia moaned as she shook her head. She looked around blankly, confusion etched on her tired features. "What? Where are we?"

Fralia's words trailed off when her eyes landed on General Jeniq, who stood silently by Queen Bariwa's side, his arms folded in front of his chest. He did not look happy.

Fralia tried to stand, but the wolfman demon forced her back down on her knees. "Father? We're innocent. We're not criminals or traitors."

General Jeniq pursed his lips. "I know about the Dragon Riders, Frali. I just wish you didn't get yourself involved in this mess."

"Father, what are you talking about?"

"It is a great shame that the offspring of one of my most trusted generals turned traitor," Queen Bariwa said with a sigh. "When I invited your family to dinner once, you impressed me with your intellectual and magical talents, talents I believed would serve me quite well in the future. Yet you recklessly threw away that promising future to side with a young Relic Hunter and a foolish old hermit who filled your head with stories of nonsense."

Fralia looked completely heartbroken, but Old Snow, who was now sitting up and rubbing the back of his head, looked at Queen Bariwa and smiled. "My nonsensical stories couldn't even come *close* to yours, Your Majesty. No disrespect intended."

Queen Bariwa scowled at Old Snow. "I should have killed you ages ago, old man. A mistake I fully intend to correct."

Hal looked from Old Snow to Queen Bariwa and back again. "You know the queen, Old Snow? I thought you were just a hermit who lived by yourself in the Desolate Tops."

Queen Bariwa shifted her gaze to Hal. "Is that what the old fool told you? I shouldn't be surprised. He always was a bad liar. I just didn't realize how much old age and isolation from the rest of humanity had degenerated his mind."

"My mind is as sharp as ever, my *queen*," said Old Snow. "It is yours, I am afraid, that has grown weaker. Constant exposure to the darkness of the Nameless One has been known to do that to humans and dragons alike."

Queen Bariwa glared at Old Snow. "Silence yourself right now, or else I will do it for you."

Old Snow smiled. "Do what you want. I've lived a good, long—"

Old Snow did not even get to finish his sentence before Queen Bariwa pointed her scepter at him. A flash of green and red energy erupted from her scepter, and the magical cage in which Old Snow sat glowed even brighter than before.

Bands of magical energy lanced out of the floor and ceiling of the cage and wrapped themselves around Old Snow's arms and legs. Old Snow cried out in agony as the energy chains seared his skin, filling the air with the scent of burnt flesh.

Watching Old Snow twist and turn like that was enough to make Hal's stomach flip. Even Surrels and Anija looked horrified by the torture.

Finally, after several seconds of pure agony, Queen Bariwa lowered her scepter. The magical chains unwrapped themselves from Old Snow's limbs and retreated, leaving the hermit lying on the cage floor, panting hard. His arms and legs were covered in thick, ugly looking burn marks.

Hal glared at Queen Bariwa. "Is this how the queen of Malarsan treats her subjects? I was always told that you were a defender of the weak and the poor, the provider of the old. All I saw was coldblooded torture of an old man who had done nothing wrong except refuse to let ancient history be forgotten."

Queen Bariwa turned her gaze to Hal. "Old Snow is a traitor just like you, only far worse than you could ever hope to be. He betrayed me ten years ago, giving up his place by my side. I thought him dead for years until just recently, but I am not displeased to see him again, for he gives me a chance I dreamed of to finish what I started."

Hal's mind raced with the implications of Queen

Bariwa's statement. "Was Old Snow once a knight or a Relic Hunter of some kind? Maybe even a general?"

Queen Bariwa sneered. "He was my husband, King Rikas Bariwa, the former king of Malarsan."

Hal's jaw dropped. Even the Four Generals exchanged surprised looks with one another.

Surrels suddenly laughed, a sound which startled even the demon holding him. It certainly drew the irritable attention of Queen Bariwa, who said, "What do you find so amusing, my former Black Soldier?"

Surrels, clearly trying to do his best to control his laughter, said, "What a *hilarious* joke, Your Majesty. An old hermit who lived up in the most desolate mountains on the farthest edge of your kingdom is actually the long-lost, presumed dead King Rikas? Even I didn't realize you had a sense of humor *that* good, my queen."

Queen Bariwa's eyes seemed to glow with rage. "Do you think I would lie or joke about a matter as important as this, my former Black Soldier? If so, then it's a good thing you decided to join the rebels. I can't imagine the damage an idiot of your magnitude would have inflicted on the Black Soldiers if you had continued to serve among them.

"No," Queen Bariwa continued. "I would not lie nor joke about my former husband's true identity. I would recognize Rikas anywhere, anytime, regardless of what guise or alias he may use. Although I find his current one very amusing."

Old Snow suddenly stopped moving. "You. Can't. Save. Her." Old Snow's words came out with agony as he looked at the queen. "Our. Daughter. Is gone."

There was a moment of hesitation in the queen's eyes, but then it passed. "You don't have the right faith. I have never abandoned mine." She took a deep breath and turned to face Hal and the others. "With that out of the way, it is time we move onto the real subject: Your fates."

Hal snorted. "What is there to discuss?"

"Your father, if I recall correctly, was killed by a dragon."

"No, he wasn't," Hal said. "He was killed by a demon. On *your* orders."

Queen Bariwa's eyes narrowed. "Who told you that?"

Hal shook his head. "Doesn't matter. What does matter is that I've been angry at the wrong people for all these years."

Queen Bariwa looked for all the world like she was very bored. In fact, a soft smile even played across her aged lips, tightening the skin on her face and making her look more skeletal than she normally did.

"Very well," said Queen Bariwa. "If there is one thing I have learned while ruling this country, it is that once a truth is spoken, it can no longer be *un*spoken."

"*Why*? What did my father do that made him such a threat to your rule?"

Queen Bariwa shook her head. "The same thing you did, my son. He was a threat to my rule. So I had him eliminated."

Hal scowled. "That has to be the least helpful answer anyone has ever given."

"I am not trying to be helpful," Queen Bariwa replied. She waved her scepter. "But there's one other thing I have learned from my life and it is this: Everyone has a price. And I think I know what yours is."

With another wave of her scepter, Queen Bariwa opened a portal to the right of her throne. It shifted and swirled, its changing colors and textures difficult to look at.

"Bring out the dragon," Queen Bariwa barked to the portal.

Two Black Soldiers emerged from the portal, dragging thick chains until the creature emerged.

His scales were cracked and chipped. His wings lay limply on his back. Some of his teeth had been knocked out and he walked with an obvious limp. He smelled of blood and mud and looked like a dead dragon walking.

In short, Hal had never seen Keershan look so pitiable – or close to death.

Chapter Thirty-Three

Hal glared at Queen Bariwa. "What did you *do* to Keershan?"

Queen Bariwa smirked. "Ask General Jeniq. He should be able to tell you."

Hal turned his gaze to General Jeniq, who was determinedly not looking at Keershan. Fralia also looked at General Jeniq and asked, "Father, did you do that to Keershan?"

General Jeniq nodded. "I am currently the only general in the capital, so when I heard about the dragon attack, I joined the battle immediately. I would have killed the dragon, but Queen Bariwa ordered me to spare him."

"He's not just a dragon, you bastard," Hal growled. "His name is Keershan."

General Jeniq met Hal's gaze. "He was a threat to our people. So I took him out. Same as any other dragon."

Hal was surprised to see a lack of triumph in General Jeniq's eyes.

"As you can see, young Halar, your pet dragon is currently indisposed," said Queen Bariwa. "Should you reject my offer, I will have him put to death. And, while I am no Rider myself, it is to my understanding that the death of a Rider's Steed is almost as painful as dying yourself. You might not even survive it."

Hal's resolve was shaken by seeing Keershan in such a sorry state. Taking a deep breath, Hal looked at Queen Bariwa again. "State your offer. I'm listening."

Queen Bariwa smiled. "It's quite simple. Swear your fealty to me, forsake your friends, and help me end the dragon menace once and for all."

Hal's eyes narrowed. "You want me to help you destroy the dragons? I've never killed one."

"I didn't say 'destroy,' Halar," said Queen Bariwa. She wagged a finger at him. "As the saying goes, there are many ways to skin a cat, so there are many ways to end the dragons as a threat to our people."

"And what would that be?" said Hal.

"Isn't it obvious?" said Queen Bariwa. She rested her chin on her hand, her eyes practically glowing with excitement. "You are the very first Dragon Rider in ages. You have successfully bonded with a dragon, even if it's very small and weak. You are proof positive that the relics can be used to control them."

"It's not about control," Hal said. "We're a team."

Queen Bariwa laughed. "A team? Please. Humans and dragons cannot be a 'team.' We are mortal enemies, and our eternal conflict will end only once one wipes out the other. And I, for one, intend for humanity to be doing the wiping out."

"But we *were* allies once," Hal said. "Friends, even. Isn't that why your Defacers have gone around the kingdom, covering up all evidence of the Dragon Riders, to avoid awakening your subjects to the pointlessness of this war?"

Queen Bariwa shook her head. "If you think *that* is the reason I have sent out the Defacers, then you are sorely mistaken. The Defacers don't *merely* deface ancient historical paintings or burn old books and scrolls."

"They don't?" Hal exchanged a puzzled look with Fralia, who was trying—and failing—to use her magic to escape. "But what else do they do?"

Queen Bariwa grinned. "They *memorize* the information and bring it back here, where it is then recorded for my use."

Old Snow, who had been rather silent during the entire conversation, suddenly spoke up in a weary, pained voice. "You're not just destroying information about the Dragon Riders. You're gathering it. For your own purposes."

"Indeed," Queen Bariwa said with a nod. She tapped the side of her head. "Every single bit of information the Defacers gathered about the Dragon Riders and their final battle with the Nameless One is right here. I am, perhaps, the only living human who knows the complete and true history of the Dragon Riders. And knowledge, as the ancient saying goes, is power."

"What are you going to do with that power?" asked Hal.

Queen Bariwa smiled, a chilling expression on her aged features. "If you choose to pledge your allegiance to me, then I will show you exactly what I intend to do."

Hal scowled. "Is that it, then? In exchange for me and Keershan serving you, you'll spare us?"

Queen Bariwa nodded. "Of course. We both get what we want. You and your dragon get to survive to see another day while I get the first Dragon Rider in ages to serve me."

"Why do you want me so badly?" Hal asked. "I thought you were trying to wipe out the Dragon Riders."

Queen Bariwa put a hand on her chest. "But you would not be a mere Dragon Rider if you served me. You would be the first of the new Dragon Rider Corps of the Malarsan Army. Proof to the army that the relics work, that humans can control dragons, and that by doing so, we will make ourselves stronger than any other army in the world. If we had even a hundred dragons at our command, the mighty Glaci Empire would fall."

Hal bit his lower lip. "So that's your goal: Weaponize the relics and dragons. Use them to conquer the world."

Queen Bariwa shook her head. "Ah, if *only* it were that simple. In truth, while world domination is certainly one of my goals, it is, in its own way, a means to a greater and deeper end. Much, much deeper."

"What could be greater than world domination?" Surrels asked. He glanced at the ceiling. "Are you planning to conquer the stars after that?"

"Not quite," General Mokoa said with a chuckle. "She said *deeper*. Not higher. Think about it. What did the old legends say lies below the earth?"

Keershan said, in a weaker than normal voice, "The corpse of the Nameless One."

"Precisely," said Queen Bariwa. She glanced at the floor. "Castle Lamor was built on top of his body to prevent anyone from reaching it. But I *have* reached it. I am trying to resurrect the Nameless One of old, he who once ruled the entire world with an iron fist. And I cannot do that without the relics."

Fralia looked at General Jeniq with terror and confusion in her eyes. "Father, did you know this?"

Again, General Jeniq did not meet her gaze. "I did, yes."

"We all did," said General Mokoa, folding her arms in front of her chest. "It's what we've been working toward for the past ten years."

"Didn't you know about the demons that have been trying to kill us?"

"I know it doesn't make sense to you, but in time, it will. I promise."

"Assuming your daughter lives long enough to understand, that is," General Mokoa said, flashing General Jeniq a smirk.

General Jeniq shot General Mokoa a murderous glare. "I was promised that Fralia would not be touched."

"She won't, Kolass," Queen Bariwa said in her usual regal tone. "She may need to hand over her robes and give up her position as a Minor Mage, but unlike the others, I will not put her to death for her crimes."

"Wonderful," Surrels muttered.

Hal leaned forward. "Why do you want to resurrect

the Nameless One? How do you even resurrect a demon god, anyway?"

Queen Bariwa shook her head. "You misunderstand me. I'm simply the one providing the resources for the process."

Hal frowned. "Wait, if you weren't the one who came up with the idea in the first place, then who did?"

"That would be me," a deep, dark voice said from behind them.

Startled, Hal looked over his shoulder and felt his heart sink into the pit of his stomach.

Standing in front of the doorway to the throne room was another demon, this one quite familiar to Hal. Clad in a red hood and robes, leather hiking boots partially covered in dried mud, a bow slung over his shoulder, the Archer looked no worse for wear for the fireballs it had taken from Keershan earlier. He was holding Hal's relic bag.

"Dark Priest," Queen Bariwa said, her tone noticeably more subdued. "I didn't think you'd be here. I thought you were communing."

The Archer shrugged. "I finished five minutes ago, so I decided to come and see how the interrogation was coming along. I thought they'd all be dead by now."

Without warning, the Dark Priest slammed his fist into Hal's face, knocking him onto his side.

"Hal?" Fralia said beside him, her voice sounding somewhat distant. "Hal, can you hear me?"

Blinking, Hal felt his senses coming back to him. The Dark Priest stood over him, his fist slightly bloody. Malicious green eyes peered out from the hood.

"He is still alive if you are worried, mage," said the Dark Priest. He glanced at the blood on his fist. "Although drawing blood was pretty easy, I must say."

Hal spat out blood at the Dark Priest's feet. "How close are you to resurrecting the Nameless One?"

"We are only missing three more relics to subdue the dragons and use their energy to bring the Nameless One's soul back from the beyond."

The Dark Priest stood up, hauling Hal to his feet. Letting go of Hal's hair, the Dark Priest turned around and walked away, obvious smugness in each step.

"Bariwa, why are you okay with this?" Hal asked, staring at Queen Bariwa in horror. "The Nameless One is pure evil. If he is brought back—"

"What do I care?" Queen Bariwa snapped. She gestured at the Dark Priest, who had stopped at the foot of her throne. "The Dark Priest claims that the Nameless One's return will make Malarsan a force to be reckoned with. Not even the dragons will be able to stand against us. Besides, how many of those old legends about the Nameless One are accurate, anyway?"

"More than you realize, Marial. And that's not why you're serving him. You want—"

A blast of cold air sent Old Snow staggering back a step, cutting him off.

Hal turned his gaze to General Jeniq and the other generals, who had all been oddly quiet during this discussion. "Generals, you must realize just how crazy this sounds. Do you really want to help resurrect an evil demon god that only seeks to destroy humanity?"

General Mokoa brushed her hair back. "If this will end the dragon menace, then it will be worth it."

The other generals nodded, except for General Jeniq.

Probably trying to figure out whether he should save his daughter or let her get killed with me and the others. Bastard.

Then Queen Bariwa lowered her arms and met Hal's gaze. "What will your choice be, then? Will you swear allegiance to me and to the Nameless One for the rest of your days, or will you continue to fight against us and perish along with all of your friends?"

Hal bit his lower lip. He wanted to tell Queen Bariwa exactly where she could put that scepter of hers. But then Hal looked at his friends kneeling beside him, fear and anxiety on their faces. He looked at Keershan, who was looking worse and worse with each passing second.

And finally, Hal looked at Old Snow, the hidden king turned hermit, who looked more pathetic, perhaps, than the rest of them put together. He lay on the floor of his cage, his head lolling to the side.

Without uttering a word, Old Snow pointed a finger from Hal to Keershan. It was a subtle gesture, one that even the Dark Priest did not seem to notice. Hal certainly didn't know what to make of it.

Old Snow frowned. He then mouthed one word, a word that Hal instantly understood: *bond.*

Chapter Thirty-Four

Hal knew what Old Snow meant. He didn't agree with it, but he knew exactly what Old Snow was trying to tell him.

And hell, it's not like we have any other choice. We'll probably die either way. Better to go out fighting.

Hal closed his eyes, which immediately prompted Queen Bariwa to say, "What's the matter, Halar? Have you become tired all of a sudden?"

Without opening his eyes, Hal said, "I'm thinking, Your Majesty. I'll have your answer soon enough."

Queen Bariwa did not respond, but Hal could sense that she didn't approve of his response one bit. That normally would have bothered Hal, but after everything she'd put him through today, he didn't care much for her opinions.

And, of course, Hal had lied straight through his teeth. He wasn't *just* thinking. He was trying to draw upon his bond with Keershan, to try to borrow some of

Keershan's power to save himself and his friends from Queen Bariwa.

That meant Hal was trying to do it *without* his relic. In fact, Hal didn't think it would work at all. Even if relics technically weren't needed to access the bond between Rider and Steed, that did not mean that Hal's bond with Keershan was developed enough to work without the relic.

But it does *exist,* Hal told himself. *You felt Keershan's pain earlier when General Jeniq took him down when you weren't wearing your relic. Remember that pain, that fear, that terror. Focus on it. Use it as the bridge between you and Keershan.*

Hal drew upon that memory of Keershan's pain. He remembered the shock to his system, the pain he'd experienced as if it was his own. He directed his thoughts toward Keershan, forgetting about his bloody lip, the heat of the throne room, the cold chains weighing his body down, his sweaty, shirtless body, everything to focus on his bond.

And then Hal suddenly felt it. The connection between their minds. The bond. It felt like a two-way pipeline now existed between Hal and Keershan's minds, allowing Hal to see Keershan's thoughts and vice versa.

Hesitant, Hal asked, *Keershan, can you hear me?*

Keershan's response did not immediately come, and when it did, it was much weaker than normal.

But it *did* come and Hal could hear Keershan's voice as clear as day.

Hal, is that you? How are you talking to me without your relic?

Never mind that, Hal said. *I need your power if I'm going to save us.*

Us?

Everyone. You, me, Fralia, Old Snow, even Surrels and Anija. We need to do what we did back in the Forgotten Temple. Do you remember that?

I do. Keershan sighed. *I'm so weak. I don't know how much I can give you.*

That's fine, Hal said. *You don't need to give me much. We're stronger together than we are apart. Just give me what you can and I'll make it work.*

Keershan was silent for a good while, although Hal could tell that their bond was still intact. It was just that Keershan was pondering Hal's request, which seemed odd to Hal, as Keershan usually was so eager and excited to experience their bond.

Finally, however, Keershan said, more confidently than before, *All right. What do you need?*

Hal smiled in real life. *Fire. Strength. Speed. Durability. Flight if you can manage it.*

Not sure about that last one, Keershan said, *but the others… You got it.*

With that, Hal felt a sudden warmth rush through their bond and into his body. It was the exact same intense heat and flame which Hal had felt in the Forgotten Temple, only even stronger. It was like Keershan had unleashed an entire furnace inside Hal's body, warming up his skin, burning away the pain and fatigue that Hal's body had accumulated over the past day or so.

In its place, the flame left nothing except burning certainty, strength, and confidence. His limbs felt thicker and stronger and he felt as if there was nothing he couldn't do.

Even the Dark Priest seemed to notice because Hal heard him say, "The Relic Hunter. Something seems different about him."

"He must have fallen asleep," Queen Bariwa said. She then directed her next order to the demon behind Hal. "Wake him up."

Despite his eyes being closed, Hal could hear—if not sense—Snakeling behind him raise a hand, aiming for his neck. Yet it wasn't his human senses that let him notice that. It was Keershan's, which were now his. It gave Hal a more complete picture of the room in which he knelt, knowing the position of everyone.

That included the demon behind him, which brought its hand toward his neck with lightning-fast speed.

But Hal was faster.

Without making a sound, Hal snapped the metal chains binding his body, whirled around, and caught Snakeling's falling hand. A look of pure shock crossed Snakeling's inhuman features, but Hal slammed his palm into its mouth.

Red-hot flame erupted from Hal's hand into the demon's mouth.

Then Hal yanked his hand out of the demon's body, grabbed it by the throat, and hurled it over his shoulder at Queen Bariwa.

The dead demon crashed onto the steps of the throne. Smoke floated out of its open mouth, its teeth melted together, its throat and chest blackened.

Hal didn't stop there. He thrust his hand out and unleashed a stream of fire from his palm toward the demons holding his friends hostage. He formed the fire into a single line and burnt their heads off. The now headless demons collapsed on the floor.

"There's your answer, Your Majesty," Hal said. He raised his hands. "And it's a big, fat *no*. I'll never work for you or your demons."

The queen sneered at him. "I won't just kill you. I'll kill your dragon, your friends, and perhaps your entire tiny little village as well."

General Jeniq looked at Queen Bariwa in shock.

Hal's temper flared. "Touch my village—especially my mother's house—and I will burn you to ash."

That got Queen Bariwa's attention, causing her to look toward Hal, an amused grin on her face. "I would think twice about so brazenly threatening my life, young Halar."

"You're outnumbered."

Queen Bariwa's grin twitched slightly. "How so?"

Hal pointed a finger at his friends. Bolts of pure flame launched toward them, shattering their chains. Fralia, Surrels, and Anija stood up. Old Snow was still stuck in his cage, but even he was smiling now.

One of the Black Soldiers holding Keershan's chains was on fire. He ran around like a madman, screaming his head off, desperately—and futilely—trying to beat the fire off his body. He only seemed to make the fires worse, however, and eventually just stopped and fell flat on the floor, his clothing, skin, and hair slowly but surely burning away.

As for the other soldier, he was lying on the floor underneath Keershan's right claw, which dug deeply into the Black Soldier's back. He looked even deader than the other one.

And Keershan himself stood, looking far better than he had even a few minutes ago. His scales were still cracked in a few places, but other than that, the dragon looked like he'd nearly made a full recovery already.

Keershan opened his mouth and unleashed a full stream of dragonfire.

A thick half-barrier of stone erupted in front of Queen Bariwa and the generals. The dragonfire washed over it, burning so hot that Hal could feel it from a distance. Surprisingly, the barrier remained standing, even though Hal could see it melting under the heat.

"Stop!" Fralia cried out. "Keershan, stop!"

Keershan closed his mouth abruptly. The flames vanished, revealing the half-melted barrier, the liquid stone dripping onto the steps of the throne.

"The barrier is self-repairing. See?"

Hal noticed pieces of the stone floor flowing into the barrier, slowly but surely repairing the damage Keershan's flames had inflicted. It was almost organic, like the wall was a living creature. "How—"

Without warning, the wall fell.

Revealing that the entire throne was missing, leaving only a very stone-faced General Jeniq standing there. The other generals' transparent forms had disappeared as well, and the Dark Priest was nowhere to be seen.

"What happened?" Keershan said in surprise. "Where did Queen Bariwa go?"

General Jeniq gestured, "I used my Earth magic to help the queen escape through a hidden passage beneath her throne. As we speak, she should be inside her own private dragon shelter, where she will be safe from you."

"The army is on its way right now, isn't it?" Hal asked.

General Jeniq nodded without lowering his sword. "It is. Or will be soon, once Queen Bariwa gives out the order. There are approximately ten thousand soldiers, five thousand mages, and a thousand guards stationed in the capital at the moment. Do you really think you can beat them all, even with your dragon?"

Hal felt his burning confidence starting to waver.

General Jeniq, however, shook his head. "But you probably won't have to fight the army or even the city guard. No, your odds of survival, much less victory, would be a hundred times higher if you had to fight them."

"Then who are we actually fighting?" asked Hal.

General Jeniq raised his sword above his head. "Me."

With that, General Jeniq slammed his sword onto the floor. The entire room shuddered as though an earthquake had hit. The chandelier overhead swayed dangerously while thick cracks appeared, causing parts of the ceiling to fall down.

And then General Jeniq erupted from the platform toward Hal, riding a pillar of stone, his drill sword glowing with moulash. His eyes with anger.

Chapter Thirty-Five

Keershan launched through the air and body-slammed the general into the wall on the other side of the chamber. He bounced off it as if it was rubber and landed on his feet more or less unharmed.

Keershan wasn't done yet. Standing on the pillar which General Jeniq had summoned, Keershan unleashed another stream of dragonfire onto the war mage. In a flash, General Jeniq formed a dome-like stone barrier around himself.

Hal placed a hand on Fralia's shoulder. "I need you, Surrels, and Anija to free Old Snow from his cage."

A massive shadow suddenly fell over Hal, and he looked over his shoulder in time to see General Jeniq's drill sword coming toward him like a falling tree.

Hal wouldn't have been fast enough to dodge that attack. But thanks to his bond with Keershan, Hal was able to leap forward at the last second and hit the floor. When the sword crashed into the floor, it caused the whole room to shake and shudder again, widening the cracks forming everywhere and even causing chunks of the ceiling overhead to collapse entirely. One of the banners along the wall fell onto the floor while others just barely clung to the nails they were affixed to.

Rising to his feet, Hal whirled around and launched a fireball at General Jeniq. The war mage deflected it with his sword, sending the fireball flying out through a nearby window.

Twirling his drill sword in his hand, General Jeniq said, "You have quick reflexes. I see why you were such a successful Relic Hunter. I imagine you could have been a captain at some point, like your father was."

Hal scowled. "What do you know about my father?"

"A lot, given how he was in my squad," General Jeniq replied. "Although I am disappointed his son became the first new Dragon Rider in years and has willingly sided with the dragons."

The flapping of wings overhead was followed by Keershan landing beside Hal, baring his teeth at General Jeniq while digging his claws into the floor.

"Trust me, General, I never thought I'd work with a dragon, either," said Hal, glancing at Keershan. "But somehow, I do. Funny how life works that way sometimes."

General Jeniq launched forward, swinging his sword faster than Hal's eyes could follow. Hal and Keershan had to jump to the side to avoid his wide swings, which were so fast that the air from them alone nearly knocked Hal back.

General Jeniq turned on Hal, swinging his sword

while advancing. It was all Hal could do to keep just out of the range of General Jeniq's sword, which now looked less like a sword and more like a windmill of death that would chop him to pieces if he let it get too close.

Hal bumped into a pillar and immediately ducked to the side. He was just in time, too, because General Jeniq's sword followed a second later and slammed into the marble pillar hard enough to make the whole thing shake. General Jeniq must have gotten his sword stuck in the pillar, however, because he struggled to remove it.

Sensing an opening, Hal rushed forward and slammed his fist into General Jeniq's gut. Although General Jeniq had a thick layer of armor underneath his flowing brown mage robes, Hal's fist was driven by the strength of a dragon, which let him hit faster—and harder—than he normally could.

The blow sent General Jeniq staggering, forcing him to let go of his sword while gasping in pain. Hal followed it up with another right hook, striking General Jeniq in the chest, sending the Dragonslayer falling backward onto the floor.

And General Jeniq *kept* falling, sinking into the stone floor like it was water, and disappearing before Hal's startled eyes.

The cracking of stone overhead made Hal look up. One of the pillars supporting the ceiling had somehow tipped over and was crashing down toward them. Keershan immediately body-slammed Hal to the side, sending Hal flying. Hal hit the floor and rolled several feet until he slammed into the wall, where he lay for a moment, dazed by the impact.

Then a loud smashing sound could be heard, and Hal felt more than heard Keershan's cry of pain.

Looking up, Hal saw Keershan lying underneath the stone pillar. The small dragon was clearly trying to free himself, but it was just as clear that the tons of stone covering him were too much even for Keershan to move on his own.

Rising to his feet, Hal said, "Keershan! Hold on. I'll be there in—"

Unfortunately, Hal didn't get to finish his sentence before huge stone hands emerged from the ground and grabbed his legs, forcing him to stay where he was. The stone hands held him with a grip tight enough to nearly cut off circulation to his legs, but Hal still tried to free himself anyway.

"Don't," a voice said before Hal. "You'll just hurt yourself."

Startled, Hal looked up to see General Jeniq standing before him, arms folded in front of his chest. Where the massive man had been hiding up until now, Hal didn't know, but he didn't care. He just raised his hands and summoned two fireballs, ready to throw them at General Jeniq.

But then two stone hands emerged from the wall behind him and clamped down on both of his arms, pulling them behind his back at an almost unnatural angle with intense pressure. Hal grunted in pain, letting the fireballs in his hands dissipate due to the pressure destroying his ability to concentrate.

"Don't try that either," General Jeniq said. He patted his chest, making a soft clinking sound where his hand touched. "Not that your fireballs would have done you much good. Both my mage robes and armor are enchanted to be fireproof."

"Then why did you hide from Keershan's firebreath earlier?" Hal snapped. "Were you afraid your enchantments wouldn't work?"

General Jeniq shook his head. "While my equipment is indeed fireproof, it doesn't mean *I'm* fireproof or that I can't be hurt or burned with fire. Protection does not give one license to be an idiot."

Hal scowled. He struggled against the stone hands binding him but found that even his dragon strength was no match for the stone strength of the rock hands constricting him. "You're making a mistake. The queen—"

"Must be protected at all costs," General Jeniq said grimly. He pointed the tip of his drill sword at Hal's face. "I wish I didn't have to do this, Hal, but you leave me with no choice. Sparing you would only delay the inevitable. The only way I can end this now is by ending *you*."

Hal stared down the tip of the drill. He'd heard of General Jeniq's legendary and unique drill sword, but never in his wildest dreams did he imagine he would find himself at the other end of it.

General Jeniq brought his drill sword down on Hal's head… and stopped.

Fralia stood in his way, her arms held out to her sides, tears trailing down the sides of her face.

Surrels and Anija supported Old Snow between them.

"What I do, I do for you and your siblings." General Jeniq sighed. "The reason I've sided with the demons is because I want *her* back, and they said they could bring *her* back."

Hal frowned. "Who is 'her'?"

Fralia rubbed the tears out of her eyes in shock. "My mother died five years ago," Fralia said quietly. "She was alone in the house, tripped, and cracked her skull in the bathroom. No one knew until hours later, by which time it was too late to save her."

General Jeniq looked at his feet. "After her death, I went to all of the archmages I knew, delved deep into the Library's most archaic books, but I could never find a spell or ritual that would allow a mage to resurrect another person. Reanimating the dead is the closest thing, but that's more like controlling a puppet than bringing back a real human being."

Then General Jeniq raised his head, a hopeful look on his features. "That's when the queen approached me. She said she knew of a power that *could* bring back a human being from the dead. She said it was a magic that even the archmages didn't know about, a magic so powerful it was beyond what mere humans could achieve. So long as I helped gather relics and made sure the Defacers had room to work, the Dark Priest promised me that the Nameless One would reward me with Aila. He would bring her back for me and we would never be apart again."

General Jeniq's voice cracked slightly as he spoke. His earlier facade of a strong, stoic wall of a man was starting to break down the more he talked. Hal almost felt bad for the guy. He certainly couldn't imagine what was going through Fralia's mind as she listened to her father's explanation for his behavior. Her back was to Hal, making it impossible to see her face. Her body language was stiff as well, making her look a bit like a scarecrow.

General Jeniq held out a hand toward Fralia. "I know you miss your mother as well, Frali. If you join me now —or at least get out of my way—then I can make sure that Queen Bariwa doesn't have you put to death like your other companions. We could see Aila again. Our family would be complete. You, me, Aila, and your siblings. Together at last. What do you say about that?"

Fralia again was eerily silent. Hal tugged at his bindings, but found that they were just as strong as ever. Not that he made a serious effort to escape.

He was waiting for Fralia's decision, which was the most important decision in the world right now.

Finally, Fralia walked up to General Jeniq. She stopped in front of him, took a deep breath, and slapped her father in the face.

Keershan gasped, while Surrels and Anija's jaws dropped. Even Hal couldn't believe his eyes. Old Snow, still hanging between Surrels and Anija, simply nodded as if he expected that.

No one looked more surprised, however, than General Jeniq himself. His face was frozen in pure shock, his head tilted to one side as if Fralia had permanently adjusted the position of his neck.

"Father," Fralia said, wiping the tears from her eyes. Her tone suddenly became angrier. "You *idiot*! I miss

Mother as well. When she died five years ago, it felt like my whole world had fallen out from under my feet. It didn't help that you became more and more distant as well." Fralia poked General Jeniq in the chest. "But the answer *isn't* to bring back Mother, which I doubt even the demons could do. The answer, Father, is that you should have been more present in the lives of me and my siblings. Rather than retreat into yourself or make some sort of pact with demons of all things, you should have *been* there for us."

"I supported you and your siblings in your goals, gave you food, water, and shelter, and even paid for your admittance into the academy."

Fralia nodded gently. "Yes, and I still appreciate that. But your soul was never really in it. You were always distant and more involved in your work than with us. You didn't even *come* to my graduation."

General Jeniq cringed. "I needed to lead a campaign against the dragons in the Eastern Lakes that day."

"See?" Fralia asked, poking her father in the chest again. "It was Queen Bariwa, the same woman who promised to bring Mother back, who consistently kept you from being there with us when we needed you most. What in the world makes you think she—or the demons—will let you be a family man after the Nameless One is resurrected?"

Fralia's question hung in the air like a thick dust cloud. There was no avoiding it, and even Hal felt the sting of it.

For several tense seconds, not a single person in the

room spoke. Now the most important decision in the world belonged to General Jeniq.

General Jeniq dropped his drill sword onto the floor. His massive shoulders drooped, and tears started to glisten at the corners of his eyes as he looked down at Fralia.

"I'm sorry," General Jeniq whispered, although Hal could hear him just fine. "Frali, forgive me."

Fralia, who also had tears running down the sides of her face, smiled and spread her arms. "It's okay, Father. I know you just wanted to do the right thing and help Mother. I'm still here for you. How does a hug sound?"

General Jeniq smiled through his tears. "Like something I haven't had in a long time."

With that, General Jeniq raised his arms to hug Fralia…

Before an arrow struck the base of his neck, and he collapsed onto the floor.

Chapter Thirty-Six

A THUNDEROUS EXPLOSION ECHOED THROUGH THE throne room as General Jeniq crashed to the floor.

"Father?" said Fralia, kneeling beside her fallen dad, shaking him. "Father!"

"Don't bother, girl," a slimy, serpentine voice said from the other side of the room. "He isn't long for this world."

The Dark Priest stood on the platform where Queen Bariwa's throne had once been. His green eyes gleamed brightly under his red hood, his hand already reaching for the next arrow in the quiver on his back. Hal's bag also hung over one shoulder, the relic's shape vaguely visible through its leather surface.

"Why?" Hal asked. He glanced at the fallen General Jeniq and Fralia, who was trying to staunch the bleeding. "Why did you kill him? I thought he was on your side."

The Dark Priest sneered. "Because he was becoming a liability. What are you going to do? Cry and call me names? A useless gesture, but then, you humans are known for doing useless gestures in the face of absolute power and—"

The Dark Priest did not get a chance to finish its sentence because Fralia thrust her hands forward.

Winds powerful enough to rip the roofs off of houses descended on the room. The ashes of the dead demons were flung into the air while Hal's hair whipped about his face. Keershan put his claws on his head, while Surrels, Anija, and Old Snow struggled to remain standing in the face of the whirling wind. Even Hal felt like he was about to get blown away, despite General Jeniq's stone hands still holding him down.

Their struggles were nothing, however, compared to what happened to the Dark Priest.

The tornado smashed into the Dark Priest's body full force, sending it flying backward into—and *through*—the stone wall. The sound of smashed stone filled the air as the Dark Priest's red robes vanished into the night sky beyond, leaving a demon-shaped hole in the wall of the throne room.

The blow had also knocked Hal's bag off of the Dark Priest's shoulder. The bag fell onto the ground with a *clunk* and rolled a couple of times before coming to a stop several feet away from Hal.

Once the Dark Priest was gone, Fralia's hands stopped glowing, and the powerful winds ceased. She then fell to her knees and, resting her head on General Jeniq's back, started sobbing.

Hal just stared at the demon-shaped hole in the wall for a moment before he heard tumbling stone. Looking over at the source of the sound, Hal saw Keershan had finally managed to pull himself out from underneath the fallen pillar. The dragon limped over to Hal and Fralia with Surrels and Anija, holding Old Snow between them, coming to join them as well.

Fralia continued to sob, prompting Old Snow to push himself out of Surrels's and Anija's arms and kneel beside her. He draped an arm over her shoulders and said, "There, there. It won't be easy for a while, but you have done your best. It is enough."

Hal wasn't sure if Fralia found that comforting or not, but her sobbing did die down slightly at Old Snow's words. She didn't look up at them, but that was fine.

Hal knew what it was like to lose his father. He knew she needed time to grieve.

Keershan looked at Hal and frowned. "Hal, you look stuck. Can you free yourself?"

Snapped out of his thoughts, Hal looked at the stone hands gripping his limbs. He tugged at them again, this time finding that they were not as strong or tight as they had been before. With a few well-placed tugs, Hal broke his arms and legs out of the bindings, the remnants of the hands crumbling to dust.

"Huh," Hal said as he rubbed his wrists, trying to get feeling circulating through them again. "When General Jeniq was alive, I couldn't break them at all."

"Makes sense," Keershan said with a nod. "Most human magic stops working when the caster dies. So without General Jeniq's support, of course it would weaken."

Hal raised an eyebrow at Keershan. "I thought you didn't know anything about human magic."

Keershan shook his head. "Fralia explained how human magic worked to me on our way to the capital. I'm far from an expert, though, even if I do know more than your average dragon."

Hal put an arm over Fralia's shoulders. She leaned into his chest and continued to sob, while Hal patted her on the back. He glanced at Old Snow, who gave Hal one nod, dusted himself off, and stood up.

"Well, this is sad and all," Surrels suddenly spoke up, "but don't you think we should be leaving? Preferably soon? The demon might be dead, but Queen Bariwa is still alive. I'm willing to bet the entire treasury of the Kingdom of Malarsan that soldiers, mages, and guards are on their way here even as we speak."

Anija thrust a thumb at Surrels. "I'm with this bloke. Longer we stay here, the more likely we all get arrested or, far more likely, executed on the spot. And whilst I can't speak for you blokes, I don't want to die."

Hal glared at Surrels and Anija, but Old Snow sighed and said, "You're both right. Although we might have survived this fight, that does not mean that the war is anywhere close to being over. For the time being, we need to retreat."

"Retreat?" Keershan repeated. "To where?"

Old Snow opened his mouth, but the earth shook. Instinctively, Hal grabbed his relic bag.

Surrels looked at the others uncertainly. "Am I crazy or is the ceiling shaking?"

No one was able to answer Surrels's question because

at that moment, a huge, clawed hand smashed through the ceiling, sending chunks of stone flying everywhere. The chandelier broke free and crashed on top of the fallen pillar, shards of glass flying in every direction, causing everyone to duck and cover.

Everyone, that was, except for Hal, who was staring up at the hole in the ceiling. Or rather, at the monstrous face which poked through the hole, glaring at them with glittering green eyes.

It was the face of a dragon. Almost. Slimy, black scales covered a serpentine face with twisted ram horns punching out of its skull. A slippery tongue licked across its lip-less mouth, the tongue as red as blood. It stank of feces and death, its stench almost overpowering.

And its eyes were fixed on Hal, meeting his gaze as unblinking as a statue.

"What the *hell* is that thing?" Surrels asked in a high-pitched voice. "Another demon?"

"Worse, human," came the Dark Priest's deep yet amused voice. "It is the last face you will ever see."

The creature ripped the roof open wider. Its body was thin and emaciated. With scales as black as tar and skeletal wings, it looked like a corpse that had clawed its way out of the grave. Claws as long as swords jutted out unnaturally from its hands and feet while a snake-like tail whipped back and forth in the air behind it.

And seated upon its neck, a cold, amused grin on its face, was the Dark Priest.

No. 'Seated' implied the Dark Priest sat on a saddle of some sort or that it had legs at all. The Dark Priest seemed to be fused from the waist down, more like a cancerous growth than a rider.

The Dark Priest's robes were torn and hung loosely on his frame. He'd ditched the hood, however, allowing Hal to see his demonic yet eerily human face at the same time.

Surrels yelped while Anija's jaw hung open wide enough to fit a law book. Even Old Snow appeared taken aback by the appearance of the creature.

Hal looked at Keershan. "Do any of the legends of the Dragon Riders mention this *thing*?"

Keershan shook his head slowly, his eyes also locked on the demonic monstrosity. "No. Not a single one."

"That is to be expected," the Dark Priest said. He patted the monstrosity's neck. "Even the Nameless One himself had never imagined a beast such as this, though I am sure he will be pleased once he sees my ingenuity in creating this monster."

"I don't get it," said Surrels. "Where did you even *get* something like this?"

The Dark Priest grinned. "You can thank the late General Kolass Jeniq for this beast."

"Damn it, damn it, damn it," Surrels said, running a hand through his hair. "Out of all the ways I thought I'd die, getting roasted alive by a zombie dragon is the very last way I thought I'd go!"

Hal scowled. He didn't like their situation, either, but at the same time, he knew they couldn't just run. The Dark Priest and his necrodragon would kill them before they could escape.

Hal's eyes drifted over to Keershan and he mentally asked, *Keershan, are you feeling well?*

I think so, Keershan replied. His wings raised slightly off his back. *The Healing Aura has healed most of my serious injuries. Why do you ask?*

Hal looked up at the necrodragon again. *Because we're going to fight that thing. Together. As Rider and Steed.*

Keershan simply nodded. *Do you have your relic?*

Hal pulled out the relic from his bag for Keershan to see.

Good, Keershan said. He knelt down. *Then hop on when you're ready.*

Hal nodded again and looked at Old Snow. "Get everyone to safety. Keershan and I are going to take on the Dark Priest."

Fralia looked up at Hal. "Are you sure about that, Hal?"

"Hey, if the kid is going to distract the monster long enough for us to escape, then that's his prerogative," Surrels replied. "His funeral."

"Agreed," Anija said with a nod. She smiled at Hal. "Nice knowing you, freak."

Hal frowned. "With friends like these …"

"I'll offer as much wind distraction as I can," Fralia said.

"Ah. Fine. I'll see what mayhem I can make," Surrels said, looking to Anija. "Maybe the thief wants to help."

She shrugged. "Better than standing around to die."

"Go," Old Snow said, gesturing at the necrodragon. "May the gods be with you and Keershan."

Hal nodded and ran over to Keershan. Before he

jumped on him, however, Hal realized that he lacked a sword. His old sword had been confiscated from him when the demons captured him and his friends in the sewers, so Hal was currently without any sort of weaponry.

Looks like I might need to rely on Keershan's power. Hal glanced at his empty hands. *Maybe that will be enough, but I feel very naked without some kind of weapon of my own to use.*

That was when Hal's eyes fell on General Jeniq's drill sword. It lay a few feet away from Hal, looking quite abandoned now that General Jeniq was no longer around to use it.

Without hesitation, Hal snatched the drill sword from the floor and hefted its weight. It was much heavier in his hands than his old sword had been, perhaps twice as heavy. Hal could only wield it thanks to his bond with Keershan granting him strength beyond what a human normally had.

Should be more than useful for killing a demon and a dead dragon. Hal glanced up at the necrodragon. *And I can avenge the Dragonslayer as well.*

Putting his relic back on his head—this time willingly and with full knowledge of what it meant—Hal hopped on Keershan's back. He was surprised at how easily he slid into place, his legs finding purchase in grooves running along Keershan's side. He felt quite secure on Keershan's back, almost as if the two of them had been made for each other.

Making physical contact with Keershan suddenly enhanced Hal's senses. He could see, hear, smell, feel, and taste far more clearly than before. What little exhaustion and pain he'd been suffering vanished in a wisp of smoke, leaving him feeling as strong as a dragon. Even Keershan, when he rose to his full height, stood a little straighter, as if he, too, felt like this was natural and right.

The Dark Priest appeared to notice because his grin faltered slightly. Only slightly, however, before it returned, this time with the Dark Priest showing all of his crooked, sharp teeth.

"So the Dragon Rider has finally accepted his destiny," the Dark Priest said. "I would congratulate you on doing what so many mortals fail to do, but unfortunately, that makes you the enemy. And all Dragon Riders *must* be killed."

Hal did not say a word. He didn't even think. He and Keershan shot into the air toward the Dark Priest and the necrodragon without hesitation.

Chapter Thirty-Seven

Hal felt only a split second of reluctance when Keershan took off into the air for the first time. Only a split second. Then it was replaced by a sense of thrill, of *rightness*, like this was what Hal had been born to do. He instinctively held onto Keershan's back with one hand, the other holding the drill sword tightly. Wind screamed past Hal's head as they shot toward the necrodragon, everything a blur.

And Hal could tell Keershan felt the same way. He sensed Keershan's confidence and calmness, the feeling that Keershan knew this was where he needed to be as well. It was as if they had both finally found their place in the world, had finally come to understand their destiny as individuals and together.

They had truly become Rider and Steed.

Hal even saw fear in the Dark Priest's eyes. This was the first time any demon had seen a real Dragon Rider in ages. It probably didn't even know what it was dealing with.

But it soon would. And it would regret it.

Then the Dark Priest screamed, "Kill the Rider!"

The necrodragon opened its mouth. Some sort of white energy started building up in its throat that Hal thought at first was fire, but somehow he sensed that it was something else entirely.

Regardless, neither Hal nor Keershan let it scare them away. On the contrary, Hal mentally ordered Keershan to fly faster, which the dragon was all too happy to do.

Size was often an advantage in a fight. The bigger fighter usually won.

But sometimes, size could be a disadvantage. It made you slower, less able to quickly react. Against a nimble opponent who knew what he was doing, a bigger fighter might find themselves down before they even realized what happened.

Hal's next attack wouldn't be enough to down the necrodragon for good.

But it sure would hurt.

Gripping the drill sword in his hand tightly, Hal lifted it to the side and, as they passed the necrodragon's hideous face, he slashed his sword along its cheek.

The drill sword was sharper than Hal expected. It cut through the necrodragon's scaly face with ease, carving a thick wound in its right cheek. Greenish-black blood flew out from where Hal dragged the sword while Keershan was breathing fire along the necrodragon's neck.

The necrodragon immediately yanked its head and

neck away from Hal and Keershan, which was fine by Hal, because it let them escape through the opening and out into the nighttime air.

Soaring through the sky, Hal gaped at the sight of the capital. He'd never quite seen the city like this, all the way from up in the air, like some sort of…

Dragon, Hal thought.

Buildings and houses glittered below, the streets no longer packed with citizens fleeing for shelter. Yet somehow, even from up here, Hal could see soldiers and mages and guards running down the streets, clearly heading toward Castle Lamor. He could see them as easily as if he was down there with them, right in their midst.

Dragons have great eyesight, Keershan informed Hal. *It's how we're able to see things all the way on the ground.*

But Hal didn't have time to ponder that or appreciate the view. The sound of claws tearing through tile, followed by an unnaturally deep rumble, made Hal look over his shoulder.

The Dark Priest and the necrodragon had turned to face Hal. The necrodragon looked even worse than before, with the nasty gash in its face from where Hal had slashed it, its skin burning from Keershan's dragonfire. He was surprised that the thing was even still capable of moving with an injury like that.

Then again, if it's a zombie, it probably can't *feel pain,* Keershan said. *Zombies are basically just puppets, after all.*

You sure know a lot about zombies for a dragon.

The things you learn while researching forbidden knowledge about history.

Hal shook his head, smiling despite himself. He was glad the necrodragon was focused on them. It meant his other friends could escape unscathed.

The necrodragon flapped its wings once, twice, and then launched itself upward. Its unnatural roar—like bones breaking—filled the air. Hal noticed several soldiers and civilians on the streets below stop and look up at the sight with gaping jaws.

Looks like we've got an audience, Hal said to Keershan.

Keershan chuckled. *Guess this is your chance to show off, huh?*

Hal rolled his eyes. He urged Keershan to wheel through the air and fly back toward the necrodragon. He wanted to keep the fight in the sky for as long as possible. Otherwise, he was worried about what kind of collateral damage a creature like the necrodragon could inflict on the innocent people below.

The necrodragon flew much faster than it moved. It soared through the air like a feather, wings only occasionally flapping to keep it afloat. Its throat shone an unnatural whitish color, no doubt the built-up energy from its previous attack. Hal still didn't quite know what the necrodragon's breath attack would look like, but he didn't want to find out if he could avoid it.

But the necrodragon clearly didn't care about Hal's wants, because it opened its mouth. Hal had only a split second to yell, "Move!" before the breath was unleashed.

Keershan banked to the left, almost throwing Hal off his back. The next moment, the necrodragon launched its attack.

It *looked* like fire. It was hot and bright, illuminating the night sky, its flames dancing.

But even Hal could sense something off about it. Its texture looked more like water or perhaps blood, and it left behind a trail of embers that seemed to burn the sky itself. Like the necrodragon itself, the necrofire should not have existed.

Thanks to Keershan's quick maneuvering, they managed to avoid it. But it struck a house below and blew up the entire building. Screams of horror rose from the streets below.

Hal, we need to avoid that thing, Keershan thought as they soared, keeping a good distance from the necrodragon, which had cut off its breath attack and was now wheeling around toward them. *If we get too close, we'll get blown up just like that building and the people who were inside it.*

Hal grimaced. *Agreed, but we can't just run away from it, either. Especially if its attacks will hurt people and damage the city. We* need *to kill it and we need to kill it* now.

How? Keershan asked. *None of the legends about the Dragon Riders mentioned something as grotesque as this. I wouldn't even know where to begin to kill a corpse.*

An idea suddenly hit Hal in the head and he said, *Keershan, maybe we don't need to kill a* corpse. *Maybe we just need to kill—*

The stench of rotting flesh suddenly entered Hal's nostrils and he looked over his shoulder.

The necrodragon was nearly upon them now, so close that Hal could see the greenish-black blood leaking out of its neck wound. The Dark Priest was attached to the necrodragon like a parasite, grinning its crooked grin, murder and hate in its eyes.

Keershan, Hal said, briefly turning his attention back to the dragon. *I've got an idea, but you're going to have to trust me.*

Better make it quick. That necrodragon is getting too close for comfort.

Hal waited patiently, listening to its wingbeats approach.

Finally, Hal spared a look over his shoulder and saw the necrodragon was now within reach of them. It raised a claw to slash at the two of them, a move that would no doubt kill them instantly if it hit.

Go up! Hal roared in Keershan's mind. *Now!*

Keershan didn't even hesitate. The dragon suddenly shot upward, forcing Hal to tighten his thighs around Keershan's sides and hold on tightly with one hand. Behind him, he felt the whistling air of the necrodragon's claw as it narrowly missed his back by mere inches.

Hal pushed a mental image of the two of them doing a wheel-like arch backward over the necrodragon's head. Hal could sense that Keershan was surprised and doubtful, but he followed the command.

At the apex of their flight, Keershan flew backward, passing over the top of the necrodragon's large head. At which point, Hal let go and fell down.

Hal's focus was on the necrodragon's head. If he could just make it—

Hal landed on the necrodragon's skull feet-first. Its head felt solid yet fragile under his boots, and he could sense the creature already starting to shake its head to throw him off.

But Hal launched himself down the necrodragon's neck, dragging his sword through the creature's rotting flesh on his way down. Greenish-black blood exploded, and Hal felt the hot liquid slash against his skin.

Hal didn't slow down or scream in pain. He just kept carving a clear downward trajectory toward his real target: The Dark Priest, who stood defenseless on the base of the necrodragon, its eyes wide with surprise.

That makes two of us, Hal thought.

Three, Keershan chimed in. *Crazy human.*

Hal reached the base of the necrodragon's neck and, wrenching his sword out of its flesh, swung the drill sword at the Dark Priest's neck.

The Dark Priest caught his wrist and twisted it, forcing Hal to drop the drill sword onto the back of the necrodragon. Hal groaned as his arm twisted.

"Foolish human," said the Dark Priest, raising his voice to be heard over the howling winds. "Cocky, arrogant, and even suicidal. Just like your father."

Hal stopped resisting. "You knew my father?"

The Dark Priest grinned the most ghoulish grin imaginable. "Not only did I *know* your father, but I killed him, too. He was starting to catch on to the queen's plans. In that dragon nest, he saw and heard things he shouldn't have seen or heard. And because he refused to keep quiet about it, I had to put him to death."

Hal felt numb. All his life, he'd wanted to avenge his father's death, to kill the one who'd taken his father from him, and now here he was, standing before his father's killer.

But then, heat filled Hal. White-hot rage, like nothing

he'd ever felt before in his life, flowed through his veins. It was hotter than his blood and made his skin start to shine.

Even the Dark Priest noticed, although it did not seem to grasp the significance, because it twisted his arm even further and said, "Get angry, Rider. Not that it will do you any good. After all, anger will never bring your father back."

Hal scowled. He stared straight into the eyes of the Dark Priest and said, in a hard voice, "No. But it will help me avenge him."

With that, Hal channeled dragonfire down his arm, causing it to explode into flame. The fire burned the Dark Priest's hand, causing it to screech in pain and yank its hand off his arm. He grabbed the drill sword and, channeling fire through it, slashed it across the bottom of the Dark Priest's robes, the part where the Dark Priest was connected to the necrodragon.

The drill sword cut through the Dark Priest's lower half. The Dark Priest gasped one last time before his severed body fell.

And with it, the necrodragon dropped straight toward the city below.

Chapter Thirty-Eight

For a second, Hal found himself floating in midair.

But then in the next, he plunged toward the city below, not far behind the necrodragon and the Dark Priest, the wind blocking everything except his own screams.

Then Hal landed on something rough and scaly and gasped in surprise. He looked down to see that Keershan had managed to intercept the fall and was now flying him back up into the sky.

As they rose up, Hal could not help but look one last time at the falling necrodragon. He caught a glimpse of the Dark Priest's furious, pain-filled expression, briefly—ever so briefly—illuminated by the light from the moon above.

And then both the necrodragon and the Dark Priest crashed into the streets of the capital, the sound of breaking wood echoing as the necrodragon smashed into a stall and storefront.

You okay, Hal? Keershan asked as they flew.

Hal nodded, rubbing his forehead. *Thanks to you.*

Keershan snorted. *I don't know if I should be impressed or terrified by that plan.*

Hal grinned. *It worked, didn't it? We're both alive. Let's head back to the castle before someone notices another dragon flying in the sky.*

Keershan swooped down toward the ruined throne room at the top of Castle Lamor and landed on the floor. As soon as Keershan touched down, Hal jumped off of the dragon's back and stretched his limbs.

"Hal! Keershan!" Old Snow said as he, Fralia, Surrels, and Anija approached them. He clasped a surprisingly strong hand on Hal's shoulder. "Good job, my boy, good job. For a moment there, I feared you might not succeed."

Hal smiled back at Old Snow. "So did we."

"But we did," Keershan added. "Even if we had to lose our minds to do it."

"The Dragon Riders of old were said to be a bit strange," said Old Snow with a chuckle. "But I am glad you both survived. That's what's most important."

Fralia nodded without a smile on her face. "Yes. If you don't survive, then what's the point?"

Hal noticed Fralia's eyes drift briefly to her father's corpse, which still lay where the Dark Priest had left it earlier. His feelings of triumph suddenly became far more subdued.

Then Surrels stepped up and said, "Yes, yes, congrats to Hal and the dragon for saving the day, but you do realize that the queen is still alive and that the army is probably heading this way even as we speak?"

Hal shook his head. "Not going to be a problem. It looked like everyone got distracted by the necrodragon's death. I think we should be okay for now."

"Actually, Surrels has a point for once," Old Snow said, looking around at everyone and taking his hand off of Hal's shoulder. "The dead necrodragon won't keep them distracted forever. Eventually, they'll send men up here to see what happened, and after everything that went down tonight, I don't think any of us are in any condition to fight a whole army."

Hal almost disagreed. He felt as energetic and powerful as ever. The idea of mowing down an army of enemy soldiers sounded good to him—were they not people he'd once felt a part of.

A glance at the rest of the party told him that he was probably the only one who felt that way. Fralia still looked depressed about her father's death, Surrels and Anija seemed like they were going to have a heart attack any second now, and Old Snow was clearly still limping from his own injuries.

"All right," Hal said, rubbing his forehead. "Then I guess we should leave for now."

"But where should we go, exactly?" Anija asked, looking around at everyone. She gestured at the hole in the ceiling. "We're probably the most wanted men and women in the whole kingdom now. Ain't nowhere that will be safe for us going forward. Even the Tops probably ain't safe for us."

Keershan licked his lips. "Well, who says we need to

stay in the kingdom? What if we go somewhere that the queen can't reach, no matter how hard she tries?"

"And where would *that* be, dragon?" Surrels asked in annoyance. He gestured at the sky. "The heavenly abode of the gods?"

"No," Keershan said with a shake of his head. "Dragon Valley. The place where I was born and raised."

"Dragon Valley?" Surrels repeated in horror. He gestured at himself and the others. "We'll be dead meat."

"They'll listen to me," Keershan insisted. "If they see me with you, they'll spare you. Trust me on this."

Hal frowned. He tried to read Keershan's mind for more information but suddenly found that he no longer could. It felt as if Keershan had blocked their mental connection for some reason.

"I think Keershan's plan is a good one. Many people likely saw you and Keershan tonight. That means rumors of the return of the Dragon Riders will soon spread throughout the kingdom. The dragons must also know about the return of the Dragon Riders." Then Old Snow clapped his hands together and said, "All right, everyone. Hal and Keershan can fly out of here while I can lead everyone through Castle Lamor's secret escape routes. We'll meet up on the other side of the city's walls and then head east to Dragon Valley."

Hal nodded. He'd forgotten, in all of the revelations tonight, that Old Snow was King Rikas. It was something he'd have to grill him on later, but now, he knew, was not the time for that.

Saying goodbye to his friends, Hal hopped on Keershan's back again and the newest Dragon Rider and his

Steed took off into the night sky, heading toward the east, toward Dragon Valley, and their destiny.

Grab the next book in The Lost Riders: The Rider Rises

The Lost Riders will return…

With the truth of the queen's deception revealed, Hal and his team must find new allies to stop her.

Their journey brings them into Dragon Valley, but they quickly learn that all is not well. A dark danger has come to Keershan's home, poisoning the dragons. If they want to find the help they need, they must first save the dragons—but the dragons no longer trust humans.

With war coming, they must choose a side. Could it already be too late?

Series by Jasper Alden

The Lost Riders

Similar Series by D.K. Holmberg

The Dragonwalkers Series

The Dragonwalker

The Dragon Misfits

The Dragon Thief

Cycle of Dragons

Elemental Warrior Series:

Elemental Academy

The Elemental Warrior

The Cloud Warrior Saga

The Endless War

Made in United States
Troutdale, OR
04/19/2024